I0640212

Shocking Deceptions

Penrose & Pyke Mysteries, Book 9

Rose Pascoe

Published by Flax Bay Books, 2025

Copyright

SHOCKING DECEPTIONS

Copyright © 2025 Rose Pascoe. All rights reserved.
Written by Rose Pascoe
First edition September 25, 2025.

This is a work of fiction. Names, characters, places and incidents are either the product of the author's imagination or are used fictionally.
Without in any way limiting the author's exclusive rights under copyright, any use of this publication to train generative artificial intelligence (AI) technologies is expressly prohibited.

ISBN: 978-1067024369 (Softcover POD)

978-1067024352 (Epub)

Publisher: Flax Bay Books, New Zealand

Cover design: Rose Pascoe
Cover images from Adobe Stock Images

Contents

Shocking Treatment

Grace Penrose Pyke ran the end of her stethoscope over a bulging mound of stretched skin. The baby booted the offending object with its tiny foot, pushing up a small molehill of flesh.

The anxious first-time father recoiled. "There it goes again. Is there something wrong?"

"Not in the least," Grace said. "Your baby is perfectly healthy and active, as it should be."

"I told him it was only the baby's foot kicking." The expectant mother ran a hand over the bump, tickling and chasing the foot across her swollen belly. "My gorgeous little football player. Do you have children, Mrs Penrose Pyke?"

"Not yet." It was Grace's standard reply, but sometimes she wondered if she would still be saying it when her hair was grey. She went across to her desk to check the patient file. "You're due at the end of next month. Is that correct?"

"That's right. The little devil better not come early or questions will be asked by the local busybodies."

"Nine months after our wedding night," her husband said, with undisguised pride. He leaned close to his wife's ear. "Maybe I could give her husband a few helpful tips on how to show his woman who's in charge."

Unfortunately for him, Grace had excellent hearing, and she was more than a little tired of being offered helpful and unhelpful advice on her perfectly splendid love life. She smiled sweetly. "How kind. You'll find my husband at the Central Police Station with the detective team. You can't miss him. Six feet tall, jet-black hair, looks like he could knock a prize fighter clear out of the ring."

5

The husband's smug grin vanished, but his wife's eyes lit with silent laughter.

Grace had invited him to join his wife in the consultation room because she held the radical view that a well-informed and engaged father would make a better parent and husband. Normally, the father-to-be remained in the waiting room – or in a nearby tavern – and she was beginning to see why. His wife was delightful, but he had been difficult from the moment he was informed that a female medical student would be examining his wife. Hopefully, he wouldn't complain about her. Now in her final year of medical school before qualifying as a doctor, Grace couldn't afford to make mistakes or ruffle feathers, especially given her well-deserved reputation as a magnet for trouble.

She forged on in the firm, professional voice she adopted with reluctant patients, not giving him time to comment. "Your wife is in excellent health, but the last few weeks before birth can put a great deal of strain on the mother's body. It's your job to ensure your wife gets plenty of rest. She must put her feet up as much as possible, especially if she is feeling unwell or tired. Don't hesitate to come in again if you have any concerns."

The husband nodded obediently, perhaps fearing that Grace would send her husband around to knock him out of the ring if he disobeyed. "Thank you, doctor. Come along," he said, helping his wife up as if she was made of Waterford crystal. "Home to put your feet up, my dear."

The mother beamed a smile as she passed by Grace, who was holding the door open for them.

Doctor Andrew Harvey watched on as they left. Harvey had been the only local doctor willing to take Grace into his general practice, so that she could complete the required practical hours before qualifying as a doctor. His willing acceptance put him in line for sainthood in her eyes. It helped that Harvey and his wife were friends of her Great-Aunt Anne, with whom Grace had lived for most of her time in Dunedin.

Aside from being a loyal friend, he was a fine doctor. Doctor Harvey would be a great loss to the community when he eventually retired, if he ever did. His bushy whiskers had long since turned white, but he kept up a small practice because he couldn't imagine life without patients under his tender care – although he insisted it was because his wife would be driven mad to have him under her feet. Having met the perpetually cheerful Mrs Harvey, Grace didn't believe the excuse for a second.

"You have an excellent bedside manner, Grace," Harvey said, "especially with the mothers and children. I do hope you will consider going into general practice. Your skills are wasted on the dead, although I know the police surgeon and your detective colleagues would disagree."

Grace finished cleaning her instruments while she considered her answer. "I've loved my time here, but I enjoy working for the police surgeon too. To be honest, I'm not sure where I see my future. I lie awake at night wondering what path would be best. Until I worked with you, I had almost convinced myself that the other doctors were right when they assured me that patients would never accept a woman doctor. Whereas corpses don't object to my appalling lapse of judgement in being born female."

In fact, the women and children had mostly been accepting of her, once Doctor Harvey assured them of her skill. However, the male patients flatly refused to see her. Grace doubted that would change anytime in the next century. Still, stranger things had happened. Women had finally been granted the right to vote the previous year, against the odds, and Grace was no longer the only female student at the medical school.

Doctor Harvey waved her through into the waiting room ahead of him. "In the few weeks you've been here, I have heard nothing but praise for you from the patients. Indeed, I have new patients enquiring about joining the practice every day, all of them women. I am beginning to wonder if I have given insufficient thought to the specific needs of the female of the species all these years."

7

"That is very gracious of you to say, Doctor Harvey."

Grace glanced around the empty waiting room. Although it was only mid-afternoon, her elderly mentor preferred to limit his hours. Especially on Friday afternoons, when he joined a group of fellow septuagenarians at his club for drinks, cribbage and gossip – or lively intellectual discussion, as he preferred to call it. But not tonight, because Mrs Harvey had insisted they attend the charity auction to support the hospital.

The early finish suited Grace, too. She had an essay due on the latest developments in drugs used during invasive medical procedures. With the rapid advances in sedatives, anaesthetics, and muscle relaxants over recent years, even the most experienced surgeons struggled to keep up with best practice. Fortunately for Grace, she was on friendly terms with a surgeon and the hospital pharmacist, both former clients of her husband's private detective agency. With their help, most of the essay was already written. With luck, she'd have time for a long, hot soak in the bath after dashing off the final conclusions, and she'd still be ready in time to go to the auction.

Doctor Harvey went into his office while she jotted a few notes and filed the last of the patient records for the day.

The door to the surgery crashed open, ruining her hopes of an early escape.

A frizzy-haired young woman in a maid's uniform flashed the whites of her eyes at her, before looking past her. "Is Doctor Harvey still here?" She didn't wait for an answer before galloping through the message, shrill panic echoing in every word. "My mistress is dying. The doctor must come at once."

"Who is your mistress?" Grace asked, grabbing her medical bag.

"Mrs Eugenie Atkinson. Please hurry."

Her panic summoned Doctor Harvey from his office. "Hello, Ellie. Is it Mrs Atkinson's heart again?"

"Yes, Doctor, but real bad this time. She'll die if you don't come quick."

8

"I'll be along in two shakes of a lamb's tail. I need you to run back as fast as you can and tell Mrs Atkinson to take slow, deep breaths until I get there."

"Deep breaths? She can't hardly breathe at all." The maid contorted her face and hands, breathing in short, desperate pants to demonstrate the terrifying symptoms.

"Tell her to do exactly what I said, Ellie. Long, slow, deep breaths. That goes for you, too. Now go."

Ellie raced away on youthful legs, strengthened by Dunedin's steep hills and her work carrying heavy basins of water up and down stairs. The doctor gathered his hat, coat and gloves at a less frenetic pace, anticipating the autumn chill, before ushering Grace out the door.

The maid's panic had Grace bouncing on the spot while she waited for Harvey to lock the door behind him. She wanted to urge him to hurry, but she resisted, knowing he had half a century more experience of medical crises than her, as well as half a century more wear to his joints.

"You can go home, if you wish, Grace," Harvey said, as he made his way down the street at what, for him, was a swift pace.

"I'd like to come if I may."

Harvey nodded and increased his pace at the sight of the cable car ready to leave the terminus. The Roslyn cable tramway, built thirteen years earlier in 1881, had saved many thousands of weary Dunedin residents a steep climb after a long day of work or shopping in the central city.

Once they settled into their seats, Harvey briefed her on their patient. "Mrs Atkinson has regular episodes of minor heart palpitations, exacerbated by panic attacks. Naturally, one cannot ignore such symptoms, because one day her addiction to cream and butter will prove fatal. But sometimes, I wonder why she bothers to seek my advice, because she routinely ignores my suggestions in favour of the latest fad in quackery. Some patients would rather trust a patent potion or an enchanted talisman bought from a

9

fairground quack than accept that a sensible diet and a healthful daily walk in the fresh air would cure their ills."

Their destination lay on York Place, not far from the six-way intersection with Rattray and Arthur Streets. Ellie, the maid who had delivered the urgent message, was on the front porch, beckoning them to hurry. Upstairs, they found a woman of ample proportions lying on a wide bed. A trembling lady's maid fanned her, while urging her mistress to breathe deeply and slowly.

Their aid had failed to revive Mrs Atkinson, whose condition had deteriorated. She lay as stiff as a corpse, although clearly alive and in pain, her breathing rapid and shallow. Her hands formed rigid claws, grasping at her chest. Grace now understood Ellie's panic. If Doctor Harvey hadn't been with her, she might have panicked too.

Harvey moved with unprecedented speed, pulling open the top buttons of his patient's heavy linen nightgown, which fastened high and tight around her bulging neck. To the onlookers' horror, he grabbed one of the many lace-edged pillows and pulled the pillowcase off, wrapping it around the patient's mouth and nose to form a bag for her to breathe into. Mrs Atkinson's eyes bulged into terrified orbs.

"Calm breaths now, Mrs Atkinson," Harvey murmured. "I know it feels frightening, but regulating the airflow is the best cure for your condition."

Gradually, the frantic puffs of breath into the pillowcase slowed, and the tension in the patient's face and extremities subsided. Grace, who had been monitoring her heartbeat, felt the hammering, erratic staccato ease to a rapid rhythmic thrum.

Finally, Doctor Harvey removed the pillowcase from her face. "How are you feeling now, Mrs Atkinson?" he asked, his soothing bedside voice further balm to the panicked servants.

If the doctor was expecting the patient to be grateful to him for saving her, he was sorely mistaken. Although, from the look of kindly resignation on Harvey's face, Grace suspected he knew what was coming next.

Mrs Eugenie Atkinson's hand clasped her gown together at the neck and glared at her saviour. "What were you thinking, man, trying to smother me when I was having a heart seizure?"

"Your heart palpitations set off an episode of extreme hyperventilation, madam." Otherwise known as a panic attack, although Doctor Harvey was too kind to use such words. "May I ask what you were doing prior to the onset of the symptoms?"

"I was preparing for an evening out, when my heart felt as if it was about to explode. It was so severe, I was sure I would die this time."

"Was your bath particularly hot?" Grace asked. She had noted the dampness of the patient's skin, and the strong aroma of bath salts, which suggested Mrs Atkinson had been in her bath when the symptoms manifested. The hasty donning of the nightgown in the mid-afternoon, as indicated by the buttons being in the wrong holes, suggested she had clung to standards of decorum in covering herself for the doctor's visit, even while suffering severe heart palpitations.

Mrs Atkinson noticed Grace for the first time. She appeared startled that this unknown woman had the temerity to ask a personal question.

"Mrs Penrose Pyke is in her final year of medical training," Doctor Harvey said, "and is ably assisting me. Were you in the bath, Mrs Atkinson? Excessively hot water might have brought on the heart palpitations, which led to your … hyperventilation."

"Nonsense, I bathe at least once a week and this has never happened before, although sometimes I do feel a little fluttering of the heart." Mrs Atkinson flushed an unbecoming shade of crimson, and her eyes darted to the two maids. "And I resent the interrogation about my personal habits."

11

"We don't wish to pry," Harvey said, "but it is vital to understand what triggered such a serious episode in order to prevent it from happening again."

The silence that followed suggested a reluctance to admit the full truth. Mrs Atkinson sent a haughty glare at the maids. "Why are you girls hovering over me like a pair of ghouls when there is work to be done?"

Doctor Harvey waited until the maids left before continuing. "Have you been taking the medication I prescribed for your heart?"

"Of course, I have," Mrs Atkinson said, but her eyes refused to meet the doctor's gaze. "Well, perhaps not as regularly as it said on the bottle, because I was feeling so much better. Until today."

Doctor Harvey closed his eyes, no doubt counting to ten as he despaired at his patient's logic. Did she not consider that she was feeling better *because* she was taking her medicine regularly and thus she needed to keep taking it? "Have you been taking anything else?"

Again, the sideways flick of the patient's eyes. "Nothing but a tonic my sister-in-law's cousin swears by. An entirely natural herbal remedy can do no harm, surely. It's only liquorice root."

"Please do not take it again," Harvey replied through gritted teeth, his tone brooking no argument. "It is precisely the wrong remedy to take for your condition."

Aware that her presence was unwelcome, Grace left the patient's bedside. She took the opportunity to assess her surroundings. The lady's boudoir was decorated in a style Marie Antoinette might have approved of, had she been forced to move to a less than palatial house at the far side of the world. Gilt, or some facsimile of it, adorned far too many surfaces for Grace's taste, from the decorative elements of the ceiling to the edges of the many mirrors and the heavy drapes.

In the adjoining room, she found a large bathtub, still full, surrounded by a scatter of bathing paraphernalia. Bath salts, sponges, towels, perfumes and lotions, as well as discarded underclothes and a tea gown festooned with ruffles and lace. A broad, belt-like garment caught her attention. Grace assumed it was a support brace for a weak back until she picked the belt up and realised it was soaked through.

The belt, made of canvas webbing, seemed heavier than a normal corset. Turning it over, she saw the reason. It was studded with metal discs and wires underneath the fabric. The fastening strap had been ripped loose. It took only seconds to ferret out the box this intriguing specimen came from, which announced the device as an "Electropathic Belt" from the Medical Battery Company in London. The label advised that *All Suffering Men and Women, and All in Search of Health*, should wear one.

The instruction sheet inside the box was short on actual instructions but waxed lyrical about the device's life-giving efficacy. In short, the wearer of the belt was promised a miraculous return to full and energising vitality within a few short and delightfully pleasant sessions. It made no mention of not wearing the belt in water, presumably because the manufacturer had never considered the possibility of such stupidity.

Grace took a moment to reflect before berating their patient for her foolishness. Perhaps it was unfair to blame Mrs Atkinson. The everyday person knew little about electricity, at least in the sense of having personal experience of using it. Grace knew more than most, both from her medical studies of the mechanism of muscle contraction and from the dinner discussions between her husband and his Aunt Lily, who loved nothing more than to embrace the latest advances in science and technology.

However limited their experience of electricity, everyone had a view on it, since the topic was constantly in the newspaper for one reason or another. For some, it was the Devil's work, usurping the natural order of existence. For others, it was literally a shining light heralding the future. Already, a few shopping emporia touted electric lights as the latest innovation, drawing vast crowds to witness bright, flicker-free illumination, which highlighted the wares on display and the imperfections of the viewers alike. It seemed every week there was renewed talk of electrifying the street lighting and tramways of Dunedin, so as not to fall behind other cities.

Doctor Harvey found Grace with the box in one hand and the belt in the other, still contemplating the marvels and oddities of the era. She held them out for his inspection.

"Lord, give me strength," Harvey muttered. He traipsed back into the boudoir with the wet belt dangling from his fingers. "Mrs Atkinson, did you wear this electrical device in the bath?"

The lady scorched Grace with a glare for invading her private space. "The doctor who prescribed the cure told me to wear the belt during calm repose. What better place than reclining in a nice hot bath?"

Seeing the dark cloud hovering over her doctor's brow, she became defiant. "All the most forward-thinking medical specialists in London are embracing Galvanic Therapy over the old-fashioned reliance on pills and potions, you know. England, with her superior medical schools, is far ahead of the colonies in such matters, naturally."

Grace cringed at the words, which were likely parroted from the mouth of the charlatan who sold her the device. Mrs Atkinson might as well have been waving a red, white, and blue flag at Doctor Harvey, who had trained at the world-leading Edinburgh Medical School in Scotland, and who was assiduous in keeping abreast of medical discoveries, despite his advanced years.

She decided to speak up, to rescue her mentor from an uncharacteristic loss of temper. "Mrs Atkinson, did the person who sold you the device mention that water and electricity can be a lethal combination? Water and flesh are highly conductive, especially in the presence of bath salts and perspiration."

"Well, no. But —"

"And did he examine you and take a full medical history to ascertain whether you suffered heart problems or similar contraindications? Electrical stimulation is exceedingly dangerous in such circumstances."

"Well, no. But Doctor Crabtree assured me that every condition could benefit from stimulation of the life forces to enhance vitality. He said there was no risk whatsoever."

Grace wanted to shatter their patient's complacency by mentioning one of the recent and appalling innovations in the field – the use of an electrified chair to kill convicted murderers in New York – but she didn't wish to risk the patient having another seizure. Besides, the high voltage needed to ensure death was a far cry from a few small batteries, which would be very unlikely to cause harm to a dry person with no heart problems.

She took a leaf out of Harvey's book and tried to speak calmly, rationally, and with authority. "Electricity can kill as well as cure, Mrs Atkinson. Please promise never to use this device again, under any circumstances. If Doctor Harvey hadn't rushed to your aid and used his comprehensive medical knowledge to save you, the consequences could have been extremely serious."

Indeed, the so-called doctor who sold Mrs Atkinson the device could have faced a malpractice investigation, or even a charge of manslaughter, if Doctor Harvey hadn't saved the day. The grim set of Doctor Harvey's jaw suggested he wasn't about to let the charlatan get away with it.

Despite her terrifying experience, Mrs Atkinson would not hear a word against Doctor Crabtree, insisting her episode was caused by the prescribed medication. By the time they left, Grace's ears were burning. Another point in favour of working with the police surgeon – corpses didn't argue with their doctor. She hoped her husband was having a better day than she was.

Elusive Criminals

Charlie Penrose Pyke arrived at the Dunedin Central Police Station in the middle of the afternoon. His services as a private detective had been hired to find a lost necklace, and the police had allowed him to look through files of recent burglaries and thefts to identify potential suspects. A shockingly large pile of files, because there had been a recent spate of burglaries. He'd come in today to tell the police team they could strike one crime from their caseload, because the necklace had been found underneath the cushion of an armchair. A frustrating, but not uncommon, outcome.

He was settling down for a quick chat with his best friend, Detective Sergeant Declan Kelly, when the far from dulcet tones of Detective Inspector Wallace boomed across the room.

"Pyke, Kelly. Got a minute?"

"Yes, sir," they both replied, leaping to their feet. Charlie's border collie, Blaze, jumped up too, ready for action.

Wallace hadn't yet got in the habit of calling his former detective constable by her married name, just as Charlie would never stop calling Wallace "sir". They'd settled into a comfortable new relationship to their mutual benefit, helped by the fact that Charlie's partner in the detective agency, Alistair Stewart, was Wallace's oldest friend.

"Sit," Wallace said, prompting all three to sit. Blaze sat by Wallace's chair, where she knew she would receive a thorough patting. For all his hulking authority and severe countenance, the detective inspector had a soft spot for dogs and children. "Not sure if Kelly has told you, but we've had a spate of burglaries recently."

"He mentioned it," Charlie said. "Spread out across the city and so cleverly executed that the offences were not always noticed at the time."

16

Declan Kelly shifted his muscular bulk in the chair, his frustration over the unsolved burglaries showing in his agitation. When he and Charlie were together, the two of them usually fell into friendly banter, with Declan's Irish accent to the fore. Today, he was very much the detective sergeant with his mind on serious matters. "We thought it was an inside job at first, because there were no signs of forced entry at any of the houses. However, that's been ruled out because we cannot find any links between the victims. The similarities between the burglaries suggest they must be the work of the same expert burglar or a well-organised gang of burglars. Has there been another one, sir?"

Wallace shook his head, but the angled grey clouds of his converging eyebrows signalled bad news all the same. "The Chief Inspector has expressed concern that we have no leads, let alone a suspect. He is not happy."

An unhappy chief inspector was a fearsome sight, as Charlie remembered all too well from his time in the police force. Little wonder Detective Inspector Wallace looked like he was sitting on a prickly gorse bush. Wallace was not a man who liked to let criminals get the better of him, and few did.

Wallace did not like to ask for help either, but Charlie and his business partner owed him a favour. "Alistair and I are at your service if you would like our assistance to put these rogues behind bars, sir."

"Appreciated, Pyke. When they next strike, could we use Blaze to track the scoundrels to their lair?"

"Of course. I'll even throw my services in as a bonus, if required."

Wallace gave Blaze's ears a last rub. "We could do with a dog like her on the team permanently. In fact, I'd happily trade the latest raw recruit they sent me for a border collie. Twice the brain cells for a fraction of the bother and cost."

"The same thought crossed my mind," Charlie said. "Blaze and I have been interviewing candidates to sire a litter of pups, but we

17

have yet to find a male border collie with the necessary detective skills. You can have first pick of the litter if you like. I can see to their training."

Having resigned himself to the possibility he and Grace might not have children, Charlie had seized upon the idea of breeding from Blaze and training the pups for detective work. He knew far more about training dogs than babies, anyway. In his limited experience, young humans seemed unable to grasp even the simplest of commands, such as coming to heel when called.

"That would be marvellous!" Wallace shocked him with the intensity of his smile, because he so rarely bestowed one. "We'll pay you well, of course. A dog of her exceptional talent is worth her weight in gold."

Charlie wished he could see the look on his old friend Duncan MacEwen's face when he wrote to tell him of Blaze's latest triumph. Duncan had given the collie to Charlie and Grace as a wedding present because she was worthless as a sheepdog, not knowing Blaze was destined to become an exceptional tracking dog.

"Contact me as soon as the next burglary is reported," Charlie said. "The fresher the trail, the better. If that's all, sir, I'd better go. We're going to the hospital charity auction tonight, and my darling wife informed me I'll be sleeping with the dog for a week if I'm late."

Wallace grunted. "Take my advice, Pyke – choose the dog. Last time we went to that darned auction, I had my arm twisted into buying a portrait of the Queen after a mix-up with the lot numbers. My wife insisted it would be disloyal to the Crown to stash it in the attic, so I had to live with old Vic glowering at me for an entire year. I swore I'd never go to the auction again."

Charlie headed home in a cheerful mood, whistling a ditty as he enjoyed the last of the weak autumnal sun, and vowing to avoid unwise purchases. For the life of him, he could not see why buying items one didn't need at an excessive price could be classified as a highlight of the social calendar. However, Grace's Great-Aunt Anne had assured him it was more amusing than it sounded, as well as raising much-needed funds for the hospital. Besides, attendance was obligatory, Anne said, using the honey-on-steel voice that brought politicians to their knees and loosened the purse strings of many a donor to Lavender House. After using up their store of excuses in previous years, this year Charlie and Grace had agreed to attend.

To his surprise, his wife wasn't home yet. She'd be cutting it fine to get ready in time. Not that he was complaining, as it meant he could indulge in a long, hot bath. With the detective agency ticking along nicely, Charlie relished these indulgent interludes in his busy life. A few years ago, a splash of cold water in between shifts as a beat constable was all he managed.

As he dried himself off after the bath, he poked his abdominal muscles with his finger, wondering if he was going soft. He was upstairs getting dressed when the front door banged open, sending Blaze into a frenzy.

"Anyone home?" Grace's light steps pattered up the stairs with her habitual speed.

"Upstairs," Charlie called.

He sucked in a breath in order to button the old shirt across his belly. He'd had an enforced rest after breaking a minor bone in his foot almost three months ago during a harrowing kidnapping case, and it showed in his waistline. If he was like this before he reached twenty-five years of age, what would he be like at fifty? No more second helpings of their housekeeper's excellent cooking, Charlie vowed, and definitely no thirds.

On the positive side of the ledger, he'd enjoyed the time off from chasing criminals to get his desk in order and ruminate on plans for the future. He had even taken a few painting lessons, which were deeply satisfying, even if he hadn't come close to Freya's mastery

19

of colour and technique, let alone the brilliance of the painter she had learned from. The painting Freya had given them after the kidnapping case had pride of place opposite their bed, where he and Grace admired it every morning when they weren't otherwise occupied.

Grace breezed into the room, flinging a damp cloth bag into the empty basin by the washstand. "Sorry I'm late. Last-minute drama. A patient electrocuted herself, unintentionally. I need to ask your advice about it, but not now. The Drummonds will be calling for us any minute." As she walked past him, she sniffed. "You smell good enough to eat, unlike me. I haven't eaten all day."

Charlie caught his wife around the waist. "Shall I fetch some food to keep you alive, rather than risk your nibbling on the tender parts of my anatomy?"

Grace eyed him up. "Mm, don't tempt me. Anyway, there'll be a supper at the auction."

After stealing a kiss, Charlie helped his wife change into an old but respectable evening gown. For unspecified reasons, Anne had told them not to wear their best attire for the auction.

"Suffering saints," Grace huffed as they struggled to get the gown done up, "Lily is going to have to let the seams out again."

"You are more beautiful than ever, if that is possible," Charlie murmured as he loosened the laces as far as he could.

Grace pulled at the tight bodice. "If I keep on with this eating regime, I'm going to be so front-heavy I'll topple over. I'm worried my handsome husband will be crushed under the weight."

"I'd like to see you try," Charlie said, unpinning her dishevelled hair and combing out the glossy dark strands down to her waist. He couldn't resist slipping his hands around her again, admiring her new curves.

"No time for that, Pyke." She swivelled in his arms and stretched up to put her lips to his ear. "Later, if you buy me something nice at the auction." When he ran his lips up her neck slowly but surely, she said, "Better yet, let's forget about the auction and tell the Drummonds that we have an urgent investigation to attend to."

"I would if I thought we could get away with it. We'll have to console ourselves that at least there will be dancing after they have emptied our pockets." Dancing with Grace was a delight Charlie could never get enough of. He turned his wife around and piled her hair up. Grace could slice open a human body or pick a lock with absolute concentration and precision, but she was all thumbs and frustration when it came to the art of styling hair. To his surprise, he found the task soothing, and the results would have done a marginally competent lady's maid proud.

With a mouth full of hairpins, Charlie mumbled it was good to see her looking so well. She was still so slight that two of her could fit within his broad shadow, but it was a vast improvement on what she had been like at the end of the previous year, when she had been gaunt and exhausted. His wife was now glowing with vitality, with curves in places they had never been before.

Grace splashed herself with rosewater to cover the fact that she hadn't had time for a bath. She'd always been a hard worker, but this final year of her medical degree had put her under even more pressure than normal.

He took the opportunity for another lingering kiss on her neck while putting on her necklace. "Next year, we will no longer be announced as Mr and Mrs Penrose Pyke. You will be Doctor Penrose Pyke, the third generation of doctors in the Penrose family."

"If I pass my finals," Grace said, holding up crossed fingers.

Charlie checked he had his pocketbook, having been warned that they would not escape the auction without being landed with one or more items. Anne had promised to brief them on auction etiquette on the way. And, right on time, he saw the Drummonds' carriage coming down High Street.

During the drive, Anne explained the complicated and unspoken rules of the charity auction. In short, whereas the hospital charity's

21

Christmas ball was an opportunity for attendees to impress with their finery, it was best to don last year's fashions and modest jewellery for the auction, as if to say, "yes, I'm well-to-do, but times are dreadfully tough this year". The whole auction seemed to be a subtle game, aimed at getting rid of possessions one didn't like, whilst at the same time avoiding being stuck with someone else's cast-offs.

Anne's enthusiasm was infectious. Her stiff gait and ever-present walking stick might give her away as a woman in her mid-seventies, but she had the mischievous *joie de vivre* of a child and a scalpel-sharp mind and tongue. Her second husband, Kenneth Drummond, an eminent retired barrister, matched her in wit and intellect.

As they drew up outside the Scottish baronial splendour of Garrison Hall, at the bottom of Dowling Street, Anne summed up her advice. "You must spend enough to be generous to the hospital charity fund, without getting carried away by the excitement. Read the auction list and have a target in mind. I've got my eye on items for Lavender House, so you better not outbid me. Above all, do not drink too much, for alcohol can be deadly to your pocketbook."

"Heed that advice," Kenneth Drummond said, as he handed the ladies out of the carriage, "or you may end up with an enormous set of antlers in your drawing room, as I did last year."

Anne laughed with the glee of a woman who might well have had a pre-event sherry or two. "That specimen has been put up for auction every year for at least a decade. Speak of the devil, there it is again."

A slight but muscular man in his twenties staggered up the steps with an enormous set of red deer antlers mounted on a heavy oak base. Charlie went to his aid to prevent any of the waiting auction-goers from being gored before they could spend their money. They deposited the spiky beast on a table groaning with an astonishing assortment of donations. The man nodded a brief thanks, before dropping his head again and shuffling sideways through the door, presumably for another load of auction delights. Charlie wasn't sure if the man felt out of place because of his ill-fitting suit, which looked too baggy to be his own, or if he felt self-conscious because of the uneven triangle of the port-wine birthmark that slashed across his face from eye to cheek. Both probably.

Charlie returned to the entrance, where Grace and the Drummonds were waiting in the queue to show their tickets. Anne exchanged a few words with the couple ahead of them, while Grace chatted to an acquaintance further down the queue. The couple speaking to Anne moved off as Charlie returned, having shown their tickets. They entered the foyer, where they shed their outerwear into the arms of a manservant, who accepted the garments as if he was used to being treated as a clotheshorse. The manservant didn't so much as blink as he retreated the ten paces to the cloakroom and deposited the coats, before standing in the foyer with the other servants, awaiting his next command. At least he wouldn't end up with antlers on his wall, Charlie thought, as he helped Anne with her cloak.

"Mr and Mrs Vale," Anne said, seeing Charlie watching the couple. "Not part of my social circle. Mrs Vale is taking her turn on the auction committee, as all respectable society ladies must do when their shoulder is tapped. Everyone who is anyone must be seen to be here, but I suspect Matthew and Rosannah Vale are unwilling participants."

"Their sour faces certainly suggest it," Charlie said. The Vales were a handsome couple in a quiet, respectable way, without the loudness of manner or dress that would make them memorable in this diverse crowd. "I take it that Mr and Mrs Vale do not care for such frivolous activities?"

"Oh, it's not the auction itself," Anne said. "They do not care to be seen in the company of Mrs Vale's brother when he is performing."

"Is Mrs Vale's brother a musician?"

23

Anne shook her head. "He's been persuaded to take the role of auctioneer, although I doubt it took much arm-twisting. The chairwoman of the auction committee, Mrs MacDonnell, insisted that Crabtree would be the perfect candidate. I suspect she is right, because I've heard the man could sell mutton to a sheep farmer. You have been warned."

Grace came up behind them and took her great-aunt's arm. "Crabtree? That name came up at the surgery today. Is he a doctor?"

"Barnabas Crabtree calls himself a doctor," Anne said, "but he is little more than a silver-tongued showman, if you ask me. I'm surprised you haven't heard of him, Grace. He's been advertising the latest advances in Galvanic Therapy in the *Otago Daily Times* in recent months."

"When do I have time to read a newspaper? My head is ready to explode with all the extra assignments they are piling on us for our final year of medical studies."

A waiter interrupted to offer them a selection of drinks from a silver tray. Charlie took glasses of fruit punch for himself and Grace, heeding Anne's warning about the hazards of alcohol. He had taken a gulp before he realised his mistake. The punch was spiked with rum. Before he could warn his wife, Grace was whisked away by Doctor Harvey to join a group of doctors. Her focus was soon on the discussion rather than the drink she was glugging down to quench her thirst.

"Battleship approaching on the starboard bow," Kenneth Drummond whispered in Charlie's ear. "On guard, Charlie. Mrs MacDonnell has scented new blood."

A woman in a dark red gown bore down upon them, her ample bosom adorned with a diamond necklace and her coiled hair topped with peacock plumes. Apparently, the sombre dress code did not extend to the chairwoman of the charity committee. "Greetings to you all. And who do we have here?"

"Allow me to introduce Mr Charles Penrose Pyke," Kenneth said. "A newlywed forging his way in the world, so take pity on him, Mrs MacDonnell."

The lady gave him the triumphant smile of an admiral giving the order to fire on a weaker vessel. "The poor folks in need of hospital care they cannot afford are the ones we should be pitying tonight, don't you think, Mr Drummond?" She turned to Charlie, sizing him up. "Would you be the Mr Penrose Pyke who has featured in the newspaper for your *highly successful* detective exploits?"

Charlie bowed his head. "You cannot believe everything you read in the newspapers, Mrs MacDonnell."

"You are far too modest, Mr Penrose Pyke. I am sure our dear Mrs Drummond will not let you escape without joining in the fun of bidding."

"So I have been informed, Mrs MacDonnell," Charlie replied. "I am told it is best to make a spectacle of oneself in pursuit of a favoured lot. It will be my honour to contribute to the welfare of the sick and impoverished."

Her full-throated laugh boomed in his ear. "Splendid. That's the spirit. As the chairwoman of the committee, it is my role to swoop on naive new attendees to wring money out of them. However, it seems my work here is done."

Charlie waved a hand at the packed hall. "You have done a splendid job of organising the event, Mrs MacDonnell. I'm told the auctioneer you chose has a silver tongue."

"Doctor Crabtree is an absolute marvel." Mrs MacDonnell cast an adoring glance at the man on the stage. "My lumbago is vastly improved since I consulted him, which is nothing short of a miracle after the suffering it caused me. There are rumblings within the medical fraternity about his pioneering approach to medicine, but if you ask me, they could learn a thing or two from a man of his talent. He trained in London, you know, so we are very fortunate to have him on our far-flung shores. If it hadn't been for his father being struck down by apoplexy, he would be tending the *beau monde* in Harley Street."

"Every cloud has a silver lining, as the saying goes," Charlie said, because his hostess had paused, obviously expecting words of appreciation for the doctor's talents.

"Quite so. And now, if you will excuse me, duty calls." Mrs MacDonnell gave him an encouraging pat on the arm, then sailed off to hunt down fresh targets.

Anne watched her progress. "What a marvellous chairwoman she makes. The hospital charity will make a record haul tonight, if I am not mistaken."

Charlie was surprised to find that he was enjoying himself. He drained his glass and recklessly accepted another. He shook hands and exchanged pleasantries, working his way over to Grace's group of doctors in time to catch the end of their conversation.

"One of my patients severely compromised his recovery by stopping his prescribed medication on Crabtree's advice," Doctor Beechworth was saying. "And now, Doctor Crabtree put your patient's life at risk, Andrew. Enough is enough. We must act without delay."

Beechworth was speaking to Doctor Andrew Harvey, which meant the patient he referred to was probably the one who caused Grace to be late home. The base of Charlie's spine tingled – always an ominous sign. He ought to have known better than to indulge in the flood of contentment he'd been feeling all day. Whenever he felt his life seemed perfect, a particularly gnarly case came along to jerk him back to reality.

Doctor Harvey's fluffy white whiskers bobbed up and down as he nodded his agreement. "Absolutely. However, we must proceed with caution. In my patient's case, it's fair to say the risk arose mainly from the patient's foolish use of the electrical device. Before we act, we must find out exactly what this so-called doctor is selling and what treatments he is advocating, because we cannot shut his operation down without evidence of fraud or malpractice. After all, there may be some merit in using electricity for certain medical conditions. I'm old enough to remember the reluctance of doctors to accept many marvellous medical advances of our age. We'd still be relying on leeches and pooh-poohing germ theory if the naysayers had their way."

"What do you suggest?" another doctor asked.

Doctor Harvey nodded towards Grace. "Mrs Penrose Pyke has kindly volunteered to investigate. She can attend one of Crabtree's public demonstrations and buy an electrical device to test without raising suspicion, unlike the rest of us."

"I will visit his surgery too," Grace said. "Doctor Crabtree has donated a consultation to the auction, which will be perfect for our plan. Once we know whether he is a charlatan, we can act."

"I'm not sure that putting Grace at risk is a good idea in light of –" Doctor Beechworth didn't finish the sentence because he noticed Charlie had joined them. "Although if Grace's husband has agreed to let her investigate, I can have no objection."

The other doctors agreed. Grace gave Charlie an apologetic shrug that left him with a sinking feeling in his stomach. Not that he would have stopped Grace from investigating, even if he had been asked. He hadn't married a strong-minded, intelligent woman with the aim of curbing her talents, although occasionally he wished they could discuss such matters before she agreed to venture into the lion's den.

The group of doctors broke up, leaving Charlie and Grace with Doctor Harvey.

"Good evening, Charlie," Doctor Harvey said. "I've told Grace she can investigate during practice hours, so as not to cause any inconvenience to her home life or medical studies. Can you start tomorrow, Grace?" He handed her a newspaper clipping.

"By all means. I must admit I am intrigued." Grace liberated another glass of punch from a passing tray and glugged it down.

"Go easy on the punch," Charlie said. "There's more rum than fruit in it, and we don't want to end up with those red deer antlers."

27

He read the clipping over her shoulder. It was an advertisement for a demonstration tomorrow morning at eleven o'clock, promising: *A Dazzling Display by a World-Leading Professor of Galvanism direct from London! Be Amazed By The Latest Medical Marvel! Cure All Ailments Using the Latest Developments in the Life-Enhancing Healing Energies of Electricity! Guaranteed Safe And Efficacious!!*

What a load of bollocks, he thought, although he couldn't help feeling intrigued too. However, his main concern was Grace's safety. "I can't come with you tomorrow. Promise me you'll take someone with you. Aunt Lily has an interest in electricity."

"Of course," Grace said, but her thoughts were clearly elsewhere, leaving Charlie to wonder what recklessness she was planning.

Silver Tongue

Grace excused herself and hurried to the fresh air of the foyer, cursing the idiot who put rum in the fruit punch. No wonder she'd been feeling increasingly dizzy during the doctors' discussion.

Fortunately, the only people in the foyer were the young man who'd carried the deer antlers and a man he was engaged in conversation with, whose spotless attire and portly figure suggested he might be a butler or valet. Hopefully, they would ignore her. She took a seat, leaning forward with her head in her hands.

"May I be of assistance, madam?"

Grace looked up at the smooth, ageless face of the butler-valet. The combination of alcohol and the compassion in his eyes loosened her lips. "A glass of water would be greatly appreciated, thank you. It seems some prankster dosed the punch with rum. I haven't eaten all day, you see …" Her words trailed off into embarrassment, because the poor man appeared mortified at hearing the details of her disgrace.

The manservant hurried away, returning with a glass of water and food, which was presented to her artistically arranged on a plate, complete with cutlery and napkin. He still seemed embarrassed, perhaps at his inability to conjure up a table laid with a snow-white tablecloth, silverware, and candles.

"You're an angel, thank you." Grace hoped he'd leave her alone so she could tuck in with unladylike haste, to calm her growling stomach. When he didn't leave, she felt obliged to say something to break the uncomfortable silence. "I hope you didn't get into trouble for raiding the supper table early."

"Not in the least, madam. My employer's daughter, Mrs Vale, was in charge of arranging supper, and, er, the drinks." The pallor of his face flared red at Grace's inquiring glance. "I feel obliged to

29

apologise on behalf of my employer. It seems the lady's brother added the rum without her knowledge to, er, encourage lively bidding. Mr and Mrs Vale intend to leave as soon as the auction begins. I'm sure, in the circumstances, they would be willing to take you home in their carriage."

She was touched by his thoughtfulness, especially as he had nothing to apologise for. "Thank you for your gracious offer, but I have no doubt the food and water you provided will restore me. I wouldn't want to miss the excitement of the auction."

The manservant departed to a discreet distance, his friend having left. Grace tucked into the food, which had the desired restorative effect. As she ate, she recalled the earlier conversation with Anne about Mrs Vale and realised the errant, rum-toting brother was none other than Doctor Crabtree, auctioneer and potential charlatan. It seemed he was destined to disrupt her peaceful life.

The rum incident could be laughed off as a prank had it been the work of a foolish young scallywag, just as Mrs Atkinson's near-death experience could be put down to foolishness had she purchased the electric belt from an unqualified salesman. However, Grace's blood boiled to think both incidents were caused by a qualified doctor, who ought to have known better. Doctor Barnabas Crabtree had better watch his step, because she would be starting her investigation tomorrow, and she wasn't in a forgiving mood.

When she finished her repast, she took the plate and glass back inside the hall and found a seat next to Anne, moments before the auction began. Charlie was sitting with Doctor and Mrs Harvey, two rows behind her. Judging from the lively banter between him and Mrs Harvey, Charlie hadn't been alarmed by his wife's absence.

Mrs MacDonnell stepped onto the stage and gave a rousing, but thankfully short, speech on the desperate need for funds to create a hospital worthy of the fine city of Dunedin. After introducing the auctioneer and heaping praise upon him as if he were royalty, she said, "Pocketbooks out everyone, and don't forget I can see every last one of you from up here."

And then the auctioneer was off and running, beguiling the audience with encouragement to spend up for a worthy cause under the guise of amusing banter. Grace had to give Doctor Crabtree his due. With his natural showmanship, she had little doubt that his business selling medical devices would be a tremendous success. Grace glared and ladies giggled, as he swiped back flowing locks from a patrician face and flashed a set of unnaturally white teeth every time he made a well-received joke. The combination of excitement, laughter and excessive quantities of alcohol worked its magic; the coffers of the hospital charity would get a much-needed boost, while the attendees enjoyed an amusing night out.

Belatedly, Grace realised the auction was several lots in and she hadn't yet done her duty by bidding. The next lot was a gorgeous peacock shawl in a Chinese style. From what she could see, it was the perfect replacement for her much-cherished, but worse for wear, silk shawl, which had been Charlie's first gift to her. To her surprise, the bidding was spirited. She was about to shout out another bid, when Anne nudged her in the ribs. Grace looked around, seeing her husband leap to his feet and shout out a truly outrageous bid, which drew applause from the audience. Grace gave him a rueful grimace, and the shawl was his.

"Thank you for your marvellous generosity, young man," the auctioneer boomed. "I'm sure some fortunate young lady will be delighted with your purchase."

The portion of the audience who had spotted the determined bidders and knew they were married burst into jovial cheers, to which Charlie bowed. His was by no means the only outrageous bid of the evening. Anne, who must have ignored her own advice to go easy on the alcohol, laid claim to a gorgeous mahogany cradle for an eye-watering price. She seemed delighted to have won the bid and muttered an aside to Grace about there being an influx of babies at her Lavender House women's refuge.

31

The deer antlers were next up. Grace shrank in her seat to avoid the eagle eye of the auctioneer. To her surprise, Mrs Harvey won the bid against less than spirited opposition. Indeed, the audience let out a collective sigh of relief, knowing that they wouldn't be landed with the antlers this year.

The following lot was a personal consultation with Doctor Crabtree, which Grace snapped up, in the interests of her investigation, after outlasting a bevy of eager ladies. The auctioneer professed his humble appreciation, while failing to conceal his delight that his services were considered so desirable. According to one of the other doctors she had talked to earlier, Crabtree had only been in town for a few months, but he had already built up an enthusiastic following. "Fervent acolytes" was the term the doctor had used, which is not a term that should be associated with a reputable doctor, in Grace's opinion.

When the last item was dispatched to a new owner, the chairs were cleared for supper.

Charlie met her at the auction table, where they paid for their purchases. He wrapped the beautiful shawl around her shoulders. "Aunt Lily bought it from the Chinese handicrafts group, thinking it would be perfect for you. Shall we get supper before you collapse from hunger?"

"Would you mind terribly if we went home now?" Grace said. "I hate to drag you away from the supper and dancing, but that dratted punch has left me feeling woozy."

Galvanic Display

The next morning, Grace tumbled out of bed at an early hour, fighting back nausea and cursing Crabtree's rum. She stumbled downstairs and emptied the contents of her stomach in the water closet.

In the kitchen, she made herself a strong pot of black tea and nibbled on a slice of gingerbread. Neither was permitted by the eating regime she had been testing over the past three months, but it was all she could force down to settle her innards. Besides, the eating regime had worked spectacularly. Almost too well. From being lethargic and excessively thin, she had blossomed into a round-cheeked version of her former self, with a renewed vitality that owed nothing to spurious medical devices.

But vitality was far from evident this morning. Grace had planned to finish her essay, then go to the medical school library to read about the therapeutic uses of electricity before attending the demonstration at eleven o'clock. However, all she wanted to do this morning was to take her tea and curl up in a ball somewhere warm and dark.

Blaze got up from her blanket by the coal range, nosing up against her and whining softly.

"Hungry, Blaze?" The collie pushed her nose against Grace again, making her wonder if their highly intuitive dog was sympathising with her mistress's self-inflicted illness. "Or are you excited about meeting an eligible suitor?"

"The latter, I hope," Charlie said. "Are you unwell, Grace?"

Grace jumped at his voice. Despite his size, her husband moved as silently as a panther. Or a dancer, depending on the circumstances. "Just getting an early start," she said, ignoring his question. "You're up with the birds, too."

33

"I thought I'd take Blaze to the breeder early. I'd like to get back in time to join you and Lily at the *Dazzling Display by a World-Leading Professor of Galvanism direct from London.*" Charlie bent down to scoop food into Blaze's dish, then stepped aside before he was bowled over by his loyal canine companion. "Forgive my cynicism, but I can't help being suspicious of anyone promising a *Guaranteed Safe And Successful Cure for All Ailments*, especially when the proclamation is followed by multiple exclamation marks."

"Perhaps you underestimate the *Latest Developments in the Life-Enhancing Healing Energies of Electricity!!*" Grace said, fluttering her fingers in the air like a music hall chorus girl.

Charlie's return smile didn't reach his worried eyes. When his hands slipped from his hips to the base of his spine, Grace wondered if her husband was feeling the tingling sensation that warned him of trouble ahead. Or maybe it was simply that his shirt was over-starched.

"I hope you will be careful, my love," he said. "Electricity can be extremely hazardous. As can charlatans who feel their livelihood is threatened."

"I'll be careful. I'm a perfectly healthy young woman, after all. His devices cannot be harmful, or elderly and ill patients would be dropping like flies."

"You're too precious to lose, dearest wife. Promise you won't see this charlatan on your own."

"I won't. There's no need for you to hurry home, Charlie. I'll take Lily with me, I promise." She pointed at the teapot. "Tea's still hot. I'm going back to bed." Grace gave Blaze an encouraging rub around their ears and wished her well in her search for true love, before shuffling upstairs to snuggle under her blankets.

Grace woke up with a jerk at the sound of the front door closing and the clock chiming. Ten chimes – she'd better get moving.

34

The tread on the stairs was far too delicate for Charlie and lacked the characteristic thump of her Great-Aunt Anne's walking cane. After the extra sleep, Grace's brain was functioning again, if somewhat sluggish. She put two and two together to equal Lily Stewart, her husband's petite, clever aunt. In looks, Lily took after her Chinese father, while Charlie was the image of his English father. He must have gone next door to arrange for Lily to escort Grace to the demonstration of electrical devices.

Not wishing to be caught indulging in an outrageously long sleep-in, Grace poked her head out the door and called down the stairs. "Just getting ready, Lily. Can you give me ten minutes, please?"

Within the hour, Grace and Lily entered the hall with minutes to spare before the start of the demonstration of galvanism. Of the few remaining seats, they chose off-centre seats in the third row, not wanting to draw attention to themselves but wanting to be close to the action. The hall was more often used for plays and recitals than scientific demonstrations, but Grace suspected Doctor Barnabas Crabtree would exploit the melodrama of the location as ably as any Shakespearean villain.

A booming drumroll cut across the chatter of the audience. The gaslights around the hall dimmed. In a blaze of light, the maroon velvet curtains parted to reveal an electrical apparatus in the middle of the stage, drawing a gasp of excited anticipation. The hall plunged into darkness seconds later. Just when they thought it must be a fault with the lighting, the stage blazed with an intensely bright, flickering light, as if miniature bolts of lightning were arcing between the two rods across the apparatus. The audience erupted in gasps and squeals. A woman in front of them shrieked and hid her face against her companion's shoulder.

"A simple voltaic arc between two carbon rods," Lily whispered with a touch of asperity. "Humphrey Davy demonstrated the effect at the turn of the century. The same principle that powers electric arc lights used for street lighting in more advanced cities."

Before Grace could reply, the arc light flickered out, and a spotlight illuminated a figure at the far side of the stage – Doctor Crabtree, his long locks swept backwards and gleaming. Given the dramatic introduction, Grace expected Crabtree to be wearing a top hat and swirling cape lined with scarlet satin, but the doctor was clad in a medical coat, stiff and searingly white in the bright light. He paused to pose with his fingers on an outthrust chin, the light catching his handsome profile. Behind Grace, a lady swooned.

After a long pause to build anticipation, Crabtree's voice boomed in the deep, entrancing cadence that had worked so effectively to separate last night's auction attendees from their hard-earned savings.

"Welcome, ladies and gentlemen. You are about to witness a dazzling display of one of the foremost wonders of modern science. I am Doctor Barnabas Crabtree. After seeing for myself the astonishing power of galvanism to heal, I set about training under the foremost specialists in London to become a fully qualified Professor of Galvanism. And now I am back in my hometown and at your service."

He raised his hand, and the electric arc sparked to life again. "And God said, 'Let there be light,' and there was light. And God saw that the light was good."

Clever, Grace thought. Opponents of the experimental use of electricity on the human body argued that it was ungodly. Doctor Crabtree was astute enough to nip that powerful criticism in the bud.

"God made fire and lightning," Crabtree said, "which can be terrifying to us mere mortals. But He also gave man the power of invention, to harness fire and lightning for the betterment of society in this great age of scientific innovation. When my grandfather was my age, he gazed in awe at his first sight of a steam engine. Now, we cannot imagine what life would be like without steam engines to carry us between cities at astonishing speed or power the machines that drive a veritable revolution in technology."

Crabtree paused for the audience to nod their agreement. "By the time you have grandchildren, ladies and gentlemen, they will look back and laugh at how uninformed people feared electricity. Folks who quiver at sensationalist journal articles of corpses being reanimated, or lurid novels featuring Frankensteinian monsters. But not us. We know this is mere artifice intended to shock. Those gathered here today understand the truth is far more uplifting. We are witnessing the birth of a revolution in medicine."

Grace recognised the ruse as one used by astute salesmen and fraudsters alike. Make the audience think they are smarter than the average person for believing in whatever was being sold to them; make the audience feel they are on the cusp of a revelation – a secret given to them alone. She remained deeply suspicious. The very idea of a doctor touting his wares in a public forum was reason enough to label the man a quack, since such behaviour was considered unethical within the medical profession. Still, she didn't wish to judge him prematurely, because it was also true that some doctors recommended electrotherapeutic treatments within the regulated confines of their practices using devices sourced from reputable companies.

Another drum roll covered the rumble of a second apparatus onto the stage, wheeled by an assistant dressed entirely in black, making him almost invisible.

"Did you know that the body makes its own electricity?" Crabtree said. "It is our life force, giving us the wholly natural vitality we need to live our best lives. My medical electric devices enhance that natural force. Allow me to demonstrate. Who is willing to test my statical machine?"

Doctor Crabtree selected a young man with long hair from the few brave souls who tentatively raised their hands. The man bounded onto the stage and exchanged a few words with Crabtree.

"Please give a round of applause to a courageous young man, Bob from South Dunedin." Crabtree directed the man to sit on the glass platform of the machine. "Shall I turn it on, ladies and gentlemen?"

When the cheers and applause subsided, Crabtree faced the audience and put a finger over his lips to silence them, out of sight of his volunteer. "Bob, I want you to tell us if you feel anything."

Crabtree nodded to his assistant, who turned a knob on the machine. Bob fidgeted as he waited for the electrical charge to pulse through his body. His nervousness turned to puzzlement when the audience broke into raucous laughter and applause.

"Do you feel anything, Bob?" Crabtree asked.

"Maybe a kind of buzzing. It don't hurt none."

The doctor winked at the audience and held up a mirror to show Bob what the audience was laughing at. The volunteer's hair rose straight upwards, as if each strand was attached to an invisible wire hung from the ceiling. Bob's jaw gaped at the sight. He tentatively lifted a hand to his electrified hair, not quite believing what the mirror reflected.

"There you see it, ladies and gentlemen, electricity moving through the body, causing the hair to rise without the least discomfort to the patient. Completely safe and yet endowing the body with incredible powers."

Crabtree took a gas burner from his assistant and held it out. "Hold your finger to the end if you dare, Bob."

When Bob's trembling finger ignited the gas to produce a spurt of flame, Grace had to put her hand over her ears to shut out the thunderous cacophony of gasping, hooting, cheering, stamping, and applause. She had to admit it was a dazzling spectacle, even if the display had nothing to do with medicine.

"Are there any young ladies in the audience who would like to kiss this young man? I assure you, sparks are guaranteed to fly!" Crabtree laughed at the chorus of squeals. "No? Perhaps for the best. Step down, thank you, Bob."

38

After Bob received due applause and returned to the audience, Crabtree gripped the lapels of his white coat and adopted a serious expression. "But this is mere amusement. My life's mission is far more vital – nothing short of curing illness and revitalising spirits. Who among us could not benefit from that?"

Crabtree went on to list an astonishingly comprehensive range of conditions that would benefit from the application of electricity, from arthritis, back pain, and constipation, on through an entire alphabet of malaise, from gout to hysteria, indigestion, ladies' complaints, nervous exhaustion, paralysis, rheumatism, and sciatica.

As an almost-qualified medical doctor, Grace remained highly sceptical that one method could cure so many diverse conditions. However, the Professor of Galvanism made it sound believable when he explained how gentle applications of electricity could move through the body, soothing the knotted muscles and damaged nerves that caused pain and illness.

"But don't take my word for it. Can I have Mr Ebert and Mrs Fernyhough onto the stage, please?"

A middle-aged man ascended the stage and told the audience how he had been paralysed in one shoulder for fifteen years before he sought help from Doctor Crabtree as a last resort. He circled his arms to show the miraculous difference the course of treatments had made, while praising the doctor for this miracle. Mrs Fernyhough gave a similar testimonial, going so far as to call Doctor Crabtree an angel sent from heaven for curing her after years of crippling sciatica. They returned to the audience to thunderous applause.

"And, of course," Crabtree said, waving a thick wad of letters, "I have hundreds of written testimonials from my Harley Street practice in London, as well as from appreciative patients here in Dunedin, which you are welcome to peruse later. But you don't want to hear words of praise and profound gratitude, do you? You are here for a practical demonstration of the curative powers of galvanism."

The audience, having been goaded to a pinnacle of excitement, cheered and stamped their feet, while a brave minority jumped up, waving their arms to be the chosen one.

"My goodness," Doctor Crabtree said, feigning astonishment, "so many willing volunteers! I need someone who suffers mild aches or a lack of vitality to test my restorative 'Electropathic Belt'. The gentlest of electrical currents, scarcely more than a tickle, will pulse pleasantly into the body to unblock the sources of pain and distress. Perhaps the lady in mauve?" he said, pointing to a middle-aged woman at the end of the second row.

The lady shuffled forward, her pinched face a combination of nerves, embarrassment, and doubt under an elegant mauve hat. First, Crabtree established that he and the woman were strangers to each other. He then held up a broad belt, which looked similar to the one Grace had removed from Mrs Atkinson's house yesterday. The lady went behind a screen with a female assistant who looked familiar. After a moment's reflection, Grace recognised her as Mrs Rosannah Vale, who had been at the auction. Anne had said Mrs Vale was Doctor Crabtree's sister, but also that she did not care to be seen in the company of her brother when he was performing. From the sour pinch of Mrs Vale's lips, she was not here by choice.

"While we wait, perhaps I could show you my range of health-giving devices," Crabtree said, holding up each new marvel as he spoke. "The Electropathic Belt is just one of many curative marvels I offer to you. Here I have a Pocket Magneto Electric Machine for general vitality, one of my many medical batteries of every strength and size for home use, complete with cables and probes for simple application to the affected area of the body. All products can be used by menfolk too, providing a marvellous enhancement to manly vitality."

Crabtree emphasised the last two words and paused to let the hint sink in. More than a few necks craned to see the device, both

40

men and their wives. The doctor obliged by walking to and fro, holding the portable battery aloft for all to admire.

"Gentlemen, your other needs are not forgotten! These electrical socks are perfect for rheumatism and gout, while keeping the feet warm on these cold autumnal nights and soothing away the agony of a long day on one's feet at work. This electrical hairbrush is marvellous for stimulating the scalp, banishing headaches and encouraging a glossy head of hair."

The doctor swept back his own flowing locks at this point, causing the balding man beside Grace to lean forward eagerly and sigh.

The volunteer reappeared from behind the screen in a garment that looked to be the offspring of a medical gown and a circus tent, presumably for the sake of her modesty. Crabtree stepped in front of her, explaining the procedure to her at length in a soft, beguiling voice. At first, his words were only for the volunteer, but his voice rose for all to hear at the end. "This brave lady will feel a mild buzzing and a feeling of intense well-being as the blockages within her system dissipate and vitality is restored. She will feel renewed, refreshed. Are you ready to be astonished, madam?"

The woman's obvious terror dropped away to mild worry under the spell of the doctor's persuasive tone. She nodded eagerly when he asked if she was ready.

The audience held their breath, perhaps fearing that the woman would jerk and scream once the electricity pulsed through her. Instead, they witnessed the tension in the volunteer's facial muscles dissipate before their incredulous eyes. Her expression deepened into one of apparent serenity, and then into a state of bliss, without a single jerk or scream.

"Oooh!" The woman sighed, loud enough to be heard in the breath-held silence of the front rows. "That feels ... simply divine."

Crabtree waited for the full effect to be witnessed, before shutting off the device. "And how do you feel now?" he prompted.

"Renewed, refreshed. I don't feel any pain at all."

41

The audience expelled a simultaneous breath and burst into renewed applause, while the lady went back behind the screen.

Crabtree held up his hand, both to acknowledge the applause and to draw it to a halt. "You have witnessed the power of the mildest of my devices, intended to restore vitality in everyday cases. For those of you with medical conditions, I recommend a consultation at my surgery, conveniently located near the Roslyn cable tramway. A consultation will allow you to experience intensive electrical therapy far beyond what I can demonstrate in this fine hall. I can even, for a small additional fee, attend to you in the utmost privacy of your own home. My able assistant will take appointments at the right-hand table."

Mrs Vale, who had taken a seat at the table, gave a stiff smile and opened a large leather appointment book.

"And now, dear folks, I thank you for your attention and invite you to experience the life-giving force for yourself. For today only, I am offering an extraordinary opportunity to purchase one of these miraculous devices at half the regular price! Please assemble at the left-hand table to make your purchase. Again, I thank you for your kind attention and your good sense in embracing the future of medicine."

The burst of applause was briefer this time, because of the stampede towards the tables, which the assistant in black had set up while the Professor of Galvanism was speaking. The assistant stood in the shadows of a curtain behind the left-hand table, next to a tall stack of boxes, ready to resupply the stock already laid out. Grace was startled to recognise him as the young man who had carried donated goods into the auction the night before, because there couldn't be two young men with such a distinctive port-wine birthmark forming a delta between his left eye and cheek.

"Would you mind queuing to buy one of the electrical belts, Lily?" Grace asked, "while I join the other queue to make an appointment for a consultation."

42

"Make it for me, not you," Lily said. "The name Penrose Pyke might be linked with the private detective agency, whereas Mrs Stewart will not. Besides, you are far too young and full of vitality to genuinely need a medical appointment for a serious condition."

Grace didn't argue, because the queue was growing and she didn't wish to be here all day. What Lily said made sense, and Charlie would be pleased that his wife was honouring her promise not to attend the consultation alone.

While she waited, Grace reflected on what she had seen. Crabtree was a superb salesman, without a doubt, but he also showed all the classic elements of a charlatan. The use of shock-and-awe theatrical tactics, the promise of a cure no matter the ailment, the pressure to buy now or miss out on a one-time-only deal. And, of course, that old nugget, the lure of a cheap option for conditions so mild one might not discern any real improvement after treatment, especially if one was convinced of the efficacy in advance, while subtly promoting an expensive consultation for genuine medical conditions.

The final, and most definitive, proof of a charlatan would be the use of an accomplice in the audience to fake a glowing testimonial. As luck would have it, the woman who had demonstrated the belt passed Grace on her way out, clutching her gift of a free electrical belt as her reward for volunteering.

Grace stopped her with an outstretched hand. "Was it really so marvellous, madam?"

"Oh, yes," the woman said, her eyes shining. "I only came today because I wanted to protect my friend, who was desperate to attend. Frankly, I volunteered because I wanted to show the man up as a charlatan, which just shows how wrong one can be. He truly is a marvel."

She could see the woman was completely sincere. To Grace's surprise, Doctor Crabtree's electrical belt passed the fake volunteer test with flying colours. Could she and the other medical doctors be wrong? Perhaps, despite all the inappropriate theatricality, the electrical belts really were effective. There was only one way to find out.

He pulled out a chair and helped himself to a cup of tea and a piece of shortbread, suspecting his next meal would be a way off.

Wallace nodded to Charlie, ruffled Blaze's fur, and got straight down to business. "Apologies for disturbing your Saturday morning. As I was telling Alistair, we had six more burglaries last night between the hours of eight o'clock and midnight."

"A coordinated team?" Charlie suggested.

Wallace drummed his fingers on the table. "Unknown. It could be one highly organised burglar, especially if he had inside knowledge. Either way, they were in and out in minutes, leaving few clues, and taking only small, portable valuables. Undoubtedly professionals. None of the wanton damage and random grabbing of items typical of amateurs. Exactly like the rest of the burglaries we've had lately, only all at once rather than spaced out over weeks."

"Six in one night. I imagine the city's elite are up in arms."

Wallace grunted. "The Chief is breathing down my neck, demanding the case be solved before the newspapers come out on Monday. Not a chance, of course. We've no leads, and I haven't enough men for the scale of the investigation. The victims were well-off, but not necessarily obvious targets. I'm hoping the latest victims will provide the breakthrough we need to get these criminals behind bars. Hence the need for experienced boots on the ground as soon as possible." Wallace scratched Blaze's ears. "Boots and paws."

"Blaze and I are at your service," Charlie said. "Grace will do what she can too, although she has an investigation of her own underway. A medical matter."

"Your help today would be most appreciated, to give us a fighting start." Wallace looked uncharacteristically hesitant. "I'm not sure I can thank you properly."

Charlie and Alistair exchanged nods. They both knew Wallace's team operated on a paltry budget.

47

"No need for thanks of any kind," Alistair said. "You've put plenty of work our way. It would be our pleasure to return the favour."

The tension in Wallace's jaw dropped away. "Thank you. Much appreciated, as always. DS Kelly has our men doing a door-to-door inquiry in each neighbourhood. I'd like the three of us to interview two victims each." Wallace handed out a list. "These are the people who reported burglaries this morning. It took a while for the scale of the problem to come to light, because they didn't discover the thefts straight away, what with the offender being so careful. There may yet be more victims to come."

Charlie ran his eye down the list. "All these people were at the hospital charity auction last night." Mrs Harvey, displaying an unexpected talent for sharply observed humour, had kept up a running commentary on the winning bidders in Charlie's ear the previous night.

A wolfish gleam lit up Wallace's eyes. "Well done, Pyke. That's the first useful link we've found between the victims."

"Unfortunately, it's not as strong a lead as it might sound. Attendance at the auction is practically compulsory among the well-to-do classes of Dunedin. A chance to show their charitable natures, whilst having an enjoyable time."

"Still, it cannot be a coincidence that the burglar or burglars struck on the one night they could guarantee many tempting targets would be out for the evening. The previous burglaries were one-off targets. Indeed, the burglar had been so careful that it was several weeks before we realised the crimes were linked. The local stations usually deal with property crimes, as you know."

"Risky breaking a successful strategy," Alistair said. "One last grand slam before the burglar retires to balmier climes, perhaps."

"That thought crossed my mind. All the more reason to get this case solved quickly. Do you know who organised the auction, Pyke?"

Charlie tapped the third name on the victim list. "Mrs MacDonnell. A lovely lady and an excellent organiser. I talked to her briefly last night, as it happens."

"Perhaps you could interview her this morning in that case, plus the other victim on the same street. I'll interview the top two victims personally." Wallace caught Charlie's eye and held it. "All victims will be treated with equal consideration, naturally, but you should know that Mrs Atkinson is not only a wealthy and influential widow, but also the Chief Inspector's sister, while Mr Robinson is his close friend."

"Understood, sir." Charlie studied the list of victims again. "There must have been close to a hundred people at the charity auction last night, which means about fifty households, since most of them were married couples. I don't know the victims personally, but I wouldn't have said they represent the wealthiest of the people present at the auction, Mrs Atkinson excepted."

"The specific victims must have been chosen before the auction," Alistair pointed out, "because the burglar had to know in advance which houses to target. Ask Mrs MacDonnell who saw the guest list in advance."

Charlie nodded. "If the gang was well organised, which seems a certainty, they might have had a man there on the night to pass on attendees' names. A doorman, the coat-check person, even one of the auction attendees or a servant. I'll ask Mrs MacDonnell for a complete list of people present."

"Pass it on to Kelly, who'll have them all interviewed," Wallace said. "Right, let's get talking to the victims. With six in one night, the burglar's haste might have caused him to make his first mistake."

The MacDonnells' house was a substantial dwelling on Heriot Row, halfway up the slope between the low-lying city and the Town Belt that formed a ring of greenery above Dunedin. While the house

49

was not one of the grander houses built from the wealth of the land, it was far larger than the workers' cottages on the lower slopes.

Charlie showed his police authority and was directed into a pleasant sitting room with a glimpse of the harbour. Mrs MacDonnell sat with her back to the view, a shrunken imitation of the indomitable auction organiser he had met last night. She mumbled a greeting while dabbing a lace handkerchief to swollen eyes.

Her husband paced the room, clearly furious at the violation of his domain. "The police, at last. I want this scoundrel caught and punished. Damn arrogance, breaking into a man's home and stealing every last valuable we own. My wife's pearl necklace, my diamond cufflinks, everything." He handed a list of stolen items to Charlie. "Locked away in a safe, of course, but that didn't stop the blackguard."

"He took my ring, Mr Penrose Pyke," Mrs MacDonnell sobbed. "Passed down from mother to daughter for generations. Only a garnet, but priceless to me. Thank the Lord I wore my grandmother's diamonds to the auction."

Charlie noted that the list of stolen items included nothing bulky, such as silverware or paintings. "My deepest sympathies, Mrs MacDonnell. The police have assigned every available man to the case. I regret to say that five other homes were also burgled last night while the occupants were at the hospital charity auction."

This new shock had the effect of galvanising Mrs MacDonnell from her own loss. "How despicable to use a charitable event for his own gain. What can I do?"

"The police need you to supply a list of the guests who attended the auction, as well as a list of people who helped in any way. The organising committee, as well as any workers who assisted with catering, hall preparation, coat-checking, and collecting donated goods."

"I cannot believe anyone associated with our charitable endeavour had anything to do with the burglaries." She held up the sodden handkerchief to stop his apology. "However, I will, of course, do whatever I can to assist."

"I'm sure you're right, Mrs MacDonnell," Charlie said, "but we can't ignore any possibility, especially as the burglar must have known who was attending the event. Regarding the burglary of your home, can you tell me if any servants, family or guests were at home last night while you were at the auction?"

"Not a soul. Our children are old enough to have their own homes, and we have no one staying with us. We gave our housekeeper and the two maids the night off last night. The man who does the garden was assisting me at the auction, and anyway, he lives out."

Charlie recalled the man he had helped with the antlers. "Was he the young man with the birthmark below his left eye?"

"That's him," Mrs MacDonnell said. "Jack Turner. Taciturn and a little rough around the edges, but thoroughly honest and hard-working. I call him my gardener, but he only does half a day per week with us. He's rather a Jack-of-all-trades, turning his hand to gardening, odd jobs, and so forth, wherever he is needed."

"Was Turner there throughout the evening?"

"I don't know. He carried all the donations into the hall before the auction, and I asked him to stay for a while to see to any late donations. I confess I would have been at a loss without him. Jack also helped me to collect the larger items from various donors to take to the hall, bless him."

Charlie's ears perked up at this. A man who worked in and around many households, who knew who was attending the auction and who had actually collected some of the larger items from people's homes. Prior knowledge of the victims was the key to this case, in his view. Wallace would be delighted to have a potential suspect to appease the Chief Inspector.

He addressed his next question to Mr MacDonnell. "Can you tell me how the burglar got into your home?"

51

"The devil got in through a window in my study, although how he managed it, I am at a loss to explain. I myself checked that all the doors and windows were secured before we left."

"I'd like to see for myself, Mr MacDonnell."

Charlie followed him down the hall to a small room at the back of the house. The study appeared untouched. Aside from the spread of documents on the desk, there seemed to be nothing out of place. Most burglars left a chaotic scene behind them – windows broken, drawers wrenched open with the contents strewn across the floor, locked cupboards crudely jemmied, and sometimes spiteful destruction for the sake of it. Here, the only thing amiss was the rattle of a window, its catch not properly caught.

The unprecedented care the burglar had taken suggested more victims might come to light once they noticed items missing over the coming days or weeks. Like Wallace, Charlie wanted this man caught quickly. One tiny clue left, one little mistake made, was all he asked.

"I touched nothing once I found the safe empty," Mr MacDonnell said. "In fact, I wouldn't have discovered the theft if I hadn't opened the safe to put my wife's diamonds away after the auction. A pity she wasn't wearing more of her finery. She treasures that ring above everything."

"I appreciate your good sense in preserving the crime scene," Charlie said.

The auction protocol of wearing one's least valuable jewellery had come back to bite the victims. He felt a surge of sympathy at the loss of treasured items. Part of him wanted to rush home to ensure that their own valuables hadn't been targeted, but common sense told him Blaze would never have allowed such a travesty.

Charlie examined the window, noting that there were no gouges in the woodwork or other signs it had been forced open from the outside. Not so much as a scratch. Yet the trace of a boot on the sill, and a broken twig on the bush outside the window suggested it had been used for egress. He blew powder from his fingerprint kit across the sash, with no success, indicating the burglar had worn gloves.

"Are you positive this window was securely latched before you departed, Mr MacDonnell?"

"Absolutely. I travel a great deal with my work as an importer of French furniture, which has taught me the value of attention to security."

"Excellent. It looks as if the burglar departed through the window, but he didn't break in that way. May I examine the safe?"

Mr MacDonnell opened what looked like a liquor cabinet, revealing a safe built into the wall. A key-operated Chubb safe of a vintage similar to the house, and thus not a difficult one to break into if one was a trained safe-breaker with the right equipment.

"I had the key with me at the auction," Mr MacDonnell said. "I always carry it with me, unless my wife needs it. The only other key is hidden in the attic, which was undisturbed."

Charlie closed the safe. "Your security is admirable. There can be no doubt we are dealing with an expert thief."

They went back to the sitting room, where Mrs MacDonnell was ready with the requested lists. Her list of auction donors included names, addresses, and details of items pledged, with an approximate valuation to guide the auctioneer. The beautiful shawl he had brought for Grace was listed at less than half the value he had paid. Charlie considered it money well spent when he recalled the joy on Grace's face when he wrapped the shawl around her. And, of course, the joy the donation would bring to those who couldn't afford hospital care, as Mrs MacDonnell had so ably reminded him last night.

The list of attendees was more-or-less a match for the list of donors, although several people, like his Aunt Lily, had made donations but not attended on the night. The list of helpers was shorter and included Jack Turner. Most of the rest were serving staff supplied by the owners of the hall.

In return, Charlie showed Mrs MacDonnell the list of burglary victims.

"I see what you mean," she said. "I can confirm they were all at the auction. As you see, all the victims donated goods as well. The auction is our biggest fundraiser of the year. One never knows when one will need hospital services, so people are generous with their support."

"We need to know why these particular households were targeted," Charlie said. "Can you identify any specific links between the victims? Were they friends, for example, or part of a particular social group?"

"Dunedin is a small enough city that most of us share a general acquaintance. I play bridge with this lady," Mrs MacDonnell said, pointing to one name. "And this gentleman is a member of a club my husband attends, but I wouldn't count any of them as close friends. These two, I visited in my quest for donations, but not the rest, since other committee members shared the task. There is no single link between us that I can fathom."

Charlie wasted another ten minutes asking about any suspicious activities they had noted over recent days and any doubts about the trustworthiness of their servants, tradesmen, and delivery boys, with no success. It spoke well of Mrs MacDonnell that the housekeeper and maids had been with her for years, with not the slightest problem.

"I have enough for now, thank you," he said. "Another detective may return with further questions if necessary. My last request of you is to bring my tracking dog into the house to get the scent of the offender."

"By all means," Mr MacDonnell replied. "Whatever it takes to get the swine who did this."

Charlie took Blaze through the house to get the scents of the residents, before taking her into the study and showing her the area around the safe and window. Then he took her outside to sniff the exterior under the study window. Blaze led him away from the window, following the scent around to the front of the house with gratifying certainty. She exited the gate onto the street and hesitated, sniffing first in one direction and then the other.

He directed her to the left first. Blaze took him to a bush in the corner of the adjoining property, where she whined and pointed. Broken twigs and the boot prints of a man stomping the ground to keep warm suggested the burglar had waited here for the occupants to leave for their evening's entertainment. Charlie bagged a half-eaten apple, discarded underneath the bush, along with a snapped-off end of twig lying on top of the apple.

Blaze followed the trail back to the MacDonnell's house, not stopping at the gate, but continuing on around the other side of the house to the back door. Charlie already suspected the burglar had only exited the window, rather than entering that way. Blaze's tracking confirmed an entry through the back door. Given the lack of scratches around the keyhole, and no signs of forced entry, it seemed almost certain the burglar either had a key or an inside accomplice. A key, presumably, given Mrs MacDonnell's certainty about her servants' honesty. He wasn't ready to rule an accomplice out though, because a burglar of sufficient charm might have wooed a maid in every house.

Charlie knocked at the door and was let in by the housekeeper-cook. She swore that neither she nor her girls would let a man past the door, not even the regular delivery boys. After apologising for the further intrusion, Charlie urged Blaze on. The dog padded through the house, nose to the floor, stopping briefly in the sitting room, and longer in the master bedroom, pointing to an elegant French-style chest of drawers and a matching compact writing desk.

"The burglar stopped in here," Charlie said to Mr MacDonnell, who was now following them. "Have you checked the contents of the drawers and desk this morning?"

"I have. Nothing has been taken, as there was nothing of value in either room. Or nothing easy to remove. The various pieces of antique furniture are by far the most valuable items in the house, apart from the jewellery that was stolen. Dash it, I hate to think of this scoundrel pawing through our possessions."

"We'll get him, I promise." Charlie hoped he could live up to his word. If the burglar had any sense, he'd have taken his ill-gotten gains and fled the city on the early morning train.

The only other stop Blaze made was at the study. Charlie wasn't sure if the burglar knew the layout of the house in advance, or he was sufficiently well versed in the art of burglary to know that small items of value would only be kept in a few specific rooms. Either way, if he burgled at least six houses within the space of about four hours, he must have worked swiftly and efficiently.

Charlie left Mr and Mrs MacDonnell comforting each other. At the front gate, he directed Blaze to follow the scent to the right. Her route didn't deviate until they arrived at another house further up the street. Charlie consulted his list and saw, without surprise, that this household had also been burgled.

He knocked on the door and repeated the interview and scene examination process, with near-identical results. The burglar was a man of method. And now a rich man, given the extensive list of stolen items. There was no sign of the burglar having waited and watched this household, which suggested the MacDonnells' house was the first target. Presumably, the burglar had known that Mrs MacDonnell was the auction organiser and thus likely to be one of the earliest arrivals at the event.

Blaze continued to follow the scent to a third house, where Charlie found Alistair Stewart exiting after his second interview. Alistair had a similar story to tell, although a maid had been home at this house. The maid had taken the opportunity to catch up on sleep and heard nothing. Alistair told him a nursemaid and children were at home in the first household he interviewed, but they were upstairs in a large house and heard nothing of the burglar, who restricted his activities to the ground floor and the main bedroom wing.

The common thread, aside from the charity auction and the meticulous execution of the burglaries, was that the victims were sufficiently wealthy to have valuables, while not having a large enough staff to put the burglar at a significant risk of discovery. None of the householders could identify a link between all the victims.

"Quite the puzzle, isn't it, Alistair?" Charlie said. "Unless you've found any clues, the main fact we have established is that it seems to be a single burglar, according to Blaze's nose."

Alistair shook his head. "I hope she can track this rogue to his lair, because Blaze's nose is about all we have right now."

Charlie tossed Blaze one of his homemade dog treats as a reward, which she caught in mid-air. "I do have a couple of items I'd like to examine back at the office. Could you take Blaze from here?"

They parted ways. Charlie watched them go with mixed feelings, because he agreed with Alistair's assessment that Blaze was their only hope, and he wanted to be there if she tracked the burglar to his lair. Instead, he headed home with his meagre haul of clues. A broken twig and a half-eaten apple. He could imagine the chief inspector's chilly reception when he heard about these underwhelming finds. Still, they had made progress of sorts. Wallace would be grateful for any crevice in which to drive the tip of the wedge that would eventually crack the case wide open. He'd be delighted to have a potential suspect in Jack "Jack-of-all-trades" Turner.

Apple and Twig

Grace ate a late lunch alone at home, her mind churning through what she had seen at the demonstration of therapeutic electrical devices. The entire dazzling melodrama of the show smelled as rank as month-old milk to her mind, but she was yet to reconcile her gut reaction with the many letters of enthusiastic endorsement she had perused and the shining glow of the volunteer's testimony.

Her next step would be to examine and test the electrical belt Lily had purchased. However, she was too nervous to take that step alone, having seen what it did to Mrs Atkinson's heart. Not that Grace planned to use the device anywhere near water. Unfortunately, Lily had another appointment, and Charlie still wasn't home from taking Blaze to meet her prospective mate. The border collie breeder had probably distracted her husband with a long discussion of the merits of the breed. Grace thought doctors and detectives were unbeatable in their enthusiasm for discussing their respective interests, but she was finding that dog owners could out-talk even them.

She removed the belt from its box and examined it, but it didn't mean much to her untutored eye. Grace could name every bone, muscle, tendon, and organ in the human body, detail the effects of innumerable poisons and weapons, and spot a hidden cause of death at a few strokes of a scalpel, but electricity was a new and unknown quantity.

In truth, Grace found electricity rather alarming, although she welcomed such wonderful inventions as electric light. She knew from medical experiments that the body's own electricity somehow travelled through the body to work the muscles. Grace had seen an electric probe used to startling effect to twitch the leg muscle of a dead frog during her medical studies and had read of experiments on the corpses of executed criminals. The very thought of it put her off her soup, making her profoundly grateful that the experimenters had failed in their aim of reanimating the corpses into living, breathing human beings.

The front door opened and closed. There was no scrabble of dog paws down the hall in a rush to greet her, but the tread of boots had a welcome familiarity. Moments later, Charlie caught her up in a delicious tangle of lips and arms. Before she could catch her breath for a second helping, he vanished upstairs. By the time she had dished him a bowl of soup from the pot simmering on the hob and sliced more bread, he was back.

"Half a dozen auction attendees were targeted by a burglar last night," Charlie said, catching her up in his arms again to renew his attentions.

"How awful. The burglaries, I mean. Did you go upstairs to check whether we had an unwanted visitor too?"

Charlie nodded. "Blaze would have guarded the house, but I had to be sure. The burglar showed a concerning level of expertise. Wallace has asked Alistair and me to help. And Blaze, who is with Alistair and feeling very perky indeed after meeting the dog of her dreams earlier this morning."

"Ah, the delights of new love. I can hardly recall what it was like now I'm an old married woman." Grace's breathing became unsteady as her husband worked his way across the soft skin of her neck to torment her for her untruth. A blissful tingling coursed through her body at his touch, reminding her of the look on the volunteer's face at the demonstration. She wondered if joy was a manifestation of the electrical forces within the body. If so, it was no wonder Doctor Crabtree's devices were in such demand.

Eventually, Charlie released his hold on her and sat down to attend to his stomach. Grace put the electrical belt Lily had bought in front of her husband and explained her reservations about Doctor Crabtree's demonstration as he ate.

59

"I'm sorry I missed the show," he said. "That static electricity machine must have been a sight to see. Your description sounds more like a magic act than a medical doctor's scientific display, but it is interesting that the volunteer was so impressed by the belt. Maybe there is something to electrical therapy after all."

"When you have finished scraping the pattern off the bowl, dearest husband, can you examine the belt and tell me what you think? Doctor Harvey is worried that it is outright quackery and potentially dangerous, but Crabtree's customers seem convinced of its merits."

Charlie brushed the last crumbs onto his plate and stood. "Let's take it to Lily's workroom. She and I have been discussing the merits of electricity of late. Lily didn't want to wait for the city to spend years arguing about switching from gas to electric light, so she purchased a portable electric lamp with a battery to illuminate the workroom."

It had been months since Grace had been in the workroom, having been too distracted by the pressures of her last year of medical studies. They went next door, where Charlie connected the battery to the lamp. Although she had seen a demonstration of electricity just this morning, she still gasped when he turned the lamp on.

Grace marvelled at how easy it was to read by the light. It wasn't simply the brightness; it was the lack of flicker and smell compared to a gas lamp. "If a single lamp needs a battery this size to power it, I cannot imagine how big a battery one would need to power an entire city, or even a large shop."

"City lights are not run on batteries. I know the town of Westport generates electricity using the action of water, while others use steam- and gas-powered generation. There are factories using generators of electric current in Dunedin already." Charlie took the belt out of its box. "Let's have a look at what is powering this device."

He teased apart the canvas webbing of the electric belt to uncover rows of round metal objects and wires embedded within the belt. "Small zinc and copper disc batteries wired in series," he muttered, as he detached the large battery running the lamp and attached the belt in its place. "Look at the feeble glow of the filament within the light globe, which means the batteries are not very powerful."

Charlie removed the belt from the lamp and gave it a puzzled prod. "You say one of these almost caused a woman's death? I cannot fathom how, as the current appears to be so weak, I wonder it has any effect on the body at all."

"Doctor Crabtree said it didn't have to be strong to move through the body to remove the blockages that cause pain and illness. It's not impossible, because the body has its own electrical pathways to move muscles."

"Only one way to find out, I suppose."

Grace watched on nervously as her one and only beloved husband removed his shirt and waistcoat. Gazing upon his naked torso would normally be an enjoyable distraction, purely from the perspective of an avid anatomist, naturally. But today she only had eyes for the belt being strapped on, not for the musculature underneath. Before Grace could change her mind, he switched it on.

His smile vanished as his facial muscles contorted in pain. Charlie let out a terrifying yelp, before slumping to the floor, his limbs jerking and flailing for agonising seconds before going absolutely still. Grace's years of medical training fled her mind at the sight of his unmoving body. Then, reality kicked her in the gut and forced her to act. She pulled at the fastening of the belt until it parted and broke the current. She didn't know what else to do, other than to take his pulse and start resuscitation if his heart had stopped.

Charlie opened one eye and grinned wickedly. "Don't just hold my wrist, looking petrified, wife. I was hoping you would give me the 'kiss of life' to resuscitate me."

61

Grace reeled backwards. "What happened? Did the electrical shock knock you over? Thank the Lord you recovered so quickly."

He hopped off the floor and helped her up. "I was only teasing, my love. The belt had no effect whatsoever, apart from a gentle buzzing sensation."

"Teasing?" Grace blinked back tears. "Never, ever, do that to me again, Pyke. It's bad enough seeing you injured and hospitalised on far too regular a basis, without making light of it."

"Will you ever forgive me?" he said, looking suitably remorseful for giving her a fright.

"I suppose so." Once her heart rate recovered, Grace touched the belt in his hands tentatively. "Didn't you feel any positive effect? The woman Doctor Crabtree demonstrated it on seemed to be in a state of ecstasy. You should have seen the queue to purchase these belts after the show, and all the other devices on offer."

Charlie handed her the belt. "Try it if you like, but unless I am uniquely unaffected by it, I'd say it is a complete and utter swindle. The woman who volunteered would have been well paid to simulate the miraculous effect."

"She seemed so believable, and you know I am quick to suspect a ruse when it comes to quackery. And how do you explain Mrs Atkinson's near-death experience if the current was so minimal?" Grace passed him the electrical belt she had taken from Mrs Atkinson's room, after their patient said she never wanted to see it again. "Doctor Harvey was called to her urgently on Friday afternoon. His quick actions saved her, although admittedly it was more of a panic attack than a heart attack."

Charlie bent over the second belt. "This one has larger batteries, so its effect would be stronger." He attached it to the lamp, but the lamp filament did not glow at all. "I'm no expert on these new inventions, but I cannot imagine they could hurt the patient. There is far more money to be made by selling ineffectual devices to gullible customers than in selling devices powerful enough to be dangerous. Any injury or death would cause an immediate halt to sales, which is the last thing the seller would want."

"The circumstances were uniquely dangerous in her case. Mrs Atkinson was sweating and in a hot bath. Also, she had a heart defect, which exacerbated the effect on her body, causing severe palpitations and a panic attack. I suspect she was not as close to death as she and her maid thought, although her reaction did give us all a nasty shock."

"Shocking indeed, under those circumstances," Charlie said. "I've read that the skin's resistance to electricity reduces tenfold when the skin is wet. Surely, any sane medical practitioner would warn against wearing an electrical device anywhere near water. Even a charlatan should know that water conducts electricity."

"It's possible the doctor did tell her," Grace conceded. "Patients often ignore or forget instructions, and electricity is so novel that people tend to either fear it or underrate it. The victim claimed Crabtree told her to use the device in a peaceful spot in order to find her inner calm, to achieve the maximum benefit from the electrical impulses. Not unreasonably, she felt there was nothing more calming than reclining in a hot bath."

Charlie rolled his eyes. "Idiocy. Perhaps there is no glow because the device was damaged by submersion in the bath. We would have to test a new belt of the same type to find out. And when I say we, I mean me. I don't want you testing any such devices on yourself, Grace. Promise me."

"That's a promise I am happy to keep. After seeing Mrs Atkinson ... and then you..."

"I'm truly sorry for the cruel joke, especially now I know what you went through with the patient." Charlie wrapped his arms around her. "Did you say the electrocuted lady's name was Mrs Atkinson? That's odd, because there was a Mrs Atkinson on the list of burglary victims too. I trust it wasn't the same woman."

"Our Mrs Atkinson lives in York Place, not far from Rattray Street," Grace said.

"So does ours. Poor lady. Ill-luck indeed for her to have been burgled after her near-death experience. Surely she didn't attend the auction last night after nearly dying?"

"She did. I must admit that I was amazed to see her there. However, she recovered quickly after Doctor Harvey calmed her down, and I suppose the auction is one of the social highlights of the year. I ought to have asked how she was feeling, but I was trying to avoid her last night because she wasn't pleased with my brazenness at our medical consultation."

"Speaking of the burglaries, I'd like to get your opinion on the only clues I gathered at the scene of the crime, which amounted to nothing more than a half-eaten apple and a twig."

Grace examined the apple with a magnifying glass under the bright light of the lamp. "The bite mark appears quite distinctive. Note the notches on either side, suggesting widely spaced canines. The marks of the incisors are irregular and forward-facing. I'm no dental expert, but I suspect your burglar may have misshapen or buck teeth."

"Well, that's something. It narrows down the search a little, I suppose. I hope Wallace doesn't assign me to checking the teeth of every foul-mouthed rogue in our fair city."

"Or me. Declan won't thank us if the task falls to him, either." Grace picked up the twig with forceps. "Is this a clue too?"

Charlie shrugged. "I only kept it because it was on top of the apple."

"There is a glob of something on the tip." Grace transferred a sample onto a microscope slide and smeared it across the glass, sniffing it before placing it under the microscope. "Hmm. As far as I can tell, it's a waxy substance pocked with tiny pale dots."

"A candle drip?" Charlie jiggled impatiently while waiting for her opinion.

Grace put her hand on his leg to stop the jiggling, which was very distracting to the scientific analysis of the waxy glob. "It's not the right colour or composition for candle wax. This is yellower and less dense. Where did you find it?"

"Under a bush. I think the burglar was waiting for Mr and Mrs MacDonnell to leave, and he passed the time by eating an apple. I didn't see any waxy material like a candle near the twig."

"What else would a man do while waiting that might leave a waxy trace on a stick?" Grace murmured, studying the sample again. Then she looked up at him and grinned. "Could he have been cleaning his ears? I'm not an expert on earwax, but I cannot think what else it might be."

"Earwax? Oh." Charlie sighed. "Well, it was worth a try. Short of examining every person in Dunedin for clean ears, I don't suppose it is the breakthrough I was hoping for."

"O ye of little faith. Patience, husband. Did you know that people who spend many hours in air filled with light particles can have a buildup of said particles in their earwax? I read an article about it over the summer while you were playing with the dog. The experimenter identified coalmen from their earwax alone."

"Fascinating," he said drily. After a pause, his voice rose with interest. "Are you saying those little pale dots embedded in the earwax could tell us where he worked? Remember the cement factory we visited in January? The workers were covered from head to foot in pale dust, and I'll bet their earwax was filled with it too. Or he could be a chalk miner."

Grace looked up from the microscope. "I don't have the expertise to identify the substance, but logic tells me a burglar operating within the confines of the city is more likely to be exposed to something more common. Flour, for example."

"Oh. That would be a shame, flour being lamentably common in all households."

"The amount of it in the earwax suggests a substance in high concentration in the person's workplace or living space. Bearing in mind that the burglar is most likely to be a man, it might suggest he works in a flour mill or bakery or as a pastry chef."

"If you're right, the burglar won't be roaming free for long." Charlie was already grabbing his shirt, ready for action. "We suspect the burglar had access to and knowledge of the inside of the victim's homes, which might point to a man who delivers flour from a grocer's shop, or a baker who delivers his goods directly. I'd like to return to each burgled household to see if I can establish a common link with grocers or bakers who deliver to their homes."

Grace rose too. "I'll come with you, Charlie, because the cooks and maids might find it easier to talk to a sympathetic woman than a male detective." She took a second look at his splendid torso, before it disappeared under his shirt. "On second thoughts, I'll leave the maids to you. One flutter of those lovely long eyelashes of yours and they'll be admitting the burglary themselves, especially now that you have had your life forces invigorated by the wonders of electricity."

He caught her around the waist. "If I have, I'm saving it for you."

Buck Tooth Baker

The thrill of working with his wife to solve each other's puzzles was always a source of delight to Charlie, and never more so than today. Earwax and buck teeth, who'd have thought! Even so, Detective Inspector Wallace would laugh him out of the police station if they couldn't prove the value of Grace's findings. And for that, his first stop was another member of the Southern Investigations team. If anyone knew of a local baker or grocery delivery boy with misshapen teeth, it would be their housekeeper, Mrs Brown.

They found her in the kitchen, rolling pastry for a mutton pie. She took the question in her stride and continued to roll and fold as she sifted through her store of knowledge. It took all of three seconds.

"Sounds like Gus Fenton from Fenton's Bakery on Rattray Street," Mrs Brown said. "He has teeth that would do a horse proud. Bit of a handful when he was a lad, but he seems to have settled down nicely since he married little Minnie Wood from the tobacconist shop around the corner. Minnie is a dab hand at cake decorating, but the Fenton's bread is a trifle below standard, in my opinion."

"You do have very high standards, Mrs Brown," Charlie said. "I've tasted nothing half as good as your cobb loaf."

"High quality flour and plenty of kneading are the keys to a good loaf. Home-baked is best, naturally, which is why I make my own bread. You never know what these bakers put in to bulk out their loaves or make the flour whiter. Plaster of Paris, alum, even chalk and ground bones, or so I hear. Not that Fenton's Bakery would stoop so low, I hasten to add. I suspect they merely use lower-grade flour than I do, and who can blame them given the cost of flour these days."

After he'd praised Mrs Brown's faultless knowledge of local identities, Charlie grabbed Grace's hand and danced her down the hall to the front door. At last, the potential breakthrough they so desperately needed. Handing Wallace the solution to the burglary within hours would be a fine way to repay a debt for his past support. However, Charlie didn't wish to give Wallace false hope.

"Let's visit Fenton's Bakery before we see Wallace," he said. "I'm eager to meet this buck tooth baker before I make a fool of myself based on bodily secretions and bite marks. Although I suspect Gus Fenton won't be there at this time of the day, because he would be up most of the night making bread. Or burgling houses."

They cut through side-streets and alleys, emerging near the city terminus of the Roslyn cable car. Charlie's nose caught the unmistakably pungent smell of fermenting yeast, malt and hops from Speight's Brewery, further up the road. A heady aroma to most men, but the subject of many complaints from delicate feminine noses, especially those belonging to the many temperance supporters in the city.

Before they got to the brewery, they saw a dangling iron loaf projecting out from a wall. A sign declaring the shop to be "Fenton's Bakery" topped the narrow window. Inside the window, the shelves were empty. Charlie rattled the door. Definitely closed for the day.

The woman from the shop next door stopped sweeping her doorstep and leaned on her broom to inspect him. "No use rattling the door, love, because you won't be getting no bread for a day or two. Gus Fenton up and keeled over last night." She crossed herself. "God rest his soul. Heart must have given out from the long hours of work, just like his mam before him."

Charlie was so stricken by the shock of his hopes slipping away, he couldn't think what to say.

68

"How tragic," Grace said. "Was Mr Fenton old?"

The woman shook her head. "'Twas young Fenton what died, not the old man. No more than a quarter of a century on God's earth, he was, and leaving a young widow behind. A terrible shame. I never seen a man so pale with shock as old Mr Fenton was this morning when he found Gus. Aged ten years in front of me eyes, I swear."

"Do you know where the Fenton family lives?" Charlie's premature celebration of solving the burglary now felt like a heavy ball of dough in the pit of his stomach. The potential lead was a dead end, both literally and figuratively.

"Up Canongate, in a damp hollow. A wee cottage with walls leaning into the southerly wind. But they won't welcome visitors at a time like this."

Charlie nodded his thanks. A police inquiry was the last thing the family needed, but the circumstances made it necessary. The likelihood of a young baker dying of natural causes the night he committed a spate of burglaries was vanishingly low. But first, he had the dubious honour of sharing the good and bad news with Detective Inspector Robbie Wallace, because this was very much a police matter now.

They found him in his office with Detective Sergeant Declan Kelly, Alistair Stewart, and Blaze, who had her head on Wallace's knee while he rubbed her ears. Blaze swivelled her eyes towards Charlie and Grace, but evidently found Wallace's attentions superior for now.

"Unfortunately, Blaze lost the trail when the burglar cut through the damp bush around Jubilee Park," Alistair said. "I've told Robbie and Declan that you think it is a single burglar, working fast, with either a door key or inside help, and taking only small valuables."

Wallace nodded a welcome. "Tell me you've found the scoundrel, Pyke, and I'll personally pin the medal on your chest."

"I'm hopeful I've found the scoundrel," Charlie said, "with the help of Grace, Blaze, earwax and a half-eaten apple. Gus Fenton, from Fenton's Bakery on Rattray Street, resident of Canongate. Apparently, he was less than angelic in his youth but was thought to have settled down. We'll need Blaze to confirm it's the right man because the evidence is flimsy."

Wallace raised both eyebrows at the mention of earwax and apples, but he didn't allow himself to be distracted. Instead, he jumped to his feet, disturbing Blaze's bliss. "Wonderful news. Let's go get him."

"Therein lies the problem, sir. The suspect is a dead end, literally. His father found him dead early this morning. We thought we should tell you before proceeding."

"Let's hope Gus Fenton died of guilt on top of a stash of valuables ready to be returned to grateful victims," Wallace growled. "Alistair, can you please tell Mr Peters to search for Gus Fenton in the police records and send a message to the police surgeon that we'll have a body for him to examine." His gaze shifted to Grace. "I don't suppose you'd like to take a first look, in the interests of advancing the investigation as rapidly as possible?"

Grace rubbed her fingers down her chin as if considering a tough decision. Nobody was fooled. "I suppose I could have my arm twisted. We'll explain our conclusions on the way."

Within a quarter of an hour, Blaze had picked up the familiar scent of the burglar at the bakery, and led them a short distance up Canongate, to a cottage whose walls appeared to be fighting a losing battle against gravity.

Declan crossed himself and knocked on the door. Wallace hovered over his sergeant's shoulder, a grizzly bear out of hibernation and eager for action.

The man who answered the door couldn't have been much more than middle-aged, but his face was gaunt with shock and a life hard lived. Red eyes examined their party of four and clearly didn't like what they saw. The door slammed in Declan's face, or would have, had his boot not blocked its path.

"Have some respect, copper," the man said. "We are a house in mourning."

"I'm afraid I must insist, Mr Fenton," Declan said, "although you have our sincere condolences. I'm Detective Sergeant Kelly, and this is Detective Inspector Wallace and Detective Penrose Pyke. Mrs Penrose Pyke is the assistant police surgeon, here to examine your son's body. It's a legal requirement that a doctor must establish the cause of death for a death certificate."

Mr Fenton looked around their group, rightly suspicious of the presence of so lofty an official as a police inspector. Wallace eased his way past their reluctant host, taking him by the arm as he entered the house. With a gentle hand on the grieving man's back, he guided Fenton to a chair. "I understand you found your son's body this morning, Mr Fenton."

"My Gus must have had a dicky heart like his mother," Mr Fenton said. "I found him face down in a mound of dough, stone cold, when I went to the bakery as usual at five o'clock this morning."

Charlie nodded sympathetically. He didn't envy Wallace the job of telling the grieving father his son's cause of death would be the subject of a post-mortem.

"I don't know what I'll do without Gus to do the dough preparation. My old back ain't what it used to be." Mr Fenton nodded his head towards the door to the second room of the cottage, where a pale waif of a girl stood, staring at them with cavernous eyes. "And poor Minnie, only a year married to my boy, and now a widow."

Charlie and Grace moved as one towards Minnie Fenton, fearful that she was on the brink of collapse. They each took an arm, exchanging a dismayed glance when they saw the prominent bulge of her belly under her apron. Gus Fenton's widow was within a few weeks of giving birth. Charlie propped her on a low chest of

71

drawers, there being no other furniture in the room besides the bed, which held the corpse of her husband.

Minnie had been washing his body, ready to be laid out for burial. The milky-white water in the basin must have been from the dough on his face. Gus Fenton's jaw was open, as if he had been screaming when he died. It gave Charlie little satisfaction to note the burglar's misshapen buck teeth.

Grace went over to inspect the corpse, whispering a brief prayer loud enough for Minnie to hear before she started. Charlie stood in front of Minnie, to shield her from Grace's work and also from the search being undertaken by Declan Kelly.

"I'm very sorry for the tragic death of your husband, Mrs Fenton," Charlie said. "Is there somebody I can contact to come and support you?"

"I'll go to my parents as soon as I can," Minnie said. "They own the tobacconist around the corner on Princes Street."

Charlie's presence must have soothed her, or perhaps distracted her from her grief, because she kept talking, pouring out her worries into sympathetic ears. "Me and Gus were working all hours to get the money we needed to take over the tobacconist. Ma and Pa were all for it, seeing as they're getting on in years, but we had to buy out my brothers' shares. Not that any of them had any interest in it. Gus said we'd nearly saved enough. He'd been so excited yesterday, saying it was all going to be fine and we wouldn't have to slave at the bakery no more."

What was it Alistair had said? A final grand haul before the burglar retires to balmier climes. After the hard grind of the bakery, any alternative would be balmy indeed, in Charlie's opinion. "Do you know why your husband was so excited yesterday, Mrs Fenton?"

Minnie shook her head. "Reckon he must have got another good tip on a horse. Now and then, Gus bets on the ponies, but only when he's onto a sure thing. He's won every time, and this one was going

72

to be the best yet, he said. He knew a man who had the inside word, you see."

Charlie was willing to bet Gus Fenton's lucky punts coincided with burglaries, because a horse-racing tip that never failed was as likely as a criminal with a conscience. However, he could see Minnie believed the story her husband had spun to account for the occasional riches he brought home.

"Do you know the name of the tipster, Mrs Fenton?"

"No. A man's gotta have some secrets, don't he?"

"Was it the long hours you and Gus worked at the bakery that made you want to leave?" Charlie asked.

"Hated it, we did." Minnie kept her voice low so her father-in-law wouldn't hear her. "Midnight, my Gus starts. Mixing the dough, getting the ovens lit, kneading until his hands ache. Not a minute to rest, because then there's the cobb loaves and buns and rolls to do, until his father arrives at five to help with the final preparations and baking."

Charlie felt sorry for the young couple, trapped in work they hated, although that didn't excuse Gus turning to crime. "Does Gus come home for a nap once his father arrives at the bakery in the morning?"

Minnie sniffed. "Chance'd be a fine thing. A cup of tea and a bite to eat, then my Gus is pulling loaves in and out of the ovens, stacking the shelves, cleaning the pans, and goodness knows what else. Then he makes house deliveries to the nobs until about noon."

"Exhausting work. What about you, Mrs Fenton?"

"I work from six in the morning until late. Whatever hours are needed. I make the biscuits and cakes and serve at the counter. We usually quieten down early afternoon, but then I have to prepare for the next day. Come seven in the evening, I couldn't stay awake if I tried. Not even a day off on the Lord's day for rest, because people still demand their bread."

Charlie looked up from his note-taking. "My goodness, Mrs Fenton, what a schedule you keep. You must have hardly seen your husband." He could see the appeal of a nice little tobacconist shop, with regular hours and Sundays off, and no lugging heavy sacks and scorching hot trays.

"You've no idea." Minnie dropped her hand to her belly. "It's a wonder we had time to make a baby." Suddenly, reality crashed down on her, and she burst into tears. "Choking on flour dust night and day, lugging around sacks of it until his poor heart gave out, like his mother before him. The bakery killed my Gus, sure as the sun rises. I swear I'll never set foot in the place again."

His heart went out to her. Charlie could understand why Gus was tempted by the easy money from a sideline in burglary, at the sacrifice of his time off. However, the crucial point was that Gus Fenton did have time off during the period of the burglaries between eight o'clock in the evening and the start of his bakery work at midnight, when his wife was asleep.

Charlie and Grace joined Declan and Detective Inspector Wallace outside the cottage to exchange information. Their ears still rang with the renewed sobs of Gus's nearest and dearest, after Wallace informed them that his death would be the subject of a police inquiry.

The inspector's lips formed a tight line across a rigid jaw. "It never gets any easier. Any preliminary thoughts on the cause of death, Grace?"

"I can't tell you whether he inherited heart problems," Grace said, "but I can say for sure that he didn't collapse after having a fatal heart seizure. There were traces of bread dough in Gus Fenton's nose and throat, where he tried to breathe and failed. The bruises on the back of his neck suggest he was forcibly held face down in the dough. The pinpoint haemorrhages on his face and eyelids indicate Gus died of asphyxiation."

"A murder on his patch won't make the Chief Inspector any happier," Wallace said. "We need more evidence to confirm Gus Fenton was the burglar. Kelly, what did you find?"

"No sign of stolen goods at the cottage," Declan said. "Mr Fenton gave us the key to search the bakery, but I expect Gus Fenton's killer won't have left empty-handed."

They walked back down to the bakery in a sombre mood. "What did the father say?" Charlie asked.

"Stan Fenton said his son had been in trouble for petty theft and property damage in his youth," Wallace said. "The Fenton's landlord sponsored Gus to attend a cadet corps, which aimed to transform troublemakers into worthy young men through physical training and discipline. Not simply parade-ground bashing, but sports like boxing and gymnastics. Mr Fenton was delighted at first, but it seems Gus fell into even worse company. Eventually, he was caught burgling a house. Landed him in prison about a decade ago."

"Was Gus the only one caught back then?"

"It seems so. We'll have to dig out the old files to be sure. Mr Fenton was adamant Gus had been put up to the old burglary by someone else. Someone who frightened Gus so much that he refused to name names when he was caught. After he got out of prison, his future wife, Minnie, took him in hand and transformed him into a model citizen. Or so the father thought."

"Minnie thought so too," Charlie said. "She reckoned he was making the extra money they needed to buy a better future by successfully betting on horseracing. With the help of infallible tips from an unknown person."

They arrived at the bakery, where the tragedy was written in scuff marks in flour dust, knocked over baking tins, and a face-mark plunged deep into a mound of dough, complete with prominent teeth marks.

The search for valuables proved fruitless until Blaze took Charlie into the small yard at the rear. There, deep inside the discarded flue of an old oven, he found two small bags. One

75

contained a wad of cash, and the other contained a few smaller pieces of simple jewellery. Presumably this was Gus Fenton's share of the proceeds, unless he was skimming an extra portion for himself. Charlie hoped that the cash might find its way to Mrs Fenton for her child, if she could persuade the powers that be that the money was their own savings from working at the bakery.

Charlie tipped out the jewellery, finding a ring matching the description of Mrs MacDonnell's cherished heirloom ring. If there had been any doubt about Gus's guilt, there was no longer.

But Gus was not the only guilty party. A baker working ungodly hours would be hard pressed to gain the knowledge he needed to commit the crimes. Most likely, another person had put him up to it. The man who had given him the tip-off about easy money to be made. A shadowy figure lurking behind the scenes, directing Gus Fenton to pre-selected victims on specific days, perhaps supplying inside knowledge and a key, and almost certainly taking the lion's share of the proceeds.

Gus Fenton had told his wife they would have enough to achieve their dream of buying into the tobacconist shop with this last "bet". If Gus had told the mastermind of the burglary operation that this would be his final burglary, he might as well have signed his own death warrant. Gus had become a liability, and his accomplice had become a killer.

Accomplice

Grace settled herself behind the shop counter of the bakery with an audible click of her back. She'd always been amazed at the range of clicks and groans that accompanied her elderly great-aunt's movements, so it came as a shock to hear her own body betray her so early in life.

The tiredness and unsettled stomach she had felt earlier in the day had returned too, after glimpsing the sickening face-shaped hollow in the mound of dough. Such squeamishness was a new and unwelcome development. Perhaps Doctor Harvey was right about her pursuing general practice rather than pathology.

While the men searched the bakery proper, Grace located the shop's register and compared bread delivery addresses to the list of burglary victims. Wallace emerged soon after, liberally dusted with flour and soot. Detectives in novels were always so impossibly dapper compared to the grim reality of actual police work, but she decided not to share this observation with the inspector as he coughed his lungs out. Wallace stepped outside for a breath of fresh air before returning to the search, his woolly eyebrows snow-capped peaks of flour. She didn't mention that either.

After going through two months of orders, the only name Grace found on both lists was the MacDonnell family, thereby dashing the theory that Gus Fenton had gained an inside knowledge of the houses he burgled during bread deliveries.

She persisted, and was rewarded with another matching name from an order made five months ago. One victim had purchased a large Christmas cake, to be delivered in mid-December last year. Grace struggled to see how delivering a Christmas cake several months ago could possibly provide sufficient inside information about the household to make it a burglary target, especially as no delivery man would get further than the tradesman's entrance or kitchen. She agreed with Charlie that there must be a resourceful and ruthless mastermind behind the scenes, and the murder of Gus Fenton supported the theory.

Wallace emerged from the baking area again, this time with Declan and Charlie, all brushing themselves down. From the patchwork of substances covering them, Grace deduced they had searched up the oven's chimney and inside every sack of flour – rye, wholemeal and white. For Wallace to be handling this personally, rather than assigning such labours to mere constables, Grace felt sure that he must have scorch marks on his neck from the Chief Inspector's breath.

"Find anything, Grace?" Wallace asked, as he took the brush Grace handed him and attended to his hat and coat.

"The MacDonnell household had a regular bread delivery from Fenton's Bakery, but there was only one other victim listed in the order book, for a single cake order before Christmas."

"Right, thank you. We have our burglar. Now we need to find the man pulling his strings, preferably before he hightails it out of town with a small fortune. Kelly, liaise with the constables doing the legwork, and ask Mr Peters if he has found anything in the police files about Gus Fenton or the gardener, Jack Turner. Pyke, can you talk to Mr and Mrs MacDonnell again to see if you can dig up any connection between Fenton and Turner or anybody else in the household?"

They nodded silently.

"Thank you. Your work is appreciated." Wallace's jaw tightened, and they held their breaths for the bad news that would follow. "I'll inform the Chief Inspector of progress. You've performed miracles to get us to this point. Let's keep up the momentum and pray for a few more miracles, or I'll be serving out my final years of police duty on an isolated island off the south coast of New Zealand, with penguins and icebergs for company."

Declan and Wallace hurried away, their expressions as chilly as the threatened icebergs.

Grace took a brush to Charlie's back and plucked a couple of currants, part of an old bird's nest, and some flecks of rust out of his hair. She didn't comment on the Chief Inspector's lack of appreciation for their efforts, because he knew all too well what it was like to be on his wrong side. Two years ago, the Chief had believed Charlie was guilty of murder, ending his police career.

"I could accompany you if I would be of any use," she said when her husband was more or less respectable again.

"Always, my love," he replied with a grim weariness. "You may wish to speak to Mrs MacDonnell for your own investigation, since she is a fervent supporter of your Professor of Galvanism. She credits him with improving her lumbago. She is also of the opinion that you mere medical doctors could learn a thing or two from a man of Doctor Crabtree's talent. Apparently, his prestige is demonstrated by the fact that he had a Harley Street practice. He returned to Dunedin only when his father became ill."

"Dearest husband, here was I thinking you had abandoned yourself to the joys of conversing with other ladies at the auction, when you were advancing my investigation."

Charlie took her arm. "You have repaid the debt ten times over today, identifying the burglar so quickly. I don't know what I would do without my two exceptional female investigators."

"Two?" But Grace's query was unnecessary, because Blaze was waiting for them outside with her ears pricked and her tail wagging.

They discussed their strategy as they walked, deciding that Charlie would use his charms on the housekeeper and maids to uncover any links between Gus Fenton and the staff, while Grace asked Mrs MacDonnell about the gardener and Doctor Crabtree.

Mrs MacDonnell welcomed them in. Indeed, she came close to squeezing the air from Charlie's lungs, so fervent was her embrace when she heard he had recovered her heirloom ring. "Gus Fenton! Who'd have thought he would have gone back to his wicked ways once he settled down with that lovely little Minnie from the tobacconist. The poor lass, what a tragedy to be widowed so young."

"We think the siren call of wealth seduced him," Grace said. "May I ask how you knew of Gus Fenton's wicked past, Mrs MacDonnell?"

She took them into the sitting room, ignoring the dusting of flour still on Charlie's clothes as she asked them to take a seat. "We've been customers of Fenton's Bakery for years. Stan Fenton was overcome with shame when Gus was arrested for burglary, especially after all Mr Vale had done to set the lad on the straight and narrow. Must have been ten years ago, I suppose. It was in the newspapers, too. Gus went to prison. It was quite the scandal back then."

"Mr Vale?" Charlie leaned forward intently, the servants forgotten.

"Mr Elias Vale, the Fenton's landlord. A navy man before he established his property business in Dunedin. Mr Vale ran a philanthropic venture to give the wayward young lads of Dunedin the discipline and purpose they needed to turn them into worthy citizens. He called it a cadet corps, perhaps because of his naval origins."

"Is the cadet corps still operating?" Charlie asked.

"Oh, no. The corps disbanded soon after the scandal of the burglary, as I recall. Perhaps Mr Vale felt his venture had failed to reform them." Mrs MacDonnell paused, tapping her fingers on the armrest, digging through old memories. "Now I come to think on it, Mr Vale died, so that might explain why the corps was disbanded. Elias Vale wasn't a close acquaintance of ours. Not even a distant acquaintance, to be honest. A hard sort of man, but well-meaning."

"Do you recall the names of any of the other young men in the cadet corps, especially anyone rumoured to have been involved in the burglary?"

"You would have to ask the police, Mr Penrose Pyke. I believe many young lads went through the programme. The only one I know for sure was our Jack Turner." Mrs MacDonnell must have seen Charlie's flare of interest, because she quickly added, "not that Jack had anything to do with the burglary. He was only in the cadets as an act of charity. The poor boy was an orphan in want of guidance, not one of the disreputable lads."

Grace could see Charlie wasn't convinced, and she understood why. Throwing a good apple into a barrel of rotten apples was a sure way to make the good apple turn bad. "How did Jack Turner come to work for you, Mrs MacDonnell?" she asked.

"An old friend of my husband, Mr Crabtree, volunteered as the gymnastics coach to the cadets. He saw the good in Jack and took him on as a gardener and odd-jobs man. Jack cannot have been much above fifteen years of age then. Anyway, he proved his worth, and Mr Crabtree recommended his services to us and other households. I won't have a word said against our Jack. As hardworking and honest as the summer day is long."

"Do you know where Jack lives?" Charlie asked at the same time as Grace said, "Mr Crabtree?"

Mrs MacDonnell answered Charlie with the name of a nearby boarding house, before turning to Grace. "Mr Franklin Crabtree. You know Mr Franklin Crabtree's son, Doctor Barnabas Crabtree, of course, as last night's auctioneer. We are so very fortunate to have him in Dunedin. He is one of the most eminent medical specialists ever to grace our shores."

On that cue, Charlie excused himself to talk to the servants, leaving Grace to extract more information for her investigation. "What a marvellous success the auction was, Mrs MacDonnell. As you may recall, I was the successful bidder for a consultation with Doctor Crabtree. As you can imagine, I am eager to hear more about him."

Mrs MacDonnell flushed a becoming shade of pink at the compliment to her organisation, or perhaps at the mention of Doctor

81

Crabtree. "How could I forget such spirited bidding? The hospital charity thanks you for your generosity, Mrs Penrose Pyke. I'm certain you won't regret your largesse. Doctor Crabtree is a miracle worker. After he made such a difference to my lumbago, I recommended him to all my acquaintances. We've had the honour of hosting him at our house for dinner parties, too."

"I'm reassured by your praise of the doctor's skills," Grace said. "I expect you know the Crabtree family well, as you and your husband are friends with the doctor's father."

"Franklin Crabtree was a fine man and a good friend." Mrs MacDonnell's hand pressed to her chest over her heart. "Sad to say, he never truly recovered from an apoplectic seizure a few months ago. Quite incapacitated, poor man. Unfortunately, his wife passed some years ago. Franklin's daughter, Rosannah, has been a marvellous support to her father."

"Mr Crabtree was fortunate his son came home, especially as Doctor Crabtree had such a successful practice in London. And how gallant of the doctor to agree to help at the auction."

Mrs MacDonnell nodded. "His sister Rosannah is on the hospital charity committee with me. We combined our entreaties to secure his agreement to be our auctioneer. Rosannah did a marvellous job of the supper, don't you think? Although if I catch the little blighter who spiked the punch with rum, he won't be sitting down for a week."

Grace didn't drop the revered Doctor Crabtree in the manure by admitting he was the culprit, although the image of Mrs MacDonnell spanking his rear end made it tempting. "Rosannah Vale must be a devoted sister, because I saw her assisting the doctor at one of his demonstrations."

Mrs MacDonnell reacted with the *see no evil, speak no evil* gesture of a person who does not wish to spread gossip – a sideways flick of the eyes and a fleeting movement of one hand to cover her mouth. Anne Drummond intimated last night that Rosannah Vale did not care to be seen in the company of her brother, and her hostess's reaction confirmed it.

After a fleeting pause, Mrs MacDonnell said, "Rosannah has been a great help to her brother since he returned home from London. I don't know how she finds the time."

Grace was more interested in why she did her brother's bidding, but it would be rude to ask directly. "Rosannah is married to Elias Vale's son, Matthew, isn't she?"

"That's right. Elias Vale and Franklin Crabtree have known each other for years. I believe they have a business association, which is probably how Franklin came to be helping Elias with the cadet corps. Young Matthew Vale is a lovely man. Very polite and respectable. He took over his father's property business at a young age, after his father died, and made a success of it."

The ever so slight emphasis on *Matthew* hinted that Elias was not so lovely and respectable. "I haven't met Matthew and Rosannah Vale, but I saw them at the auction last night. Jack Turner was there, too, wasn't he? What a helpful young man."

"I couldn't have done it without him," Mrs MacDonnell gushed. "Nobody realises how much effort goes into securing and collecting donations. Jack lugged everything from clocks to carpets between the homes of donors and the hall over the past few weeks, and back again into new homes this morning, all without a single complaint."

"How splendid of him. And you too, who arranged it all. The future patients of Dunedin Hospital owe you both their profound thanks." Grace couldn't think of any further questions, and she felt she had taken more than enough of Mrs MacDonnell's time.

Fortunately, Charlie returned to the sitting room at that point. They thanked Mrs MacDonnell and departed.

Back out on the street, Grace noted the long shadows, which confirmed the afternoon was seeping away into the early dusk of autumn. "I don't mind arriving home after dark if you wish to follow a lead. Do you want to visit Jack Turner's boarding house?"

"That seems the obvious next move. We'll call at Mrs Atkinson's house first. The maid told me Jack does the garden there on Monday afternoon." Charlie set off at a brisk pace, stopping at the intersection to let an overloaded hay cart rattle past. "The maids swear Jack is the kindest man they've ever met. He showed them how a caterpillar turns into a butterfly, and he puts fallen chicks back into their nests. It's not exactly rigorous evidence of character, I know, but it's hardly the act of a man ruthless enough to push a fellow conspirator's face into a pile of dough."

"In my experience, it is the boys who pull the wings off butterflies you have to avoid. Horrid little beasts. Mrs MacDonnell speaks highly of Jack too, and she's known him for years."

"I knew you'd understand, Grace. Gus Fenton's father said his son was frightened of the person who was his accomplice in the first burglary. So much so that Gus chose prison rather than informing on his accomplice. From what we have heard so far, Jack Turner doesn't sound at all frightening. Also, the maid said Jack never stepped over the threshold because of his muddy gardening boots. He had no chance to steal a key or to inspect the layout of the house. The same goes for Gus Fenton, when he delivered the bread."

"Let's visit the other burgled households to see if they know Jack before we speak to him. If the evidence still points to Jack, we can stop by the police station and suggest they bring him in for an interview. I'd also like to ask each victim whether they are a patient of Doctor Crabtree. His name, and those of his sister and brother-in-law, seem to be surfacing with suspicious regularity in both of our investigations."

"Excellent plan." Charlie took her arm and set off at a brisk pace again.

They zig-zagged their way across the neighbourhood to the next three houses, confirming only that Gus Fenton did not deliver their bread and Jack Turner did not tend their gardens. One recalled a man with a birthmark picking up a fire screen and a set of irons for the auction, under Mrs MacDonnell's instructions. Jack didn't enter the house beyond the entrance hall.

Grace dropped Doctor Crabtree's name into the conversation at each house and was surprised to find they were all patients of his. Not simply patients, but fervent supporters. Their eyes lit up as they claimed cures for everything from women's problems to headaches. One woman blushingly hinted at her older husband's improved vitality after using an electrical device.

Grace was beginning to think she was the only person in town who hadn't registered Doctor Crabtree's presence before. Her unease grew as she heard them refer to "taking the cure", "a miracle", and other such phrases more often applied to divine interventions. Two women proudly admitted discontinuing the medication their doctor had prescribed. The concerns of the local doctors had been raised in the first place by a patient who had taken a terrible turn after stopping his prescribed medication. In Grace's view, they were right to investigate his practices and shut him down if necessary.

Her feet were dragging as they headed to the fifth house, but at least the churn of her thoughts distracted her from her swollen ankles. "The coincidence of those four households being victims of both burglary and potential quackery worries me, Charlie."

"I suppose the type of well-to-do people who enjoy attending charity events might also be susceptible to the lure of a miracle cure for their ailments. Dunedin is a small city, after all, and only the well-off could afford Crabtree's services. However, I don't like the coincidence either. It seems the paths of our investigations have converged."

The next person on the list was Mrs Atkinson, who lived in York Place, where Jack Turner was supposed to be working that afternoon. Grace did not need to ask her if Mrs Atkinson was a patient of Doctor Crabtree, given the drama following the electric belt in the bath incident.

They were still two houses away when Charlie tensed. Grace couldn't see what had caught his attention.

Suddenly, Charlie called out, "Mr Turner, can I have a word with you, please?"

The click-clack of hedge clippers stopped, and a face with a port-wine birthmark appeared over the top of Mrs Atkinson's hedge. Charlie must have spotted him thanks to his greater height. The face disappeared, and Grace heard the clatter of dropped clippers, followed by feet running on gravel. Charlie stopped only to let Blaze off her leash before he ran after the dog, disappearing through the gate and up the steps.

Beyond the Gate

By the time Grace ascended the steps, all she could hear was a distant bark. The sections in the upper part of York Place stretched up the hill to Queen's Drive and the Town Belt, where only Blaze could track their fugitive. Charlie and Jack Turner were nowhere in sight. It was too late for her to follow them, partly because they had too much of a head start and partly because night was closing in and she didn't relish the thought of crashing through bushes in the dark.

Jack Turner's panicked flight had caught her by surprise. Despite his glowing references and love of butterflies and birds, it seemed they might have been wrong about his innocence. Unless he was frightened for another reason.

Grace looked up to see Mrs Atkinson's frizzy-haired maid, Ellie, on the doorstep.

"What's all the fuss?" Ellie said.

"A man's dog got loose and was chasing your gardener, I think," Grace replied, more or less truthfully.

"Must have been a brute of a dog to chase our Jack. He's a soft touch with animals. A right St Francis, he is. I've seen him move earthworms and bugs rather than cut through them in the garden. He's the sweetest man I've ever met." The maid blushed and changed the subject. "You're the doctor's assistant, aren't you?"

"Mrs Penrose Pyke," Grace confirmed, walking up to the entrance so she didn't have to raise her voice. "How is Mrs Atkinson?"

"Back to her old self, thanks to the doctor." The slight wrinkling of Ellie's nose implied that the old self was not an improvement.

"And thanks to your quick actions in summoning him. I do hope your mistress was grateful for your good sense and calm in a crisis." Grace looked around, pretending to admire the garden, which was immaculately trimmed but too regimented for her taste. "Tell me, is your gardener a good worker? Our garden is getting quite out of hand."

The maid warmed to the compliment and seemed happy to repay the favour with information. "Jack is the best in town, Mrs Penrose Pyke. I doubt he can help you, though. He already works from dawn until dusk, with hardly a minute to call his own."

"Oh, that's a shame. He comes highly recommended. I think he knows our baker, Mr Fenton."

"I wouldn't know about that. Cook makes all our bread, and Mrs Atkinson insists on using the Glasgow Bakery for any fancies. As far as I can tell, Jack doesn't have time for friends, and no interest in them either. I suppose it's the birthmark on his face that puts folk off. More fool them, I say, for he's a lovely man once you get to know him."

"Well, I must let you get on with your evening," Grace said, "because I suspect you have little time to spare. I hope Mrs Atkinson isn't too angry with Doctor Crabtree for selling her the electrical belt."

"Angry? Not likely." The maid rolled her eyes. "She put her seizure down to her dicky heart and Doctor Harvey's medicine, not that frightful belt. The mistress won't hear a word against the great Doctor Crabtree, even after what happened on Friday. He'll be strolling down the street to sup at her dinner table before the month is out, I'd wager. Anyway, she's more worried about the loss of her pearls now. Wedding present from her late husband, they were. You should have heard her tearing a strip off her brother, the Chief of Police, over the way he lets criminals rampage unchecked through the better households of the city."

No wonder Wallace had the chief inspector breathing fire on him, Grace thought. The maid gave her a rueful grimace, then turned on her heels.

"Ellie," Grace called, before the maid went inside. "If you see Jack, tell him we think he is innocent, but he needs to talk to the police to clear his name."

Ellie's freckled nose twitched at the word "police", but she didn't ask what crime Jack was suspected of, which Grace found interesting. Ellie studied her for a moment, head perked to the side and frizzy hair spilling out from under her cap. "I'll tell him," she said finally, but it was clear she didn't think it would make a difference.

If Jack distrusted the police, he might not be as innocent as he appeared. On the other hand, it might be the common fear of authority shared by many ordinary folks. Grace didn't have a chance to ask, because Ellie hurried into the house.

Charlie hadn't returned, which meant he was still chasing Jack Turner across the far reaches of the Town Belt. She shivered and pulled her heavy woollen shawl tighter around her against the icy breeze. Now that twilight was slipping into night, all heat had vanished from the air. Standing around waiting for her husband to return was far from appealing. Grace resigned herself to walking home alone.

However, Ellie's comment about the doctor strolling down the street to dine triggered a memory. Grace took out her appointment card for Doctor Barnabas Crabtree's surgery and saw it was further up York Place. The temptation to have a peek at Doctor Crabtree's house overcame her weariness.

The house and surgery were the last house on the street before it turned a sharp left and became Russell Street. When Grace reached the address, she wished she had gone straight home. The chill wind rustled the leaves of the encroaching trees and set stray boughs squeaking across the top bar of an intimidating gate, sending a shiver down her spine. Solid stone gateposts and a high stone wall

89

warned intruders they were not welcome. Through a gap in the trees, a gravel drive curved towards an imposing house, grand in both size and design.

Grace would have walked on had she not been drawn to the gate by the astonishingly bright light shining from the windows of the house. The urge to investigate the source of the illumination overwhelmed her good sense. Just a quick peek and then straight home, she promised herself. She glanced up at the spikes on top of the gate and hoped the gate was unlocked. Reaching through the bars, which were widely spaced enough that she could have squeezed through them three months ago, she lifted the latch slowly, so as not to add a metallic squeak to the disconcerting whistle of wind through branches.

Halfway up the drive, she was beginning to regret her curiosity. The bright light inside the house ought to have added a cheerful touch, but it seemed unnatural, making the twisted limbs of the trees appear all the starker without the softness of their summer leaves. What in the name of Hades is causing that brightness, she whispered to herself. There was no sign of life, so she figured she might as well keep going.

Grace was standing on tiptoes, attempting to peek through a crack in the curtains, when a rustling behind her froze her to the marrow. She whirled around, finding herself face to face with a man who had crept to within inches of her back. An older man, in his sixties, wearing a dressing gown and slippers despite the early hour. The left side of his face drooped, as did his left arm, but he had shuffled up to her as quietly as a fawn through the undergrowth.

She was about to blurt an apology when he spoke. "Did you escape too, Rosie? Shall we go dancing together in town?"

His speech was slurred, but comprehensible. Grace realised this must be Mr Franklin Crabtree, Doctor Crabtree's father, who had had a severe apoplectic seizure a few months ago. Grace had seen similar symptoms before. Bleeding into the brain could cause damage to memory and physical functioning, often on one side of

90

the body. She extended her arm to usher him out of the bushes, jerking it back when his undamaged right hand gripped her with shocking strength.

"You should go back inside the house, Mr Crabtree. It's too cold for dancing tonight."

Franklin Crabtree only tightened his grip. He gave her a crooked smile. "Never too cold for dancing, my love."

She would have to escort him into the house, pretending she had found him wandering on the street.

The click of the gate latch warned her she was too late. If she didn't move soon, she would be discovered trespassing. Boots crunched on the gravel. She hoped it wasn't the target of her investigation, arriving home, eager to escape the chill and sit down to a warm meal. Grace prised off the old man's hand and shrunk back into a thick bush by the house, holding her breath as the footsteps approached.

"Come along, Rosie, it'll be jolly to go dancing again," Franklin Crabtree said into the bush.

"Your wife's dead," a man's voice said, bluntly, but not unkindly. "Let's go into the house, shall we? Should be treacle pudding tonight, since it's Saturday. Your favourite."

"I like treacle pudding," Franklin agreed.

Grace breathed again when their footsteps retreated, although her heart still pounded so hard she thought it might burst her bodice. The front door opened, spilling light beyond the steps. Belatedly, Grace hoped the Crabtree family didn't keep a guard dog. And then, the door shut again, and she was alone with her own heavy breathing and remorse for her recklessness.

Neither man nor beast made their presence known as Grace fled down the drive, almost losing her hat and shawl in the mad dash.

The gate was locked.

Why hadn't she thought of that? It made sense that the last person arriving home would lock the gate behind him, especially

91

after a string of local burglaries. That last person wasn't Barnabas Crabtree, but it might have been Mr Matthew Vale, judging from her glimpse of the man's profile through the leaves. If it was Vale, did that mean that he and his wife Rosannah lived here with her father and brother? It fitted with Mrs MacDonnell's comment that Rosannah Vale had cared for her father after his seizure.

Grace's pulse ticked up a notch again as she tried the latch and jiggled the gate. Solidly locked. She looked around in case there was a way of scaling the fence without getting impaled on the spikes. There wasn't. Not in a long skirt, without Charlie by her side to boost her up. She had two choices: go to the house and admit to being a trespasser, thus blowing her cover for the investigation, or channel the thin woman she had been until three months ago and slide through the bars of the gate.

She inhaled deeply, then exhaled fully. It was going to be a tight squeeze. She got her head and shoulders through by angling them awkwardly, and then her newly buxom breasts, albeit with considerable discomfort. Just as she thought she would make it, her shawl caught on an arrowhead-shaped decorative iron spike.

At first, she remained calm. If she squeezed in, she could squeeze out, she reasoned. But the snagged shawl restricted her movement. Grace tugged, she wrenched, she tried forcing her way forward and then backwards. After several long, long minutes of futile wriggling, panic set in. She was completely and utterly stuck. As bad as her choices had been before, now they were far worse. Yell for help and suffer the excruciating humiliation of being discovered, or wait it out and hope she froze to death before becoming a laughing stock.

Grace cursed Matthew Vale for coming home at the wrong moment. She cursed the ridiculously secure gate and her unyielding, heavy woollen shawl. She cursed her husband for abandoning her and imagined him sharing a whisky with Wallace, having heroically secured a suspect. She cursed her newly curvaceous body.

92

But most of all, she cursed her foolish, impetuous, inquisitive, stupid, stupid self.

A Light in the Dark

Charlie cursed himself for causing Jack Turner's panicked flight, by running towards him shouting rather than calmly approaching him. He cursed himself for letting Blaze loose to chase Turner, when she was not trained for the task of apprehending criminals. He cursed the darkness and the dense trees of the Town Belt, which made following them impossible.

But most of all, he cursed himself for abandoning his wife on a dark street, miles from the safety of home. Grace had been acting a little out of character lately – a little softer, a little less forceful. Letting him be the one to test the electric belt and agreeing that Lily be the one to consult Doctor Crabtree, not to mention her unusual sluggishness in the morning. Blaze had detected something off about her too, judging from the way she hung around Grace and prodded her gently. He trusted Blaze to know. Was Grace ill again and not admitting it to him? She looked well. Indeed, she had looked radiant until last night and this morning. The new eating regime had worked wonders.

As Charlie jogged back through the trees, he whistled and called Blaze. There was just enough light to see his way down to Queen's Drive, which traversed much of the length of the Town Belt. He stumbled along, hoping he was heading in the correct direction. A bright light through the trees startled him as he rounded a corner. He had only a vague sense of where he was, but light meant civilisation, and there was a narrow side track going down towards it. To his profound relief, a single bark in the distance told him Blaze was on her way back too.

Glimpses of the extraordinary brightness through the trees told him that the light came from a grand, two-storey house. Charlie realised they must have an electricity generator, which was a first

94

for a Dunedin house, as far as he knew. He and Grace had joined half the residents of Dunedin in marvelling at the new electric lights installed in Duthie's Drapers last Christmas, which lit the store as bright as a summer's day.

The track ended at the far side of the house, on a street he now recognised as York Place. For a moment, he thought his eyes were playing tricks on him. Was that Grace behind the gate? No, not *behind* the gate, but halfway through the gate and apparently as stuck as a sow in a farrowing crate.

Charlie laughed. He couldn't help it, because she looked so darned funny, but he regretted it when he saw her anguish. His indomitable wife was on the verge of tears, a rare event. In a gush of sympathy and shame, he whispered an apology and pressed a kiss to her cheek, before warning her to hold tight.

"As if I had any choice," she muttered.

He clambered up the gate, grasped a spike and vaulted over the top of the gatepost, dropping to the other side. Grace muttered something about it being easy for tall men in trousers, which he ignored. After unhooking the shawl and pulling it off her to give her extra room to wiggle out, he pushed her from the rear. He hated being so rough in forcing her hips to the right angle to slide through, but at least she was out, even if she was sprawled face down in the freezing gravel. Charlie scaled the gate and dropped back to the other side, ready to take her in his arms and whisk her home. Blaze sat waiting, her pose submissive, recognising Grace's suffering.

As soon as Charlie pulled his wife upright, she wrenched herself away and fell to her knees again, vomiting into a pile of autumn leaves by the gatepost. He held her hair out of her face where it had escaped from its clips. When she finished emptying her stomach contents, he wrapped the woollen shawl and his coat around her, feeling terrible for having laughed at her when she was so clearly in distress and unwell.

When her shivering died down, he gently helped her to her feet, determined not to compound his error by asking how she had come

95

to be stuck in a gate. Instead, he wiped gravel off her face and handed her the only liquid he had – a small flask of brandy for reviving distraught clients – to rinse her mouth.

"Let's go home, my love," he whispered.

Grace gargled the brandy and spat. "Thank you for coming back for me."

"I should never have left you."

"I wanted to get a closer look at Doctor Crabtree's electric lights, but Matthew Vale came home and locked the gate behind him. At least, I think it was Vale."

"Rotten luck. I failed to catch Jack Turner in the dark. I was a fool to run after him and frighten him off, when I only wanted to ask about his time in the cadets." He paused to examine his wife. "Are you injured, Grace? I can carry you if you are hurt or unwell."

Grace gave him a smile that was pure sunshine in the fading twilight. "My dignity is injured. The rest of me is in fine shape. Never felt better."

Usually, he could read his wife like an open book, but now he was thoroughly confused. Unless it was a trick of the dim light, Grace looked genuinely happy, despite the vomiting and squeezing and indignity she had suffered. A touch of delirium, perhaps? For want of any other plan, he took her arm and started down Russell Street, taking the shortest route home.

"Charlie," Grace said, pulling him to a halt. "Awful as it was being stuck in that gate, it gave me time to reflect on how I was feeling. The pain of the metal against my chest, the nausea … Honestly, I think I might be the worst doctor in the world for not recognising the symptoms earlier."

Charlie cut in. "I knew you were unwell. Whatever it is, dearest heart, we'll get you the best treatment even if I have to –"

She grabbed both his hands to get his attention. "Let me finish. I'm not sick. You must promise not to get too excited, because it is too soon to be sure … but I think we might be having a baby."

After a moment frozen to the spot in shocked silence, Charlie threw his arms around her and twirled her, whooping loud enough to send the local dogs into a frenzy of barking. Fearful he might have squashed his wife and their baby, he set her down gently and kissed her, before doing a ridiculous jig in the middle of the road.

Grace had her hands on her hips, her teeth white in the darkness as she laughed. "Did you not hear the bit about not getting too excited, dearest?"

"From this moment forth, I shall be a model of discretion until you tell me otherwise," he promised, hand on heart. Charlie ignored the roll of her eyes and took her arm, setting off towards home with a smile so wide his jaw ached.

But inside he was still doing a jig, and he could tell Grace was too.

On Sunday morning, Charlie slid out of bed before Grace was awake, to make sure the fires were burning brightly enough to keep the morning chill at bay. He ought to have been feeling guilty for not returning to town last night to share the significant developments in the case with the police team, but his thoughts were too taken up with the prospect of becoming a father, after convincing himself it might never happen.

Mrs Brown was in the kitchen, singing to herself and trying not to catch his eye. Charlie suspected he had given the game away when they arrived home last night. He had said nothing, but any fool could see something was up, and their housekeeper was no fool.

"Shall I make up a tray?" Mrs Brown asked, although she had already laid out the plates and silverware on a tray and added a bouquet of tiny flowers. "Will scrambled eggs be acceptable to Mrs Penrose Pyke, do you think? Oh, and there's a message here for you from Detective Inspector Wallace."

"Thank you, Mrs Brown," Charlie said, reading the note. "I'm sure Grace would love scrambled eggs. Detective Inspector Wallace has invited Grace and me to lunch, so please feel free to visit friends after church."

"Wonderful, Mr Penrose Pyke, simply wonderful."

Charlie didn't think Mrs Brown was referring to time off, but he thanked her as normal and took the tray up to Grace. She turned over in bed at the rattling of crockery on silver and gave him a sleepy smile of such warmth that he had to blink back a tear. He helped her to sit up, plumping pillows and ensuring the blanket covered her snugly, before laying the tray across her lap with the utmost care.

Grace had a tear in her eye too, but she didn't let it show in her voice. "I'm not an invalid, my love, and you won't hurt the baby if you touch my belly. At this point, it's no bigger than a broad bean."

He exhaled slowly, marvelling at the thought. Charlie knew nothing about babies or pregnancy, which meant he had better find out fast. "Do you know when The Bean might make its appearance in the world?"

"If the pregnancy takes, which is by no means assured, my best guess is that I'll give birth around the end of November. The Bean had better be on time, because it would be a disaster if I gave birth any earlier."

Grace's final exams before qualifying as a doctor finished in mid-November. It had been the single focus of her thoughts before the tidal wave of events over the last two days. Yet, his wife looked far from stressed. Indeed, she wore an uncharacteristically dreamy expression, and her hand crept to her navel every time she thought he wasn't looking.

He ate his breakfast, scarcely tasting it. "We've been invited to Wallace's house for Sunday lunch, if you feel up to it. Do you mind if I go to the station beforehand to share our new evidence? Wallace will want to get a man to Turner's boarding house as soon as possible. I hope he's not angry I didn't pass on the news last night."

He paused, smiling sweetly. "I got a little distracted, but fortunately, I managed to contain my excitement admirably."

His wife arched a mocking eyebrow. "Oh, yes. You did such a *marvellous* job of containing your excitement, as promised. I counted no more than three silly dances, five outbursts of hysterical giggling, and not more than a dozen surreptitious glances at my navel on the way home. Poor Mrs Brown must have got quite the surprise when you hugged her like a demented orang-utan. Off you go now, dearest. I'm using the excuse for a sleep-in."

Charlie dressed for the day, humming cheerfully. He walked down to the police station, definitely *not* skipping or grinning like an idiot. Despite Sunday being a day of rest, the station buzzed like a disturbed beehive, as expected, given the Chief Inspector's personal interest in the burglary investigation. Now a murder investigation, he reminded himself, as if the stakes weren't high enough already.

He met his business partner, Alistair Stewart, heading towards Detective Inspector Wallace's office with an armful of files.

Alistair sent a meaningful glance towards an ancient clock on a nearby filing drawer, his moustache quivering with mischief. "Enjoy your long sleep-in, Charlie? I'd ask for your excuse, but the ear-to-ear grin plastered across your face tells me I'd do better not to inquire."

"Have some pity, Alistair. It is Sunday." Charlie tried to wipe the smile off his face, but it proved difficult to shift. He expected a tongue-in-cheek lecture on the policeman's lot, with pointed references to crime not stopping just because it was Sunday, but Alistair only laughed and made no further comment.

Wallace looked up from his discussion with DS Declan Kelly when they entered his office. "News, Pyke?"

Charlie almost blurted out the only news that mattered to him this morning, until he realised Wallace was talking about the case. "Gus Fenton is unknown to all but one of the burglary victims," he said, not bothering with pleasantries. "However, Jack Turner was

99

in the cadet corps with Gus. A man called Elias Vale, who was the Fenton's landlord, ran the cadets, with the help of Mr Franklin Crabtree, who coached gymnastics."

"Gymnastics," Declan said. "Handy skill for trainee burglars. Mr Peters couldn't find a criminal record for Jack Turner."

"I'm not surprised," Charlie said. "Franklin Crabtree took Turner under his wing when the cadets disbanded and got him work as a gardener and odd-jobs man. Jack is an honest, hard-working man, by all accounts. However, he does have a link with several of the burgled households through his work with Mrs MacDonnell, for whom he collected auction donations. I let Turner slip through my fingers last night, I'm sorry to say, but I have the address of his boarding house."

"A strong suspect. Excellent." Wallace pushed the scribbled address across his desk to Declan, who took the hint and left to bring Jack Turner in for questioning. "Anything else, Pyke?"

"Elias Vale's son, Matthew Vale, runs his deceased father's property business now. He was at the auction and is of a similar age to the cadets, so he may have known Gus Fenton around the time Gus was arrested for burglary a decade ago. Mrs MacDonnell is impressed with Matthew but remained tight-lipped about his father, Elias. Grace had the impression Elias wasn't quite socially acceptable."

"That's the impression Kelly got, too, when he went back to re-interview Gus's father. He didn't know any of the cadets, but he did confirm Elias Vale as his landlord and the cadet leader. A hard man, by Fenton's account. Ran a tight ship."

"Aptly put. Elias Vale was in the navy."

Wallace grunted. "You'll be pleased to know that Mr Fenton Senior has decided to sell the bakery and share the proceeds with Minnie for the benefit of Gus's unborn child. He has no heart left for the business after his son's murder. Mr Fenton will live with a daughter up-country."

"Thank you for letting me know, sir." Charlie could see his old boss was as relieved as he was that Minnie Fenton and her baby would have the funds to secure her future. Wallace was as soft as goose down when it came to children and their welfare. "Anything from the door knock or the interviews of the auction staff?"

"Nothing of note," Wallace said. "Alistair, what news from the depths of the filing room?"

Alistair rapped his knuckles on the pile of files he had dumped on Wallace's desk. "Mr Peters dug up Gus Fenton's criminal record and discovered a rash of unsolved burglaries in the year leading up to his arrest, which stopped when Gus went to prison. Similar method to the latest burglaries: carefully planned and spread out in time and place. It seems the lad was up to his old, tried-and-true tricks again. Maybe with the same accomplice. Although why they let a decade pass between is anyone's guess. Needed the money, I suppose. Before your time, of course, Robbie."

Detective Inspector Wallace had been brought in to lead the detective team four years ago, after a purge to rid the local police force of corruption. Charlie knew all about that. He had been caught up in the scandal because his former sergeant was the biggest canker of the lot. However, the investigation had also led him to a bright new career with Alistair Stewart, who was the man brought in to investigate the corruption.

"The identity of the accomplice might be in the files." Wallace eyed the pile of documents with the enthusiasm of Hercules facing a dung-filled stable. "It'll take a week to go through it all to uncover any links to the current case."

"Which is why I sent a telegram to an old acquaintance last night," Alistair said. "Sergeant Yardley, now retired, was the man who spotted a pattern in the burglaries and arrested Gus Fenton ten years ago. He's arriving by train in time for lunch."

The predatory gleam returned to Wallace's grey eyes. "The more the merrier. Let's take a well-earned break until then. Thank the Lord for all your hard work, because I've promised to brief the

101

Chief Inspector again this morning. It's a profound relief to have something to tell him. I'll have to dig out a bottle of Old Vatted Glenlivet for you when this is over."

"I'll hold you to that promise, Robbie." Alistair's nostrils quivered, as if he were already sniffing whisky fumes.

Charlie made his escape before Wallace could change his mind about the well-earned break. He'd promised Grace he wouldn't get excited or fuss over her at this early stage, but a man could be forgiven for wanting to spend a little time with his wife on a Sunday. Maybe even drop in a subtle question or two about what lay ahead. Babies were uncharted territory, and he couldn't help feeling there might be one or two of those *Here Be Dragons* notations on the map that he ought to be prepared for.

Cold Case

Grace awoke with a pounding heart to find Charlie sitting by the bed, looking at her with an expression he usually reserved for Mrs Brown's delectable caramel sponge.

At least one of them viewed her condition with pure delight. The nightmare that caused her pounding heart had featured an endless stream of babies popping out of her private parts during a lecture at medical school. Everyone had been glaring at her and her screaming babies, while she tried to reassure the professor she had the situation under control.

"I trust you won't be this mawkish for the entire seven months, Pyke." She smiled at her husband, hoping the residual terror of the nightmare wasn't obvious. An unexpected pregnancy in her final year would be a challenge, even for a person who prided herself on overcoming seemingly insurmountable obstacles. Somehow, with the support of the wonderful people around her, she would find a way.

"Would you rather I deserted you for my drinking companions at the tavern?" Charlie said. "I have a very amusing story to share with them about a woman who got stuck in a gate while trespassing."

"It's Sunday. The taverns are closed." Not that her husband ever frequented them, to her knowledge.

"Dearest Grace, if there was one thing I learned during my time working behind a bar, it's that a thirsty man can always find a drink."

"That wasn't the only useful thing you learned, as I recall." Grace patted the bed. "Why don't you join me and ask the question that is so obviously burning a hole in your tongue."

Charlie looked as if he were about to speak, but he pressed his lips together to hold it back. He slipped in beside her and soaked up her warmth. "Tell me about Doctor Crabtree. Mrs MacDonnell said he had returned to Dunedin several months ago. I'm intrigued by the coincidence of his return with the renewed spate of burglaries, especially given the similarity with the burglaries leading up to the arrest of Gus Fenton a decade ago."

"Is this a subtle way of warning me that the dazzling Professor of Galvanism is a potential suspect in the murder of Gus Fenton? I'll be careful, Charlie, not least because I distrust the galvanic therapy he's hawking."

"Please promise me you won't test the electrical devices on yourself, especially not now."

"I won't do anything to endanger The Bean," she promised. "In fact, I made the appointment for Lily, not me, and we'll be walking through an open gate this time."

Charlie exhaled into her hair. "In that case, it's the charming doctor I fear for, with you two investigating his misdeeds."

Grace had only been thinking of her investigation into Doctor Crabtree in terms of the potential for medical harm, so Charlie's warning about the man's possible link to other crimes was timely. "Doctor Crabtree would be a similar age to Gus, or perhaps a little older. It's possible they knew each other a decade ago, although I expect they mixed in very different circles."

"Doctor Crabtree's father knew Gus from the cadets," Charlie reminded her. "It's possible Crabtree Senior took his son to the gymnastics class he taught. We'll have to talk to them both."

"You might not get much out of Crabtree Senior. He suffered an apoplectic seizure that affected his brain function. It was serious enough for his son to return from London. I'll see what I can find out about them at the consultation on Monday. A large helping of flattery should work on a man like Doctor Barnabas Crabtree."

They discussed their respective cases, with a shared cast of characters, until it was time to go for lunch.

Grace had never seen Detective Inspector Wallace outside the police station, which made observing him in the presence of his wife a surprise. Wallace fetched and carried at his wife's orders, treating her as the respected high commander of the household. Seeing the brief glances and touches the two shared as they passed each other brought a warm glow to Grace's heart. She knew Wallace had a soft interior within his tough outer shell, but it was still touching to see love flourishing after so many decades of marriage.

Alistair and Lily Stewart arrived shortly after, bringing with them a stooped, red-nosed man of about sixty. Alistair introduced him as Mr Yardley, formerly Sergeant Yardley of the Dunedin Police.

The meal passed with a mix of pleasant conversation and increasingly outrageous policing yarns from decades past. To Grace's relief, Charlie held his tongue over the gate incident and the revelation that followed it. Once the plates were cleared, they retreated to the sitting room with cups of tea to begin the real work.

Wallace settled into an old armchair worn into his body shape. "Thank you for taking the trouble to join us, Mr Yardley."

"Detective Inspector Stewart told me you're hunting for a murderer," Yardley said. "A murderer who might have a link to the burglary case I was involved with a decade ago. How can I help?"

"We understand you are the man to thank for spotting the link between the burglary victims."

Yardley, obviously very much at home in the company of other policemen, sank back into the cushion of his armchair and took a sip of tea while gathering his thoughts. "The burglar was a young lad called Gus Fenton, or at least he was the one who was caught. It was obvious from the start that Gus was not the mastermind, because he had neither the brains nor the contacts to plan the burglaries. The little devil wouldn't give up his accomplice though, no matter how hard we pushed him."

"Gus Fenton's father thought his son was too frightened of his accomplice to dob him in," Wallace said.

"That's for sure. We got the man regardless. When I was going back through all the burglary files, I noticed that all the victims used the same locksmith, a man called Arthur Tillman. He had the master keys to the victims' homes, which made the burglaries a simple matter. In and out before anyone noticed, taking only small, valuable items, and leaving no trace behind to alert the victims."

"Sounds like the same method Gus used in the recent burglaries," Wallace said. "He was so quick and quiet, we wondered if he had access to house keys. Could the locksmith be out of prison and up to his own tricks?"

Yardley shook his head. "Arthur Tillman killed himself after his initial interview, before we could pin the burglaries on him. He died in his vault after taking a fatal dose of strychnine. He was found with his head resting on a sack of burgled valuables, surrounded by his keys and locks. His son discovered him, apparently. Poor lad. He was shaking like a jellyfish, from what I heard. The entire Tillman family sold up and left town after the funeral to escape the shame of Arthur Tillman's suicide and criminal activities."

"Were the police certain the locksmith took his own life?" Charlie asked.

"Tillman left a signed confession on his workbench. The shop was locked, with no sign of a forced entry or a struggle. The Inspector took a good hard look at the handwriting on the suicide note, but it was a close enough match to his normal writing, allowing for the fact it was written by a man under tremendous strain."

Alistair leaned forward, his fingers steepled under his chin. "And yet, I sense you believe the case was closed prematurely."

Yardley's shoulders twitched into a hesitant shrug. "A man confessed, the burglar was caught, the Inspector was satisfied, and the burglaries stopped. Can't get much more conclusive than that. But you're right. I had a gut feeling that the real mastermind behind the crimes was not Arthur Tillman. You know the feeling, the itch that won't go away."

They all knew what he was talking about. Charlie felt it as a tingle down his spine, and he knew Alistair Stewart talked of his knee joints aching when he was onto something, but he didn't quite know what. Charlie wondered how Wallace felt it. Given the workout his woolly grey eyebrows were getting, perhaps eyebrow itch was his sign.

"The recent burglaries are too similar to the previous ones to ignore," Wallace said, "especially with Gus Fenton as the known burglar in both cases. The deceased Arthur Tillman cannot be behind the recent crimes, which means someone else knew enough to copy the original method, or your intuition is correct, and somebody else was behind the original burglaries. Who did you suspect at the time, Mr Yardley?"

"Suspect is too strong a word. But if there was someone, he must have been connected to both Gus Fenton and the locksmith. A strong enough connection to coerce Gus into becoming a burglar, as well as having access to the master keys in the locksmith's shop."

The team leaned forward expectantly as Yardley got his thoughts in order. An old-school policeman, unwilling to jump to conclusions without hard evidence.

"Gus Fenton refused to name names even after Arthur Tillman's suicide, when it would have been easy to plead that Tillman forced him into crime. The fact that he was still too scared to talk, and that we never found a link between Gus and the locksmith … well, it seemed like too many loose ends to me. Add to that the fact that Arthur Tillman was universally admired as an honest, likable fellow. I confess, I wondered if the locksmith knew who had stolen his keys but took the blame anyway."

"A family member?" Wallace asked.

"That seemed to be the most likely explanation. The locksmith had only one son, Samuel Tillman, who was the same age as Gus.

I didn't conduct the interview with him, but I talked to the man who did. He said Samuel was a right odd stick, but clever too."

"Odd in what way?"

"Quiet and awkward around people, to the point of refusing to look the Inspector in the eye, which struck the police as suspicious. On the other hand, Samuel Tillman had no interest in the locksmith trade and few friends. As far as I gathered, the only thing he enjoyed was collecting stamps. Not new stamps – old ones. What's the point of that?"

"Rare stamps can be valuable," Alistair said.

"If you say so," Yardley said, looking unconvinced. "To be fair, Samuel Tillman had never come to the attention of the police before. Also, he didn't seem strong enough to have sway over a tough lad like Gus Fenton. There was no reason to consider Samuel a suspect, apart from his access to the master keys. Samuel and Gus went to the same school, but that in itself is not surprising, given it was the local school. They were not known to be friends, although Samuel probably visited Fenton's bakery when he was younger. All the local children did, because Mrs Fenton's cream buns were legendary back then. She died though, before Gus turned bad and joined the cadets."

"Was Samuel Tillman in the cadets?" Charlie asked.

"His name was on the register. The cadet leader had been actively trying to get local lads to sign up. However, everyone we interviewed agreed Samuel never once showed his face. Can't blame him for bunking off. A timid lad like him wouldn't have lasted an hour with that mob. Mr Crabtree told the police he had sent Samuel home on medical grounds. An act of mercy, if you ask me."

"What about the other lads in the cadet corps?" Wallace asked.

"They were all interviewed, of course," Yardley said. "Waste of police time. That lot wouldn't have narked to a copper if they had a pistol against their heads. Stood up straight like a line of battle-hardened troops and refused to say anything but their name and rank. The Inspector running the investigation did press down hard on one cadet. He kept his distance from the rest of them, which made him a potential informant on the other cadets."

"Do you recall his name?" Wallace said.

Yardley glanced at his notes. "Jack Turner. An orphan. No previous trouble with the law. He swore he was innocent and knew nothing, even after several interviews and a few nights in a cold, damp cell. Mr Franklin Crabtree spoke up for the lad, so we had to release him."

The former sergeant paused again, lowering his voice as if afraid he would be overheard. "The other possibility, as I'm sure you have realised, is that the mastermind of the burglaries staged Arthur Tillman's death to throw suspicion off himself. Tillman's landlord was a man called Elias Vale. As the landlord, he had a key to the locksmith shop. He was also the cadet leader, so he knew Gus Fenton."

"The same could be said for his business partner, Franklin Crabtree, couldn't it?" Wallace said. "He must have formed a strong bond with his cadets if he put himself out to help Jack Turner."

"True, but Franklin Crabtree was a respectable businessman without the slightest whiff of scandal about him. In contrast, Elias Vale was ex-Navy, hard as nails and not afraid to rub people up the wrong way. In fact, several people hinted the police would do well to turn their attention to him, although none of them were brave enough to accuse him openly. I wouldn't blame Gus for being terrified of him. All the cadets were. Elias Vale took discipline seriously, if you take my drift. I should emphasise that the police did investigate Vale thoroughly, on the quiet, but came up with no evidence whatsoever linking him to the crimes. In the end, he was interviewed only in his capacity as landlord and as leader of the cadets. Both Vale and Crabtree had connections in society, which meant they were treated with deference."

Yardley spread his hands wide. "Thus, case closed, not a shred of solid evidence against anyone but Arthur Tillman, and, even then, only because he left a written confession."

"And yet here you are," Alistair said. "Willing to board a train at short notice on a Sunday to assist our inquiry."

"You know how it is," Yardley replied. "A copper's hatred of injustice."

"Nothing worse than a case that keeps itching at the back of the brain," Wallace acknowledged. "Do you know what happened to Samuel Tillman, the locksmith's son?"

"Left town with his mother and the rest of the family after the funeral. As long as he was out of our patch, the Inspector was happy to see the back of him. To be fair to the lad, Samuel was odd, but he didn't seem the type to go off the rails. He swore he knew nothing about the keys or the burglary, which is partly why I didn't make a fuss when the case was closed. His father's death had a devastating effect on Samuel, so I suspect he never returned to a life of crime, if he ever was involved."

The slam of a door cut through the silence. Declan Kelly hurried in, flushed from running, with a flurry of apologies for being late. "Jack Turner has cleaned out his room at the boarding house and vanished." Declan looked around at the startled faces. "What is it? What have I missed?"

Wallace jumped to his feet, demanding details and ordering a city-wide search, which Declan had already arranged. Meanwhile, Charlie shrank into his chair, no doubt feeling guilty for not apprehending Jack the previous night.

Grace was not having that, nor was she prepared to tar a decent man with suspicion when there were other possibilities. "Gentlemen," she said, using the firm tone her crusading great-aunt used when faced with more powerful opponents. "Why are we not tracking down Mr Elias Vale, who had both the character and the power to terrorise Gus Fenton into aiding him? Or Franklin

Crabtree, for that matter. Just because he was outwardly respectable doesn't mean he isn't rotten on the inside."

Charlie had that strained expression he took on when he didn't want to show her up. He gave her an apologetic glance and said, "I must have forgotten to tell Grace that Elias Vale died years ago, and thus he couldn't be behind the recent burglaries. The same could be said of Franklin Crabtree, who is said to have been severely affected by illness these past few months. You've met him, Grace. Do you think he would be capable of organising the recent burglaries and killing Gus?"

"Doubtful, but not entirely impossible." Grace saw the query in Wallace's raised eyebrow. "I met Franklin Crabtree briefly last night. He is partially paralysed on one side, but his other arm is strong and he can walk on his own. Franklin's son, Doctor Barnabas Crabtree, is the subject of a medical investigation I am undertaking."

"Grace and I have reason to be concerned about Doctor Crabtree," Charlie said. "He is approximately the same age as the cadets, and he arrived back in Dunedin after an extended absence in London not long before the latest burglaries started. Also, his dubious medical services were used by each of the six households burgled on Friday night, and he was the auctioneer at the charity auction all the burglary victims attended."

"The Crabtree and Vale families have close connections," Grace added. "Franklin Crabtree's daughter, Rosannah, is married to Elias Vale's son, Matthew. Matthew Vale is also roughly the same age as the cadets. Rosannah was a member of the auction committee, and thus would have access to a list of donors and attendees to the auction."

Alistair leaned forward, stroking his moustache thoughtfully. "I'll look into both families' business dealings to see if they needed money. I'm wondering if one of the sons could have resurrected their father's criminal operation. Did your team talk to them as part of your investigation, Mr Yardley?"

"The sons weren't interviewed because they were not involved with the cadets," Yardley said. "As I recall, Elias Vale told the police that both Barnabas Crabtree and Matthew Vale were at boarding school."

"I don't like the smell of Elias Vale and his navy discipline," Wallace growled. "Pyke, could you sound out the Vale son tomorrow? If you sniff a rat, we'll pull him in for a formal police interview. As for Doctor Crabtree and his father –"

"As luck would have it," Grace said, "Lily Stewart and I are consulting the famed Professor of Galvanism tomorrow by appointment. We can find out more about their household without looking suspicious."

"I will accompany them," Alistair said. "Not that I don't trust the ladies' abilities, but because the more people we have, the more chance we will have to distract and deploy. From what I hear, Barnabas Crabtree styles himself as a doctor, but he acts like the worst type of charlatan."

"He has already caused at least one woman to have a life-threatening medical episode," Grace explained. "The burglaries might be his way of lining his pockets before he is run out of town by the medical authorities."

"In that case, I'll wait to hear from you before we make formal inquiries," Wallace said. "Kelly, get your team onto tracing past cadets and other associates of Gus Fenton when you can. However, your priority is tracking down Jack Turner. Even if he is innocent, he seems to be the only former cadet we can lay our hands on right now."

"Take Blaze," Charlie said.

Kelly beamed at the offer. "Between Blaze and the Kelly family network of informants, Turner doesn't stand a chance."

"You all know how much your efforts are valued," Wallace said. "My feet are itching on this one. The man behind this took a substantial risk organising the burglaries of so many houses in one night and then murdering his accomplice. He will either be lying low or getting ready to run, especially if he thinks we are closing in."

Behind the Vale

Charlie woke up on Monday morning with his arms around his wife, one hand resting on the round of her belly. Not that The Bean needed protection in the warmth and comfort of their bed inside a locked house, but he needed the practice. He could have stayed there all day, but they had already slept late, and the hour hand on the clock was now closer to eight than seven. Grace had the consultation with Doctor Crabtree today, while Charlie had agreed to arrange a meeting with Matthew Vale.

They were finishing a leisurely breakfast when Alistair and Lily arrived to collect Grace for their foray into galvanic therapy.

"Don't suppose you could squeeze another cup out of the teapot?" Alistair said. "Late night last night."

Charlie poured two cups for their guests. "Were you and Robbie Wallace doing your best to support the Scottish whisky industry, Alistair?"

"Not until we crack this case. I had a quiet word with a few contacts in the property business, who told me that Elias Vale was being pursued by debtors about ten years ago. It never went as far as bankruptcy proceedings, which means the police didn't find out about it at the time. It seems Elias Vale's debts were conveniently paid off right around the time of the first series of burglaries." Alistair passed over a page of information, including the registered address of the property business, now run by Matthew Vale.

The business address was the same as the York Place home of Matthew's father-in-law, confirming Grace's suspicion that Matthew and his wife lived with Franklin Crabtree. Charlie skimmed through the key points Alistair had noted. "Convenient indeed. If Elias Vale wasn't dead, he'd have some explaining to do."

114

Alistair finished the last of his tea and dabbed his luxuriant moustache. "Come, ladies, we have to prepare our battle strategy for Lily's appointment with a shocking charlatan." Alistair rose and took his wife's arm. "I should add that Matthew's father, Elias Vale, was not well liked by my informants. A tough-as-nails boatswain, who never learned the polite manners of civilian society. His naval nickname was 'Nine-Tail Vale' because of his enthusiasm for delivering discipline using a cat-o'-nine-tails whip."

Grace paled. "If Matthew Vale is like his father, promise me you won't go prodding the man into a fury, Charlie."

Charlie promised. Matthew Vale did not appear to be in any way fearsome, based on the glimpse he had of him at the auction. He was about to comment that Grace was the one who ought to be careful, putting herself into the clutches of a mad professor, but his wife had rushed off to finish her preparations for the day, telling Alistair she would meet them next door shortly to go over their plan.

Shortly thereafter, Charlie arrived at the central city office of Vale Holdings. A small brass plate within a column of similar plates for other businesses told him he was in the right place. There was no bell, so he pushed open the door to the foyer.

A slim, grey man, whose thinning hair made him look older than his years, looked up from his desk. "Good morning, sir. Do you have an appointment?"

"I was hoping to make one," Charlie said. "As soon as possible."

"Who was it you wished to see?" The man saw his confusion and explained. "I manage the appointments for several businesses, sir, in the interests of efficiency."

In the interests of reducing expenses, Charlie thought. "Mr Matthew Vale, of Vale Holdings."

The man donned spectacles and selected an appointment book from the row on his desk. "You're in luck. Mr Vale has an opening at ten o'clock this morning. May I have your name, please, and the nature of your inquiry?"

"Mr Charles Penrose," he said, hoping that Vale didn't know his full name and occupation. "I am relatively new to Dunedin and wish to extend my property investment holdings. Mr Vale was recommended to me."

This much could not be disputed, as Charlie owned no property at all. The house in which he and Grace lived belonged to Anne Drummond. Charlie's assets amounted to one border collie, essential clothes, half a private detective agency, and a bank account that was far healthier than he had ever expected it to be, although the likes of Matthew Vale would view it as small change. Belatedly, he wondered how much it would cost to raise a child.

With the appointment made, Charlie browsed in a shop across the street while he waited for the forty minutes to pass before his appointment. Through the glass window, he saw a messenger boy leaving at a run. When he ran out of items to browse, Charlie moved to an alley a few yards down the road, where a clear view of the office came with a freezing breeze whipping down between the buildings. He hunched into his overcoat, stamping his feet to stay warm and daydreaming of an armchair in front of a roaring fire. After ten seconds of stamping, the foot he had broken earlier in the year was throbbing again.

Darn it, he was getting soft in his old age, despite being on the right side of a quarter century. Four years ago, he would have walked across a bed of nails on hot coals for the opportunity to observe a suspect in a draughty alley as a fully fledged detective.

And why on earth was he sighing, when he felt like the luckiest man alive? But that was the nub of it. The spark of hope that Grace might be carrying their child was a double-edged sword. Utter joy and utter terror. Should he have gone with her today to the consultation? Should he have let her go at all? He could see Grace rolling her eyes at the idea that he could stop her. And Alistair and Lily were with her, so what could possibly go wrong?

Charlie immediately regretted the latter thought, because his mind filled with every conceivable thing that could go wrong during a consultation with a charlatan whose electrical device had almost killed a woman three days ago. Was Grace really so sure she had not been seen when she got wedged in the quack doctor's gate? This, naturally, led to a further rabbit warren of disquieting thoughts, the foremost of which was whether their baby had been hurt by the squeezing and pushing, despite Grace's assurance that the child growing inside her would be no bigger than a bean. He sighed and waited.

Thirty-five minutes later, a red-faced, puffing Matthew Vale hurried into the office, which suggested that he either worked limited hours, or only used the office when he had potential clients to impress.

Three minutes later, Charlie brushed the shoulder of his overcoat where he had leaned against the alley wall and returned to the foyer, where he was shown up to a small room on the first floor. Spartan was the first adjective that came to mind. A desk, a single filing drawer, and a blank wall relieved only by two slightly skewed photographs, as if they had been hung in a hurry.

And yet Matthew Vale, straight-backed and dressed in a dark suit crafted by an expert tailor, made the office look as if it was only spartan because it was designed for the efficient transaction of business. Of average height and build, with neatly trimmed wavy brown hair, Vale wouldn't stand out in a crowd, but he had an indefinable air of quiet confidence about him.

Vale rose from behind the desk and extended his hand. "Mr Charles Penrose? Have we met before, sir?"

The permanent furrow between his brows and the narrowing of his eyes told Charlie he should tread carefully, because Matthew was no fool. However, his handshake was no more than politely firm, and his brief smile seemed genuine. Matthew Vale was not a

117

man one could imagine holding his father's cat-o'-nine-tails, let alone using it. This apple, it appeared, had fallen far from the tree. Charlie wondered how this conservative man of business got along with his flamboyant brother-in-law, Barnabas Crabtree.

"Charles Penrose *Pyke*, actually," he said, not wishing to be caught in a lie. "Your man downstairs must have misheard me."

"The private detective?" Matthew Vale gestured to the guest chair. "What a fascinating life you must lead."

Charlie smiled and nodded, as if he were honoured to be recognised, when he was anything but. "My business is thriving, Mr Vale, but it is arduous and often tedious work. I would like to use a portion of the profits to invest in property, so that I do not have to linger in freezing alleys and risk my life raiding criminal hideouts forever."

"A wise move, sir. With proper advice, property can provide an excellent living with little effort on your part. May I ask how you came to hear about our services, Mr Penrose Pyke?"

Was it Charlie's imagination or had there been a slight emphasis on the Pyke, as if his explanation of the name confusion was not entirely believed? If this was a game of cat and mouse, Charlie was not yet sure if he was the feline or the rodent.

Charlie tapped his nose. "I have my sources, Mr Vale. To be honest, I have heard nothing but praise for you, but I own some doubts too. My sources tell me the business was on the brink of faltering several years ago."

Vale let out a hollow laugh through thin lips. "I cannot deny the truth of that, since you are a detective. But that was a brief episode during my father's time at the helm, and long since remedied by my subsequent success."

"Are you and your father in partnership?"

"Sadly, my father met his maker many years ago. It has been my honour to run Vale Holdings since I came of age, hopefully doing my dear father proud. In the interests of full disclosure, my father-in-law, Mr Franklin Crabtree, is a silent partner. It was he who

118

provided my father with the funds to overcome past difficulties, taking a stake in the business in return. Mr Crabtree taught me well after my father's death, and thus I was able to take over the reins at twenty-one with a solid knowledge of business practice. With Mr Crabtree's backing, I can assure you there can be no doubt about the future financial strength and success of Vale Holdings. You will not be disappointed if you invest with us."

"Thank you for your honesty, Mr Vale." Charlie appreciated his candour but noted that Matthew had failed to mention that Crabtree Senior would no longer be in a position to back the business due to his ill health. "You are married to Mr Crabtree's daughter, I believe. An excellent match, from what I have heard. May I extend my condolences on your father's passing, Mr Vale? I do hope the brief financial difficulty did not hasten his death?"

"Not at all. His death was from natural causes. My father was in the navy and kept up an exhausting regime of physical training. Tragically, he caught a chill whilst out exercising in the rain. As so many dear friends lamented at the time, *oh how the good and mighty are fallen.*"

Charlie nodded in sympathy. Matthew Vale gave every sign of being an open and honest young man, doing his best to continue his father's legacy. Charlie would have been reassured if he hadn't known that Matthew was adeptly concealing his father's faults, which were many if Alistair's informants were correct. He wondered if Matthew might be putting on a front – a more subtle and gentlemanly version of Nine-Tail Vale. He was a hard man to read, which no doubt stood him in good stead during property negotiations.

It suited Charlie to pretend ignorance in order to draw Matthew out. "An acquaintance of mine, Mrs MacDonnell, was telling me only the other day what a marvellous philanthropist your father was. I believe he ran a cadet corps to improve the lives of young men. Gymnastics, boxing, and so forth. I expect your father had you there too, building your character in his own image."

119

Matthew Vale shuddered at the mention of it, which was his most honest reaction yet. "I confess I was not one for such activities. Never went near the cadet corps, I'm happy to say, thanks to my mother's intervention. Dear Mama was not willing to have me within a mile of those young tearaways. She sent me to a boarding school instead. Fortunately, the corps had disbanded by the time I left boarding school." He nodded at the framed photograph on the wall. "I tried my hand at fencing, which is a much more appropriate sport for a gentleman than gymnastics, as I'm sure you'll agree. To be honest, I was never fond of physical activities, being of the view that academic pursuits were a better path to success."

Charlie rose to look at the photograph, which was of a fencing team outside the gate of a prestigious boarding school. The young men stood straight and proud, their foils pointing upward at the Latin motto inscribed on the lintel. The school's attendance fees must have been a stretch for Matthew's father, who was on the brink of bankruptcy, but perhaps Elias Vale wanted to maintain the appearance of wealth for the sake of his business reputation and his son's future.

"A fine school, Mr Vale. I hope to send my sons to a similar establishment one day. In my view, education is the most important asset one can bestow upon a young man, especially when one also acquires the right contacts by attending a prestigious institution." Charlie hoped he wasn't laying the treacle on too thickly, but Matthew nodded his agreement.

"How right you are, Mr Penrose Pyke. I'm sure we can build an excellent portfolio of properties for you to achieve your dreams for your sons. If I can take your details –"

Charlie was turning back to the desk, intending to make a later appointment to discuss the details of his fictional investment, when he saw a familiar face in the second photograph. He leaned closer. "By Jove, is that your wife's brother, Doctor Crabtree, in the second row? Is that how you met Mrs Vale – through an old boarding school friend?"

120

Matthew's smile held, but it stretched tight on narrowed lips. "Our families were already acquainted. I am a great admirer of Mr Franklin Crabtree, but his son Barnabas and I are very different people. Barnabas was expelled not long after that photograph was taken."

"Expelled? How dreadful. A prank, perhaps? Headmasters can be prone to overreaction when riled."

"Far more serious than a prank, I'm sorry to say. The matter is best left in the past, where it belongs. Now, sir, can we return to your investment needs?" Matthew handed him a schedule of properties, listing a brief description alongside a baffling range of numbers, percentages and ratios. "These are just some of the many properties Vale Holdings is proud to own, Mr Penrose Pyke. As you will see from the figures, the rate of return on our investors' funds is exceptional."

Charlie spent another few minutes trying to sound knowledgeable about tenancy turnover rates, return on investment ratios, and the relative attractiveness of industrial versus commercial property. In truth, all he could discern from staring at the figures was that there were many properties, bringing in a substantial sum in rent, and Matthew had the neat and precise handwriting one might expect of a trustworthy and competent businessman.

Before his ignorance became too obvious, Charlie thanked Matthew for his time and excused himself to attend another appointment. He tried a parting shot while gathering his hat and coat. "May I say, sir, it is a great shame your father didn't live to see your success or your marriage to his friend's daughter."

Matthew stood and shook his hand. "Rosannah and I were betrothed long before we married, Mr Penrose Pyke. In fact, we sealed the pact on my father's deathbed, as it was his dying wish, although we only married two years ago. My wife and I make an excellent partnership, both in business and in domestic matters."

121

Charlie tipped his hat and left, thinking that the same could be said of himself and Grace. However, he would never have expressed such a sentiment without emphasising that their marriage was built on love, rather than practicality and business advantage.

On his way out, he stopped at the foyer desk again, thanking the man for his assistance. "Excellent situation you have here," Charlie said, slipping a tempting coin onto the desk. "I don't suppose you have any available offices."

"We could accommodate another gentleman if you do not require many hours, sir." The man's hand rested on the desk briefly, and the coin was gone when he removed it. "There are only three offices, you see, hired on an as-needed basis. Very economical, and yet perfectly located in the central city."

"An admirable scheme. I shall think about it," Charlie said, waving a brisk farewell.

Three offices shared amongst so many businesses suggested none of the users had many visitors, which strongly suggested Matthew Vale's property empire was not as successful as he claimed it to be, unless he conducted most of his meetings elsewhere.

He returned to the chilly alley, where he waited until Matthew Vale left five minutes later. Charlie followed him at a distance until he saw Vale stop at the Roslyn cable car terminus, presumably on his way back home to York Place.

Of all the nuggets of information he had gleaned from Matthew Vale, the most interesting was the fact that Matthew's brother-in-law, Barnabas Crabtree, was expelled from boarding school. For one thing, it suggested there was no love lost between the two men, since mentioning the expulsion unprompted was not the act of a loving and forgiving relation. Charlie wondered how they managed to live under the same roof.

However, the main concern was that being expelled from school was a black mark against the doctor's character. Charlie had no experience of expensive boarding schools, but he suspected they didn't expel fee-paying students for anything other than the most serious of infractions, which meant Doctor Crabtree was a man with very unpleasant secrets in his past. Charlie could only pray that the potent combination of Grace, Lily, and Alistair would provide safety in numbers.

Electrifying Therapy

Grace excused herself from the breakfast table after hearing Alistair's description of Elias Vale and his cat-o'-nine-tails whip. The thought of a man like him taking charge of a group of vulnerable young men in the cadet corps nauseated her to the pit of her stomach. Although she conceded, as she threw up her breakfast, the nausea might have a more miraculous cause.

They would have to tell everyone about the baby soon, because Charlie seemed incapable of concealing his joy. Grace's hand sneaked down again to the slight mound of her previously board-flat body and had to admit her husband's unbounded delight brought tears to her eyes. That said, she seemed uncommonly prone to weeping lately, which was not helpful to the image she attempted to convey of a competent doctor.

No more ridiculous emotional outbursts, Grace vowed, before shedding a tear over the lovely arrangement of fresh flowers Mrs Brown had put on the dresser.

She returned downstairs a few minutes later, refreshed and in complete grip of her wayward emotions. Charlie had already left, so she went next door to put a plan in place for the consultation with Doctor Barnabas Crabtree. Grace also wanted Lily to brief her on the theory of electricity and its practical application, so that she could approach her investigation with the knowledge she needed. Lily, with her inquiring mind and interest in science and technology, knew more than most people on the topic, especially as she had spent yesterday afternoon researching the subject in more detail.

By the time they left for the consultation, Grace had a new appreciation for the wonders of this new field of science and could only imagine what amazing uses electricity would be put to in the future. Her own interest was in medical applications. She had spent the previous afternoon discovering that electrical therapies were more widespread than she knew, both within respectable medical practices and in more dubious settings.

Despite Grace's assurances to Charlie yesterday, she still doubted the safety of Crabtree's practices and his cavalier claims to cure everything from arthritis to hysteria. All the experiments using electricity on the human body had been conducted on men, as far as she could discern. Medical researchers, if they gave any thought to women at all, treated women as merely a smaller and weaker version of the male ideal. Anyone with the most cursory knowledge of the body would reject that assumption outright. Women differed markedly in their anatomy – their distribution of organs and fat, for example – not to mention the all-important differences in the reproductive system.

Grace doubted whether Doctor Crabtree, regardless of his medical training, understood how his treatments would affect different individuals. A small woman like Lily ought not to be subjected to the same voltage as a large man like Charlie, for instance. Mrs Eugenie Atkinson's terrifying experience was the perfect example of ignoring underlying risk factors. Grace's hand inched down towards her belly again. If Lily hadn't volunteered to undertake the consultation, Grace wouldn't have proceeded, but she would be very interested to know if Crabtree asked his female patients about the possibility of being with child before he treated them.

With their plan in place, Grace, Lily, and Alistair departed for the consultation. Before long, Alistair was directing the buggy through the tall, spiked gates that had almost been Grace's downfall two nights before. In the light of day, the grand two-storey dwelling looked benign, and the trees that circled it seemed picturesque rather than menacing. The surrounding woods and the end-of-street location guaranteed privacy, with the only neighbour scarcely visible behind a curtain of foliage.

125

They arrived early by design to get the lay of the land before the consultation. A butler opened the door. His face was so devoid of expression he might have been a life-sized butler doll. It took a second for Grace to recognise the smooth face and portly figure as the same man who had brought her water and food at the auction. She shouldn't have been surprised, knowing his association with Mr and Mrs Vale. The butler took a little longer to place Grace, and his recognition came with the merest flicker of eyelids and a discreet nod.

"We have an appointment with Doctor Crabtree," Grace said.

The butler stood aside to let them pass. "Come this way, please."

Grace heard Lily's intake of breath behind her as she entered the house. The dull day and encroaching trees should have made the wood-panelled hall a gloomy space, yet it was as light as a summer day. Electrical bulbs emitted a steady, warm light, not spluttering like gas or flickering like candlelight. Judging from Lily's rapturous expression, Grace suspected that the Stewart household would be installing an electrical system before the year was out.

The presence of such an expensive innovation as domestic electric lights, and the employment of a butler, signalled a wealthy household. The magnificence of the interior of the old house indicated that the family had been affluent long before Doctor Crabtree came back from London to establish his medical practice. Indeed, the fact that Doctor Crabtree's father, Franklin Crabtree, had sent his son to London to train, when there was a perfectly good medical school nearby, suggested the sort of wealth that cared little for the ordinary bounds of common sense. Grace wondered how the old man felt about his son coming home to practice a dubious form of medicine.

The butler glided silently up the hall, watched surreptitiously by a young maid on her knees polishing the already-gleaming woodwork of the staircase. When the butler glanced in her direction, she looked away, polishing up a fury. Grace didn't envy either of them. A house this size would require an endless round of

126

work – scrubbing, polishing, cooking, and laundering from dawn till dusk – unless Doctor Crabtree had brought back electric scrubbing brushes and ovens, along with his electric hairbrushes. What a difference that would make to the lives of women, if inventors ever turned their brilliance to such mundane domestic items.

Lily, Alistair and Grace lingered along the way, entranced by the paintings and cabinets of collectibles, which showed to great advantage in the bright light. They ignored the butler, who stood patiently by a row of ornate hooks waiting to take their hats and coats.

"Goodness me, this lighting is extraordinary," Alistair said. "How is it possible? Surely you do not have a steam-powered generator to produce the electrical current?"

"No, sir," the butler said, in the patient tone of a man used to such questions. "The electrical generator runs on gas from the town supply. Doctor Crabtree had it installed when he returned from England."

"How ingenious." Alistair must have seen Grace's keep-him-talking gesture behind the butler's back, because he looked up at the light with a puzzled expression. "Does electricity run in pipes like gas? What happens if a pipe breaks, and the electric current leaks out?"

If the butler was taken aback by the stream of curious questions, he was too well trained to show it. While he patiently answered Alistair's endless questions, Grace handed her coat and hat to Lily, and slipped away unnoticed. A single door stood open at the end of the hall, which she correctly picked as the door to the doctor's waiting room. Fortunately, nobody sat at the desk in the corner. A pair of voices drifted out from the consultation room beyond, through another open door.

Grace ran her eyes along a row of photographs and certificates, positioned to impress the most anxious and discriminating of patients. Barnabas Crabtree as a proud schoolboy standing under

127

the entrance arch of a prestigious boarding school, next to a photograph of an older Barnabas in an academic gown, and later beside various people who must have been important, judging by his smug grin.

Naturally, his framed medical qualifications took pride of place in the centre of the wall: one from a London medical school and the other from the Marylebone Institute of Electrical Medicine. Grace had to admit Doctor Crabtree had done well for himself and conceded she might have jumped to conclusions about him being a charlatan. He cannot have known that Mrs Atkinson would be so foolish as to wear the electrical device in the bath, although Grace still believed the doctor had been grossly negligent by not asking about his patient's heart condition.

She hurried towards the open door, expecting the butler to enter the waiting room with Lily and Alistair at any moment.

A man's voice, pompous, edged with spleen. "Just because I hold a power of attorney doesn't mean I can dip into Father's funds on a whim to support your husband's failing business, Rosannah. I have needs too, you know."

Doctor Barnabas Crabtree and his sister, Rosannah Vale, Grace surmised.

"Father owns half of Vale Holdings, Barnabas," Rosannah replied, her voice hissing with repressed fury. "He has a responsibility to ensure its success, which now falls upon you, since our dear Father no longer has the mental competence to handle his own affairs."

"Hasn't Father done enough over the years, pouring my inheritance into the follies of Elias Vale and his son? You'll have to wait until the old man dies, Rosannah. And don't expect me to stay in this miserable little town after the estate is settled."

When Rosannah spoke again, her voice dipped to a barely audible whisper. "You'll keep the house, though, won't you, Barnabas? It's our home."

"It's mine to do as I want with as soon as the old man shuffles off this mortal coil. Why should I house you when you have a husband to provide for you?"

Grace felt the urge to slap the condescending smirk off the doctor's lips at his callousness. She couldn't see the smirk, but it dripped from his voice like a bee sting in honey.

"You might at least do me the decency of telling me what Father has left me in his will, dearest brother, so that I know I can rely on something to build a secure future. For all I know, Father could be leaving me nothing more than a pretty set of crockery suitable for a lady of means."

"Enough, Rosannah. The new patient will be here soon. She won't want to hear you wailing like an alley cat."

Grace dashed back out to the hallway, where she stood with pulse hammering, pretending to admire a truly ugly painting of a sailing ship blazing with all cannons. Just in time. Lily, Alistair and the increasingly agitated butler, whom Alistair was now addressing as Lancaster, strolled along the hall, admiring works of art and science along the way. Or rather, the men were strolling and Lily was limping behind them with agonising slowness, since she was supposed to be consulting the doctor for her debilitating sciatica.

Alistair's hand touched the butler's as they reached the door, transferring a token of his thanks for the impromptu tour.

When Grace entered the waiting room for the second time, she saw a slim woman in her twenties sitting at the desk. The woman's neck and face were scorched red, sending up a waft of lavender scent, but otherwise she remained impressively composed. Mrs Rosannah Vale's tightly pulled back hair, and the starched white shirt buttoned to her neck, gave her the appearance of an efficient woman of business, just as she had appeared at the demonstration of galvanism two days before.

Rosannah pretended to study the register in front of her for a second longer, her lips still pinched in anger in the bright light of an electric desk lamp. Then she looked up with a tight smile and

129

placed her pen back in the inkwell, before rising to greet the new patients. If she was startled by the dapper, middle-aged gentleman and the petite Chinese lady accompanying Grace, she didn't let it show. As Grace now knew, Rosannah and her husband had bigger problems than the oddities of her brother's patients.

Rosannah bobbed her head at Grace. "Welcome, Mrs Stewart. You are the young lady who purchased the consultation at the auction on Friday night, as I recall. I am Mrs Rosannah Vale. Doctor Crabtree's sister, but also his assistant until more suitable arrangements can be made."

Given the unsuitable arrangement had been in place for several months, Grace didn't fancy Rosannah's chances of escaping the role. She nodded politely and indicated Lily. "I bid on the consultation for my aunt, Mrs Lily Stewart, who has been having problems with pain in her leg from sciatica. Her husband, Mr Stewart, wished to accompany her, naturally. My name is Grace Penrose."

Using her maiden name risked her being caught in a falsehood, but Grace did not wish Rosannah and her brother to identify her as the wife of Dunedin's most well-known private detective so early in her investigation. Fortunately, Anne hadn't introduced them at the auction, and the Vales hadn't seen Grace and Charlie together, because they had left the auction early.

Rosannah Vale's gaze rested on them for a fraction of a second, assessing the unusual trio, but her smile never faltered. "Welcome to you all. If you and Mr Stewart would like to take a seat in this room, Miss Penrose, I will take Mrs Stewart through to see the doctor." She turned to the butler. "Lancaster, have Cook send in tea for the gentleman and his niece while they wait for Mrs Stewart."

"That won't be necessary, thank you," Alistair said. "Miss Penrose and I will accompany my wife to her consultation."

Mrs Vale opened her mouth to argue, but Alistair got in first. "I must insist. My wife is of a nervous disposition."

"In that case, I ask all of you to leave your valuables in this cabinet, which will remain locked throughout the consultation. A precaution, you understand, because metallic items such as coins and jewellery conduct electricity. We follow strict medical protocols, which I am sure you will appreciate is for your safety."

Grace thought this precaution sounded more like showmanship than science, but she complied, because they were acting as ordinary first-time patients might – eager and hopeful, yet nervous of this new type of treatment using a potentially deadly force.

The butler stepped forward to open the cabinet, but Mrs Vale stopped him with a touch on his forearm. "I'll see to this, thank you, Lancaster. Could you attend to my father's needs, please?"

Grace was pleased to see that Mrs Vale treated the butler with more warmth than she had shown at the auction. She even managed a fleeting smile, which showed strength of spirit considering how angry she must feel after her argument with her brother.

Lancaster withdrew as silently as he had entered, while Mrs Vale gathered their valuables.

They had agreed beforehand to do whatever was asked of them to maintain the charade of a genuine consultation, up to the point where any of them felt uncomfortable about proceeding. Alistair divested himself of his pocket watch, coin purse, keys and cufflinks, while Grace and Lily put their minimal jewellery into their purses, which were deposited in the cabinet. Parting with her beautiful engagement ring felt like torture. Fortunately, Grace wasn't wearing the knife strapped to her ankle today. Taking that off would have raised eyebrows and probably seen them escorted off the premises.

Rosannah locked the cabinet with a key on a chain attached to her belt and ushered them into the next room.

The consultation room lacked natural light, since it had no windows. However, it glowed with a soft radiance from several lamps, making it seem more like a cozy parlour than a doctor's surgery. The effect was heightened by the comforting warmth of a

131

metal radiator, presumably supplied with hot water heated by electricity. It didn't have the welcoming blaze of a fireplace, but the steady heat and absence of messy logs and coal would make the maids' lives easier. An intimate cluster of elegant armchairs in one corner added to the cosy ambience.

Midway down the far wall, next to a sturdy wooden chair with ominous straps on the arms and legs, stood a tall mahogany cabinet. At first glance, it might be mistaken for a liquor cabinet, but for the unusual instrument on top of it. Grace had seen nothing like it before. She assumed it was an electrical device, based on the number of switches and dials, and the electrical cable snaking from the side of the cabinet.

Doctor Crabtree greeted them with a gracious smile, emphasising his firm jaw and abnormally white teeth. His hands went to the lapels of his black, old-fashioned frock coat, which gave him the look of a man of sober conservatism, as befitted a doctor. In contrast, his shiny gold waistcoat and peacock blue cravat hinted he was not so stuffy as a regular doctor. Grace gave him full points for presentation, but that was not what she was here to assess.

"Well, goodness me," Crabtree said, "a veritable crowd of eager patients."

"Mrs Stewart is the only patient," Rosannah said, before closing the door behind her with a trifle more firmness than necessary.

Lily looked up at the doctor adoringly, both because that was what they had planned and because she was a foot shorter than him. "I'm afraid nerves got the better of me, so I asked my husband and niece to accompany me."

"Fine, fine," Crabtree said. "The more the merrier. But, dear lady, there is no call to be nervous. I can promise you will feel no pain, only exhilaration and relief. Now, Mrs Stewart, take a seat and tell me what ails you. I can see from your movements that you are in dreadful pain."

They all took a seat. Lily admitted her sciatica was a great burden and had been for years. Alistair confided how much it

132

grieved him to see his wife in such pain, not that she ever complained. Grace kept quiet and waited for the doctor to ask for the relevant details, such as the location, intensity and frequency of the pain, and other relevant symptoms such as numbness, tingling, or weakness. The doctor disappointed, not that she was surprised, based on Mrs Atkinson's experience. Nor did the doctor examine Lily's spine for evidence of bone or vertebral deformation that might cause the pain.

When he didn't ask about current treatments, Lily volunteered the information. "My doctor has prescribed me pain relief, and I use a soothing rub from the apothecary."

"My dear Mrs Stewart," Crabtree said, with a light-heartedness that made Grace want to wipe the condescending smile off his face. "It is of no consequence what you take now, for I have every hope that you will need no such outdated nostrums by the end of your series of treatments with me."

Lily nodded eagerly. "That would be a miracle. But, doctor, is it entirely safe? I'm not a strong woman, and my nerves do make my heart jitter." She put a hand to her chest, fluttering it to show a rapid, irregular beat.

Crabtree took her fluttering hand and held it steady. "Have no fear, Mrs Stewart. My electrical therapy is entirely safe. You will be astounded to learn that the body relies on its own electricity to function properly. The gentle pulsing current used by my devices works in complete harmony with the body's natural systems to banish pain, unlike the drugs and rubs you are using at present." The doctor went on to outline, at considerable length, the many benefits of electrical therapy and the endless list of conditions that could be cured.

"How extraordinary that an application of electricity can cure so many ailments," Grace said, when it seemed that the doctor would never stop talking and start listening. "It really is a miracle."

The doctor cut off her next sentence with a raised hand. "It is no miracle, although it may seem so to the layman. The therapy is

133

grounded in the latest advances in medical science. In your aunt's case, a blockage of the sciatic nerve between the spinal cord and leg is causing her agony. A carefully administered application of electric current will remove the blockage and, voilà, the pain will vanish."

"Oh," Lily cooed. "To be free of pain would be heavenly."

"Naturally, I cannot guarantee a complete cure. As with any type of medical treatment, one can never be certain how efficacious it will be for a specific individual. However, I can promise that you will feel a renewed vitality, even if we cannot entirely cure the pain." Doctor Crabtree swept back his mane of glossy hair, kept longer than was fashionable, perhaps to demonstrate his superior health.

There was an arrogance about the man that made Grace want to take a pair of scissors and trim his pride, but he was no Samson and she was no Delilah. Her training urged her to distrust his sweeping promises, but she had to admit Crabtree sounded sure of himself. She didn't wish to be a pig-headed Luddite who rejected new innovations outright. After all, medicine would never have moved on from incantations and bloodletting if physicians had rejected scientific advancements.

"But is it really safe?" Alistair asked, his face rumpling like a suspicious bulldog.

"Absolutely and utterly," Crabtree said. "I can provide glowing references from a great many patients, if you wish."

Alistair looked as if he was about to demand a complete list of every patient ever treated, signed in blood, but Lily interrupted her husband. "I'm sure I will be perfectly fine. Please begin the treatment, Doctor Crabtree."

Crabtree rang a bell. "I'll leave you in my lady assistant's capable hands while the belt is fitted."

Rosannah Vale came in as her brother went out. She retrieved a box from the pile stacked against one wall. "I'll be fitting you with

134

an electrotherapeutic belt configured to your specific requirements, Mrs Stewart. If you would care to step behind the curtain, please."

Grace and Alistair exchanged doubtful glances. The belt came from a box that looked exactly the same as all the other boxes, except that the size was smaller than the much larger belt Mrs Atkinson had bought. Alistair tapped the ground nervously with one foot while they waited several minutes for Lily to divest herself of her clothes and don the belt. When Lily stepped out from behind the curtain, she was wearing an all-covering gown.

Rosannah rang the bell, and Doctor Crabtree returned, holding a thick file. "Are you ready to begin your initial treatment, Mrs Stewart?" the doctor asked.

"Initial treatment?" Alistair queried.

"Every patient and every medical condition is unique, Mr Stewart. I start with the gentlest electrical stimulation and continue the treatments at increasing currents until the patient feels sustained relief. Conditions that have taken years to develop cannot be cured in an instant, you understand. It may take weeks, or even months, for severe cases."

"Sounds expensive," Alistair grumbled.

"What price can be put on freedom from pain?" Crabtree handed over an embossed card, which appeared to be a menu of treatments. Alistair's eyes widened as he glanced down the list. The doctor quickly distracted him by placing the file in his hands. "Please feel free to read through the many testimonials from other patients, while I begin the treatment."

"Yes, of course, go ahead," Alistair said, after catching his wife's eye to ensure she was still a willing participant. "We can take the belt home, I presume."

"Naturally. I recommend twice-daily sessions of at least ten to fifteen minutes each, ideally in comfortable repose and at a time that ensures you are undisturbed. A tranquil mind is essential to achieving the best results."

135

Crabtree addressed his words to Lily, allowing Grace a chance to flip through the testimonials, which were so uniformly positive as to be almost unbelievable. She noticed Crabtree did not ask whether Lily could be pregnant. He hadn't reacted to Lily's hint about her weak heart either, or mentioned avoiding water, which suggested news of Mrs Atkinson's terrifying experience had yet to reach his ears. Surprising, given Mrs Atkinson's prickly personality, that the lady had not beaten down the doctor's door and demanded her money back.

"What if it doesn't work?" Lily asked.

"I understand your concern, which is why I will test the electropathic belt now, under scientifically controlled conditions, with no obligation to proceed with the purchase."

"It doesn't look like much," Lily said doubtfully, "and my sciatica is crippling. Don't you have anything stronger?"

"My dear lady, if you are not fully satisfied within a month, you are welcome to return the belt and become part of my intensive therapy programme, with the first consultation absolutely free."

Doctor Crabtree drew her over to the wall cabinet with the gentle touch of a shepherd urging a frightened lamb to shelter. He opened the cabinet doors to reveal a bank of what could only have been batteries, judging from the coils of wires and clips that attached them together.

"Behold, the latest and most expensive medical faradic battery designed for use by a qualified physician. Not only more powerful than anything one might purchase for home use, but also capable of specific treatments." He opened another set of doors beside the instrument to reveal long electrical cables with a plug at one end and various odd-shaped devices at the other. "These probes are specially shaped for every body part, from the nasal cavity to … ahh … the most intimate of places."

Grace's stomach turned over. She told herself it was simply a little nausea and she would not embarrass herself by being sick. Lily tipped her head sideways as if merely curious, but Grace saw

136

beads of perspiration form on her forehead. Grace knew that perspiration would exacerbate any electrical shock. Inevitably, Grace then recalled descriptions of the barbaric practice that New York had adopted of executing criminals using an electrified chair. The victim had to be strapped in to prevent convulsions that could throw him off the chair or break bones.

Crabtree must have been used to the effect on his patients, because he switched his tone from excited to soothing. "I know it looks frightening at first sight, but the current can be carefully regulated until the desired effect is achieved. Extremely efficacious, I assure you, and entirely safe."

"Perhaps we could return to the electrified belt," Alistair said, with a tremor in his voice that Grace had never heard before. He had an unsurpassed reputation as a detective inspector who remained calm in any crisis.

"May I try the … what did you call it? Farantic battery?" Lily remained astonishingly composed, even if her voice was a fraction higher than normal.

The windowless walls closed in on Grace, and her stomach rebelled. She rushed out before she embarrassed herself by throwing up.

The Invalid

Out in the waiting room, Grace flung open a window and inhaled deep breaths of crisp autumn air, scented with fallen leaves. What on earth had possessed her to volunteer for this investigation? She longed to be outside, amongst the trees, skipping along with the joy of impending motherhood, far away from this feeling of impending doom. She knew she was being irrational, but electricity was such a recent invention that she feared harm to her baby simply from being in the same room as that ominous cabinet full of batteries.

The door opened behind her, and Rosannah Vale hurried out. When she saw Grace, her expression softened with concern. "May I be of assistance, Miss Penrose? You look quite unwell. Some water, perhaps? Or a brandy, if you feel faint?"

"Thank you for your kindness, Mrs Vale. A little fresh air is all I require." Grace's instinct was to get rid of Rosannah as soon as possible so she could search for evidence, but the opportunity to talk to her might not come again. "These last few days have been such a terrible strain. I don't know if you have heard about the burglaries of several people who attended the auction …"

Rosannah's thin lips pinched into a grim line. "I heard at church yesterday. An appalling situation for the victims. Very stressful for the auction committee too, since our reputation is being tarnished by association." Anger quickly changed to sympathy. "Oh, dear. I do hope you weren't one of the victims, Miss Penrose."

"No, but friends of mine had their precious heirlooms stolen. I feel dreadful for them, but at the same time relieved at not losing my one piece of valuable jewellery, which I was foolish enough to leave on my dresser while I was out. I can ill afford to lose it, with money so tight. My aunt was already cross with me for getting carried away at the auction."

"My sympathies. The thrill of bidding does rather go to one's head, as I know from experience."

"That's what I told my aunt. She was gracious enough to concede that the expenditure was for a worthy cause. Did you get caught up in the excitement too, Mrs Vale?"

"My husband and I left early. I should have stayed, but Matthew insisted we had made more than our share of contributions in previous years. It was just as well, because I was so tired after helping to organise the auction that I was asleep almost before my head hit the pillow."

"A fortunate decision, or you might have been burgled too. Although you do have a butler to see off any intruders, I suppose."

"One would hope so, but Lancaster works hard and retires early. He didn't so much as stir when my husband and I came home. Perhaps we should get a guard dog. It's all very unsettling. I do hope the police will catch the scoundrel quickly."

"I'm sure they will." Grace studied Rosannah, but her reaction to the burglaries seemed no more than the expected distress at the auction attendees being the targets. The only sign of deception had been over leaving the auction early, which might have been because of the Vales' money troubles or Rosannah's dislike of seeing her brother perform, rather than the excuse she gave.

Grace took a seat by the window and managed a wan smile. "I'm feeling much better, Mrs Vale. Please don't let me keep you from your work. I'll rest here until the consultation is finished."

When Rosannah went back into the consulting room, Grace wasted no time in using the opportunity to scout for evidence. She started with a quick rifle through the desk. Nothing sprang to her attention, other than the total dissimilarity of the two styles of handwriting on the various documents in the desk drawers. The small, precise hand in the appointment register suggested a reserved and organised woman, while the flamboyant hand on the letters could only belong to a man who thought a great deal of himself.

139

The business finances and patient records were nowhere to be found.

With Rosannah occupied in the consulting room, Grace decided to have a quick look around the house, using the need for a bathroom as her excuse if she was discovered.

Since her time would be limited, Grace started with the closest rooms on the ground floor, hoping there would be a study or library containing accounts for the business. When a maid came down the stairs with a load of soiled linen, Grace ducked into what she hoped was an empty room. It was a bathroom, recently built, judging from the freshness of the décor. A dripping sponge and wet towel draped over the basin indicated recent use.

Muffled voices drifted through a second door on the far side of the bathroom. Pushing the door open a smidgen allowed her a narrow view of a bedroom, in which the bed took up much of the space. An older man, his skin pink from being washed, sat in an armchair beside the bed, still wearing a dressing gown late in the morning. His drooping face and loose-hung arm on one side of his body indicated partial paralysis, but the determined set of his jaw and the strength with which he fended off a hairbrush with the other arm told Grace he had plenty of fight left.

But she knew that already, because this was the man who had accosted her outside the house two nights before, when he had mistaken Grace for his wife rather than a nosy intruder. Franklin Crabtree, the father of Barnabas and Rosannah. The younger generation seemed eager for their father to die, but Grace doubted the feisty Franklin Crabtree would oblige them anytime soon.

The butler, Lancaster, also appeared to act as Franklin's valet and carer. He finished brushing his employer's remaining hair, working around his employer's flailing arm, and then bustled about the room, straightening the bedclothes and gathering plates and a cup onto a tray.

"You didn't eat your egg, Mr Crabtree," Lancaster said, in a soft voice that held no rebuke.

140

"Why am I having egg? Is it morning?"

"Yes, sir." Lancaster gently wiped drool from the left corner of the man's mouth and placed a book on his lap. "Why don't you read your book, while I tend to my other household duties? I'll return soon to dress you, Mr Crabtree."

"Aren't you going to read me the newspaper?"

"Later, Mr Crabtree. A busy morning, I'm afraid."

The cloud of confusion on the old man's face suddenly cleared, although his words were still slightly slurred by the weakness in his facial muscles. "I must walk Rosannah to school."

"No need, sir," Lancaster said. "Miss Rosannah is a lady now, married to Mr Vale. Your son is home from London too. He's busy with his medical practice this morning, but perhaps you will see him later. I'll be back as soon as I can, sir."

Poor man, Grace thought. Franklin Crabtree's memory must have been damaged during the brain bleed that left him partially paralysed, as often happened in such cases. His confusion didn't bode well for their hopes of gleaning further information from him about the previous burglaries, although it was possible that he might recall the events of a decade ago better than what he had for breakfast today.

With the gentlest of touches, Lancaster tucked a tartan rug over his patient's knees and adjusted the cushion behind his back. "You know where the bell is if you need me." He held out the end of the bellpull beside the bed as a reminder. "We'll go for our usual walk at the Imperial Ground at two o'clock when the day has warmed up. Nothing like a little fresh air and exercise to lift the spirits."

Franklin's surly pout dropped away. "Will we see the new cable car?"

"Of course, sir. We'll go up the hill in it."

Franklin smiled. "Good lad."

Grace felt like a Peeping Tom spying on an intimate scene. The Roslyn cable tramway had been installed over a decade ago, giving

141

her hope that Franklin's memory went back that far. All she had to do was get Franklin Crabtree alone during one of his more lucid periods.

Franklin was a fortunate man to have a butler-valet-carer as caring and compassionate as Lancaster. In Grace's experience, patients suffering memory loss were often treated as if they were there only in flesh and not in mind. Much like Mr and Mrs Vale had treated Lancaster at the auction, dumping coats in his arms without a word of recognition or thanks, despite the cloakroom being mere yards from the entrance to the hall.

In her opinion, they should shower the butler with praise in the hope he would stay to do a demanding job. Lancaster was wise in years but also young enough for the hard work of assisting a man who needed help with everyday tasks, such as bathing. His age was hard to judge. Lancaster's unlined face suggested he wasn't much older than Grace, but a receding hairline and a figure veering towards rotund made him look older.

Aware that Lily's consultation must be drawing to a close, Grace retreated down the hall on soft feet. When the door to the consultation room opened barely thirty seconds later, Grace rose from her hastily taken seat by the window in the waiting room as if she had never left.

"Are you feeling quite well, Miss Penrose?" Rosannah asked. "You are a little flushed."

"Perfectly well, thank you." To Grace's relief, Lily came out of the surgery looking in fine fettle, although Alistair was pale and twitching. Lily still limped, but less obviously and with a significantly diminished level of fake pain.

Rosannah opened the locked cabinet and returned their possessions, which were in exactly the same position as they had been left. They bade her farewell and went out to the horse and buggy. While Alistair untied the reins from the hitching post, Grace helped Lily to get into the buggy, then took the rear-facing seat behind her.

"How marvellous, Aunt Lily," Grace said, loud enough to be heard by the indistinct shadow behind the net curtain in the front room of the house. "I see your sciatica has been miraculously improved by the treatment."

"The electropathic belt was simply wonderful," Lily said with the enthusiasm of an evangelist. "I felt no more than a mild tingling sensation, but I can scarcely describe how much better I feel after wearing it. My pain is so greatly diminished, I feel like a new person."

Grace lowered her voice. "You are a splendid actress, Lily. I hope you did not allow yourself to be attached to that terrifying electrical cabinet with the row of batteries. Seeing it quite turned my stomach."

"Sadly, I was dissuaded by Doctor Crabtree. I had been hoping to test the full array of treatments available, but he convinced me to start with the simplest treatment first, which was the sensible approach, of course. The electrical belt worked wonders. He really is the most marvellous doctor."

Alistair flicked the reins. "Crabtree's got the gift of the gab, all right. Typical snake-oil salesman. Are you well, Grace? I wasn't sure if you were putting on an act in order to search the house, or if you really did feel faint at the sight of that monstrous device."

"A little of both, but mainly the former," Grace admitted, earning her a sideways glance and a flicker of a smile from Lily.

A heavy weight lifted from Grace's shoulders as they passed through the spiked gates to the safety of the street. Lily seemed blissfully unruffled by her experience, which was another weight lifted. Beyond the overhanging trees, the sun lit up an ordinary, everyday scene. Washing fluttered in the breeze on lines strung between trees. A cat soaked up the heat of a tin roof. Distant excited shrieks drifted along the street from the nearby high school.

When they were fifty yards down the road, Grace finally breathed easy again. "Could you stop, please, Alistair? It's a fine day. A walk will help settle my stomach before I return to work. Lily, can we talk about your treatment tonight?"

"Of course, Grace."

Alistair helped her down from the buggy. Grace waved them off, then stooped to tie her bootlace. When she stood up again, she realised this was the exact spot she had told Charlie about The Bean. Inevitably, her eye flicked back to the gate.

A man had just exited, casting a furtive glance behind him at the house. He turned up the forest path beside the house, heading for the Town Belt. Oddly, he had a sack over his shoulder. A bulging sack, such as a burglar might use to stash his ill-gotten gains.

Grace had seconds to decide what to do. The buggy was now too far away for her to call for assistance. Following the man on her own would be risky, but Grace figured she would be safe enough if she kept her distance and simply observed which direction he went. Even if he saw her, she liked her chances against a soft, indoors type like him.

Curiosity overcame her better judgement. She ran after him.

School Days

Charlie's meeting with Matthew Vale had left him with as many questions as answers. What he needed now was to talk to a person with intimate knowledge of the Crabtree and Vale families. Franklin Crabtree's wife was dead, as was Elias Vale. And Franklin Crabtree wasn't likely to be of much help from Grace's description of his condition. Thus, his best option seemed to be Mrs Elias Vale, the mother who had saved Matthew from being forced to join the cadets. And for that, he needed her address and cooperation. Fortunately, he had an informant.

He took the cable car up High Street rather than walking, because he had a strong premonition that he would be footsore by the end of the day with so many leads to follow and time pressing heavily on his mind. His broken foot had healed, but it still gave him twinges when he tried to do too much in one day. He was beginning to understand why his partner left the legwork to him, given Alistair's three decades of accumulated injuries, which inevitably accompanied a long and active police career.

As the cable pulled its load up the steep incline, he reviewed the investigation. With Gus Fenton confirmed as the link between an almost identical series of crimes now and a decade ago, they were looking for a person who was sufficiently clever and connected to plan the burglaries, as well as ruthless enough to murder Gus when he became a liability. That person must either be behind both episodes of offending, or have detailed knowledge of the previous burglaries. And then there was the matter of the keys. If the burglar had keys to each victimised household before, the same efficient method might have been used again. Either way, the coincidence of all the victims being patients of Doctor Barnabas Crabtree could not be ignored.

Charlie alighted near Kenneth Drummond's house and went to find the investigation agency's expert on Dunedin's society, Grace's great-aunt, Anne Drummond.

The maid showed him into the sitting room and left to get her mistress. In the corner of the room, Charlie spotted the beautiful mahogany cradle Anne had bought for Lavender House at the charity auction. He ran his hand over the smooth wood, admiring the workmanship, and imagining his own son or daughter tucked up under blankets. The vision sparked both joy and terror. What skills did he have to take charge of a tiny, vulnerable infant? What if his inexperience caused him to drop it on its head? He told himself he was being ridiculous. There was nothing he and Grace couldn't achieve together. Besides, Grace would be in charge of all the tricky aspects. Wouldn't she?

At the creak of a door behind him, he turned to greet Anne. "Would you like me to deliver this lovely cradle to Lavender House for you?" he asked.

A flare of pink in Anne's cheeks and her averted eyes caused Charlie a moment's confusion. Perhaps Mrs Harvey had been wrong about the cradle being bought for Lavender House. He was about to ask when another possibility sprang to mind. Had Anne noticed Grace's symptoms and deduced the cause?

Anne gave him a surreptitious *do you know what I know* look and must have read a responding *do you know that I know that you know* query in his expression. She contemplated him before answering. "Thank you for the kind offer, Charlie, but I have the matter in hand, and I know you cannot spare the time." Anne paused. "Grace seemed distracted at the auction. How is my great-niece?"

"Grace is in fine spirits. If she was distracted at the auction, it was because she is investigating the potential medical shenanigans of Doctor Barnabas Crabtree, on behalf of Doctor Harvey and a group of concerned doctors."

"About time someone did," Anne said. "Will you stay for tea, Charlie? I'm due at a meeting of the Prison Reform Society in an hour, but I have time before I leave. I sense you wish to ask me a question."

The sound of a tea trolley coming down the corridor told him it would be impolite to decline, not that Charlie had any intention of refusing. As Anne poured tea and cut him a giant slice of fruitcake, he outlined his investigation into the burglaries and the potential link with the Crabtree household. "I wondered if you know where I could find Elias Vale's wife or another close relative of Matthew Vale?"

"I know the Vale and Crabtree families," Anne said, "but not well. I visited Elias Vale's house only once that I can recall, many years ago, when it was my turn to organise the annual auction donations. In fact, I do believe it was Elias Vale who donated that ghastly set of deer antlers in the first place. Rather an uncouth man, the sort who enjoyed shooting animals for trophies rather than for meat. His wife is a lovely lady, and marvellously stoic."

Here, Anne slid Charlie a meaningful glance, which had him wondering just how hard it had been for Mrs Vale to remain stoic throughout her marriage to Elias "Nine-Tail" Vale.

"I know their eldest daughter, another charming lady. Mrs Vale went to live with her when Elias died." Anne went to the roll-top desk in the corner of the room and wrote down an address. "She lives nearby, in Belleknowes. I assume you know where the Crabtree family lives, if Grace is investigating the son."

Charlie nodded. "Am I right in thinking the daughter, Rosannah, and her husband, Matthew Vale, live with Franklin Crabtree?"

"I believe so." Anne settled back into her favourite armchair after handing him the address. "Franklin Crabtree was struck down by apoplexy several months ago, but Mr and Mrs Vale lived with him before then. I know very little about them. Matthew Vale seems a respectable man, very different from his father, and Rosannah Vale is involved with several charities. Barnabas Crabtree is older

147

than his sister, but I have never met him. I heard a rumour that his past was not entirely angelic, but I know no more than that."

"Matthew Vale told me that Barnabas Crabtree was expelled from boarding school," Charlie said, giving the name of the school to jog her memory.

Anne raised an eyebrow, indicating this was news to her. "Perhaps that is why he was shipped off to London to attend medical school, when we have a perfectly fine medical school in Dunedin. You might talk to Mr Burton, a senior master at the local high school, who used to work at the boarding school. He's a fine man. I know his mother."

Of course you do, Charlie thought, wondering what he would do without Anne's inexhaustible supply of connections within Dunedin society. A loop to Belleknowes, and on through the Town Belt to the high school, would take him close to Franklin Crabtree's house. Fortunately, Anne knew him well enough not to be offended by his gulping his tea and dashing off again.

Charlie put down his empty plate and cup. "Thank you, as always, for the inside information and the refreshments. I expect Grace will be eager to see you when the time is right. She is busy, as ever."

Anne rose too. "I shall look forward to it." She gave Charlie the usual peck on the cheek, before switching to a long, tight embrace. "I'm always here for you and Grace."

"We appreciate it." Charlie gave her a last *I know you know that I know but I know you also know better than to say* glance, before departing for Mrs Vale's residence. Keeping The Bean secret was becoming exhausting.

Fortunately, Matthew's mother was at home and willing to see him. Indeed, she seemed delighted to have a visitor. Mrs Vale insisted on ringing the bell for tea, after which she returned to her nest of cushions on the sofa as if settling in for a good long chat, no matter that her guest was a complete stranger who hadn't yet stated his business. Mrs Vale was older than Charlie expected. She must

148

have met Elias Vale relatively late in life, since Matthew was probably only in his mid- to late-twenties. She was plump and cheerful but moved with the painful gait and the stoicism of a person with an old injury.

A woman of about thirty years of age swept into the sitting room, with a sleepy child in each arm and two grizzling toddlers pulling at her skirt. With brisk efficiency, she greeted Charlie, removed a toy from a child's mouth, established that he was here to see Mrs Vale, rescued a mound of laundry before another child toppled it, asked about tea, and then departed – a whirlwind sweeping through and leaving uncanny silence in its wake. Charlie had a sudden vision of what their already-busy lives would be like in the not-too-distant future. What had he and Grace been thinking, starting a family with so little thought to the practicalities?

Mrs Vale flapped a hand toward the departing whirlwind. "Mrs Alice Newbridge, my daughter. Always in a rush. It's a busy life being a mother of four, but she loves it. I'd like to help her more, but my legs aren't what they used to be. I don't get out very often, so you must stop me if I rattle on too much. Tell me again what you wish to ask me, Mr Penrose Pyke."

"I was talking to your son, Mr Matthew Vale, this morning about property investments. Franklin Crabtree's son, Barnabas, came up in the course of the conversation. I'm afraid it is terribly indiscreet to be inquiring about him, but my aunt is planning to consult Doctor Crabtree on a delicate medical matter and I ... well, I got the impression he had been rather wild in his youth. Expelled from boarding school, I hear. I don't wish to alarm my aunt, but nor do I wish to expose her to harm. As a private detective by trade, I fear I have become overly suspicious. Your name was mentioned as a person of discretion who knew Barnabas Crabtree when he was younger."

"I understand perfectly," Mrs Vale said. "Your care for your aunt speaks well of you. I don't know why Barnabas was expelled, but my husband knew and he refused to speak of it, so it must have been something distasteful. My husband was like a second father to

149

young Barnabas, you see, having known his father since he first settled in Dunedin. Barnabas was always a charmer, even as a boy, so I was shocked to hear of his disgrace. All in the past though. He's a respectable doctor now."

"Your son was full of praise for Barnabas's father, Franklin Crabtree. I understand he was a business partner of your husband and a mentor to your son."

"A fine man," Mrs Vale said, her tone subdued. "Franklin has been a loyal and generous friend to our family through good times and bad."

Reading between the lines, Charlie took this as confirmation of Matthew Vale's statement that Franklin had rescued Elias Vale from bankruptcy by taking a stake in the business.

Mrs Newbridge came in with a tea trolley and began pouring. "What have I missed? I so seldom get a chance to talk to adults from the outside world, and I do hate to miss the gossip. Polly won't mind watching the children for a while."

"This is Mr Penrose Pyke, dear," her mother said. "We're having a pleasant chat about old times."

Charlie took his tea and thanked his lucky stars for having two such willing informants. "I was about to say that you must be proud of your son, Mrs Vale, for taking on the business at such a young age."

"Oh yes, Mr Penrose Pyke. Matthew has done splendidly to keep the business going under the guidance of Franklin Crabtree. Fortunately, he had worked in the business before my husband's untimely death. Elias was very strict about our son learning the ropes early, and Franklin Crabtree felt the same. My husband took Matthew with him to collect the rents from tenants from a very early age to instil a work ethic. Fortunately, Matthew took to the work like a duck to water. Franklin sent Barnabas along with them, too, hoping he would find a vocation. Chalk and cheese, those two boys, but the best of friends when they were lads."

150

Mrs Newbridge spluttered her tea. "How can you say that, Mama? Barnabas was a spoilt brat, and Matthew was jealous of how Mr Crabtree indulged his son. They were about as friendly as two tomcats fighting over the same patch of turf."

"Boys will be boys, Alice," her mother said. "They were fiercely competitive, but still friends."

Charlie took a calming breath to prevent his excitement from showing and guided the two women back to the critical point. "It's so important for young men to learn responsibility. I expect the boys came to know some of the tenant's lads too, while collecting the rents. I know young Gus Fenton learned his trade as a baker at his father's side, so they must have met him."

"You've got that right," Mrs Newbridge said. "Papa and Mr Fenton shouted themselves hoarse sometimes when the boys disappeared to get up to mischief with young Gus Fenton when they should have been working. I envied them their freedom, although I kept out of their way, of course. Young boys can be nasty little beasts, especially to their sisters."

Mrs Vale shook her head and smiled. "Don't listen to my darling daughter. Matthew was a little angel. Alice is only envious of the marvellous cream buns Mrs Fenton made back then. She spoiled those boys rotten, God rest her sweet soul."

"Those cream buns were heavenly," Mrs Newbridge said with a laugh.

"I liked a cream bun myself at that age." Charlie patted his belly. "Still do, for that matter. Did Matthew and Barnabas know other tenants too, such as the locksmith's son, Samuel Tillman? Or Jack Turner?"

"Tillman? Why does that name ring a bell?" Mrs Vale asked.

Mrs Newbridge shuddered, slopping tea into her saucer. "Mr Tillman was the locksmith found dead in his shop. A dreadful tragedy for the family. Inconceivable."

"Inconceivable?" Charlie prompted.

151

"The police said poor Mr Tillman killed himself, but his daughter said he would never do such a thing, and I'm sure she was right. He was a good man. A family man and deeply religious. Not the type of man to ever contemplate suicide, knowing how it would affect his family and his chances of passing through the pearly gates."

"May I ask how you came to know the Tillman children, Mrs Newbridge?"

"I was acquainted with the Tillman's oldest daughter, but only because she was at the same school. I went with a group of school friends to pay our condolences to the Tillman family. It seemed the least we could do in their time of suffering, especially as there was so much gossip about the police's interest in his suicide. The shame drove the family to leave Dunedin soon after Mr Tillman was buried."

Just as Sergeant Yardley had said, but good to have it confirmed, Charlie thought. "Did you know her brother, Samuel?"

"I never met Samuel or the other Tillman children, but I do recall the sister talking about her embarrassing little brother. I gather he kept to himself and didn't have any friends at all. Samuel Tillman definitely wasn't the type to run wild with the likes of Gus Fenton. Matthew and Barnabas were fascinated by the locksmith's trade, but never once mentioned seeing Samuel at the shop. I don't recall ever hearing the name of the other boy you asked about, Jack Turner."

Charlie nodded. It didn't seem to occur to these delightful, innocent ladies that his questions had strayed far from his stated interest in Barnabas Crabtree. Charlie faced a dilemma. He didn't wish to make his interest too obvious, but he needed to know more. Crucially, Elias and Matthew Vale, and Barnabas Crabtree, were all familiar with the locksmith shop where the master keys used in the first set of burglaries were stored.

The brief pause in the conversation was soon filled by Mrs Newbridge. "You ought to ask Rosannah if you want to know about the locksmith. Matthew's wife, Mrs Rosannah Vale, I mean."

"What would Rosannah know about a tradesman?" Mrs Vale asked.

"Oh, Mama, you must remember Rosannah's mother despairing over her lively daughter?" Mrs Newbridge turned to Charlie with a twinkle in her eye. "Clever little thing, she was. Still is for that matter. It's a great shame she doesn't run the property business to my mind, but that's a woman's lot, isn't it? Anyway, when she was little, Rosannah used to hate the boys getting anything she couldn't have. She would sneak out and walk about the town until she was found and returned. Rosannah seemed fascinated with locks. Goodness knows why. The Tillman's shop was always the first place Mrs Crabtree would send the search party. I thought it terribly amusing and brave of her at the time. Now that I have children, I understand how alarming it must have been for her poor mother."

"I'll bet Rosannah liked to sample the cream buns at Fenton's Bakery, too," Charlie said.

"My word, she certainly did, the little minx." Mrs Newbridge had a jolly laugh, and she used it generously. "Oh, the stories I could tell. Suffice to say, Rosannah always managed to get her sticky fingers on enough money to supply her cream bun desires. But that is the past, and the past is best left behind, don't you think? Rosannah is now my delightful and highly respectable sister-in-law. Matthew is fortunate to have her as his wife."

Her mother had followed the discussion with interest, and an occasional shake of her head. "Heaven's above, Alice. It seems I didn't know half of what you children got up to. And thank goodness for that. Wasn't it the baker's son who got into trouble with the law? He was a nice boy when he was little."

"Gus was heartbroken when his mother died, poor soul," her daughter said. "He got into bad company and went to prison. I know Papa was angry that the police implied the cadet corps was at fault when it was only Gus who got into trouble, not any of the other boys. Gus must have been reformed, because he is back at the bakery now and happily married, as far as I know."

Charlie should have told them about Gus's death, but now didn't seem like the appropriate time, and he didn't want to stop the flow of reminiscences. "I suppose Matthew was in the cadets with Gus Fenton, since his father ran the corps. Barnabas Crabtree as well, perhaps."

Mrs Vale shook her head emphatically. "It's the one time I put my foot down with Elias. My husband felt Matthew could do with toughening up, but I refused to let him go. It's one thing to play with an honest tradesman's son as a child, but quite another to mix with a group of troubled youngsters on the verge of manhood. I know Mrs Crabtree felt the same. Matthew was better served by going to boarding school with the sons of gentlemen. Gracious me, you must excuse me for chattering on and on about the past, Mr Penrose Pyke, when all you wanted to know was whether Doctor Crabtree is a suitable doctor for your aunt."

"Not at all, Mrs Vale. I'm fascinated by what you've said. May I ask if you recall when Barnabas Crabtree was expelled from boarding school?"

"Goodness, it's such a long time ago. I'm sure Elias was still alive, because he tried to take young Barnabas under his wing when Franklin was too angry to cope with his son. Alice, can you remember?"

Mrs Newbridge thought for a moment. "Barnabas was only at boarding school for a couple of years. He was expelled before the Tillman tragedy, because I recall him sulking at the funeral. Barnabas and Matthew finished their education at Otago Boys' High, which did them no harm at all, in my opinion. People do say Barnabas is now a changed man and an excellent doctor. He's done very well for himself, I hear. He earned a medical degree in London, where he practised until his father's illness required him at home."

"Did Matthew come home when Barnabas was expelled?" Charlie blurted the question out, hoping he wasn't opening old wounds. Matthew had implied that he had completed his education at the boarding school, not the local high school as his sister had just said.

"A month or two after Barnabas," Mrs Newbridge said, glancing at her mother. "Don't give me that look, Mama. There's no shame in Papa not having the money to pay the boarding school's extortionate fees. It's not as if Matthew was expelled. I don't think the extra time at boarding school would have made a difference, anyway."

Oh, but it made all the difference in the world, Charlie thought, because it meant that Elias Vale had lied when he told Sergeant Yardley the boys were at boarding school, when both Barnabas Crabtree and Matthew Vale were home in Dunedin around the time of the first burglaries. Moreover, they both knew Gus Fenton and Arthur Tillman.

Charlie realised they were looking at him expectantly. "Otago Boys' High is a fine school. Matthew is a credit to you, Mrs Vale. You must be delighted that he married Franklin Crabtree's daughter, who has a reputation as a capable and caring young lady."

"It was our fondest wish," Mrs Vale said. "A perfect match, both for the business and for themselves."

"Splendid," Charlie said, putting his teacup down. "My apologies for taking so much of your time. I cannot thank you enough for your assistance, ladies. My aunt will be delighted to hear Doctor Crabtree is a changed man since his youthful indiscretion."

Less than an hour later, Charlie knew exactly what that "youthful indiscretion" was. It chilled his blood to think that even now Grace might be in the same room as a man like Barnabas Crabtree.

The schoolmaster, Mr Burton, had only five minutes to spare between classes, and he didn't waste words. Barnabas Crabtree had been expelled for thrashing a younger boy with a wooden chair leg, putting him in hospital. Barnabas denied all knowledge of the beating, but other pupils witnessed the incident. The witnesses tried to downplay it as a bit of ordinary horseplay that went too far, but Charlie could see that Mr Burton was still sickened by the violence over a decade later. No wonder Franklin Crabtree hushed up the incident and sent his wayward son to England as soon as he was old enough.

Charlie didn't wait around to question the schoolmaster any further. He fled the school grounds, desperate to ensure that Grace was safe.

Jack of All Trades

Grace ran back towards the spiked gate, fearing she would lose her quarry. She was fairly sure the man she'd seen leaving the house was the butler, Lancaster, who had told his employer he would be attending to household duties. And yet here he was, sneaking out of the house, holding a bulging sack, hurrying up the path through the trees in a manner entirely at odds with his air of ponderous respectability.

With all the talk of burglary, the butler's furtiveness and the bulging sack had her leaping to conclusions, especially as Lancaster's association with Franklin Crabtree meant he might have known about Gus Fenton and his larcenous tendencies.

Grace hurried after Lancaster, keeping a safe distance between them. The path led to Queen's Drive and the Town Belt. A quiet spot, perfect for burying the contents of the sack away from prying eyes. It took little imagination to see the butler's motive for burglary. Lancaster's current position was precarious. His employer might not have long to live, and the heir was planning to sell the house after his father died, leaving the butler with neither a home nor a job. In the circumstances, Lancaster could well be tempted to feather his nest by illegal means. Perhaps he had heard his employer talking about the previous burglaries and decided to use the same method for his own benefit.

The other possibility was that Lancaster was being directed by his employer. Franklin Crabtree had definitely known about the earlier burglaries. Indeed, with his connection to the burglar and locksmith, he would have been a suspect if he hadn't been so respectable. He might look like a harmless invalid now, but who was to say what he was like a decade ago, when he coached Gus and his fellow cadets at gymnastics. A house like his was not built

157

with anything less than a small fortune. The wealth was supposed to have come from a ship chandlery business. Ships were essential to the survival of New Zealand, tucked away as it was at the far side of the earth from most of the rest of civilisation, and thus it was conceivable that such a business could build a fortune without recourse to crime. Nevertheless, her brain was wired for suspicion when it came to anything to do with the Crabtree household.

On the other hand, Franklin was now partially incapacitated, and Lancaster seemed far too nice to be a criminal. Grace couldn't imagine the butler's caring hands pushing Gus Fenton's face into a mound of dough. However, as Charlie and Alistair always said, you never know what a person might be capable of when pushed to the limit.

The thought of Gus Fenton's horrible death slowed her feet. Charlie would have a fit if she did anything too risky, especially given her new responsibility for a tiny life. However, Grace felt she ought to be safe enough if she followed at a distance and observed. She could always claim she was out for a stroll in the fresh air, which had been true before she saw Lancaster acting suspiciously.

Grace reached the top of the path where it met Queen's Drive, puffing with exertion and cursing her long skirt. Lancaster was nowhere to be seen. She stood still, holding her breath, and was rewarded with the crack of a broken branch up the hill to the left. She followed the sound cautiously, avoiding any hazard that might give her presence away on the slippery, leaf-covered ground.

Two voices drifted down to her from a thicket. Grace halted, surprised that Lancaster was meeting someone, rather than burying his loot. Had she misread the situation?

Regardless, the presence of the second man was a risk too far. She had turned to retreat when another possibility struck her. Lancaster and Jack Turner knew each other. Jack had been taken on as a gardener by Franklin Crabtree, and she'd seen Lancaster talking to Jack at the auction. What if the bulging sack was not stolen jewellery, but provisions to help a fugitive friend? After

158

Charlie had scared Jack away on Saturday evening, they owed it to Wallace to find him.

Grace looked up the slope to the thicket, which, true to its name, was thick with vegetation. If she snuck up carefully and went down on her knees to crawl under the shrubbery, she could eavesdrop just long enough to identify the second man without running the risk of being spotted. The soggy ground wouldn't do her skirt or knees any favours, but dignity and detecting did not go hand in hand.

Lancaster's soft voice became audible as soon as she ducked her head to go under the branches. "I must return to the house. I understand how hard it must be for you, but you have to hand yourself in. You've done nothing wrong."

A male voice answered. "That's not the way the coppers will see it. One look at the likes of me and I'll be banged up in a cold, damp cell again. I'd rather die than face that."

"You can't live out in the bush forever, Jack. I'll do what I can, but you'd be better off leaving town if you're not going to hand yourself in. Good luck."

Grace tucked into a ball at the sound of footsteps and snapping branches, but Lancaster left via the other side of the thicket. Now she had a tricky decision to make. If she left, Jack might disappear forever. But if she tried to talk to him, she was risking her life trusting a man suspected of murder based on the premise that he must be kind if he liked birds and butterflies.

The decision was taken out of her hands when the branches rustled nearby. A pair of boots appeared in front of her face. "What are you doing here?" a harsh voice asked.

Grace stood up and held out her hand to the young man with the birth-marked face, hoping to baffle him with politeness. Her other hand was bunched into a tight fist, ready to thrust into a vulnerable part of his anatomy if he reacted badly. Fortunately, she'd been taught how to defend herself by a couple of streetwise lads after her first adventure into the seamy side of investigation.

159

"Good morning, Mr Turner. Mrs Grace Penrose Pyke, at your service."

He ignored her hand, but he didn't run or lash out either.

"I saw Mr Lancaster leave the house with a sack," Grace explained. "I suffer from a terrible malady called curiosity. Don't be frightened. I won't force you to do anything you don't want to do, because I am sure you are innocent. However, I do think Lancaster's advice to go to the police is your best option."

Jack studied her as if she were an interesting specimen of butterfly that had turned up far from its natural habitat. "I daren't hand myself in. I've no one to vouch for me now Mr Crabtree isn't right in the head."

"Lancaster clearly trusts you, and I believe in your innocence, too. Mrs MacDonnell convinced us you are honest and a hard worker without a cruel bone in your body. She will vouch for you, as will any number of pretty maids. Mrs Atkinson's maid, Ellie, in particular."

Jack's eyes lit up. But it was only for an instant. He turned and went back to the rough shelter he had made from branches and scraps of canvas. He sat on a log and tore open the sack Lancaster had left, stuffing food into his mouth as if he hadn't eaten since he'd fled with Blaze on his heels.

Grace sat opposite him. "It was my husband who called out to you on Saturday night. We only wanted to ask you some questions about your time in the cadet corps with Gus Fenton. My husband feels dreadful for causing you to run away, because now the police are suspicious. They'll catch you eventually, Jack. It would be better if you went in voluntarily."

Jack looked up from a half-eaten bread roll. "I avoided Gus like the plague. The police treated me like scum, but I truly had no knowledge of those old burglaries." He sighed. "I can see you mean well, Mrs Penrose Pyke, but you've no idea what it's like to be alone in the world. I'd wither and die if I were put in a prison cell again."

160

Grace remembered Yardley saying the police had come down hard on the cadet called Jack Turner after the earlier burglaries, leaving him in a cold, damp cell in the hope he'd inform on the other cadets. Franklin Crabtree had vouched for Jack and given him work, which made Grace wonder why. "Mr Crabtree went to a great deal of trouble to help you back then, Jack."

"He did, and I'm grateful. I was innocent, and I suppose he felt sorry for me and maybe a bit guilty. I barely knew Gus, and I knew nothing of the burglaries he'd committed. When I heard Gus had committed a new lot of burglaries, and had been killed for it, I knew it wouldn't be long before the coppers came after me." Jack gave her a hard stare. "I'm innocent now, too."

Grace changed tack. "Did you ever meet Arthur Tillman or his son, Samuel?"

Jack shoved the rest of the bread roll into his mouth and chewed. Grace wondered if he was using the time to forge a lie, but the eyes watching her seemed more amused than fearful.

"I knew *of* them. But only after the coppers interrogated me and repeatedly asked me about them. They said Arthur Tillman was the man suspected of planning the old burglaries. Samuel Tillman and his family left town after his father died. I should've done the same."

Grace turned the new information over in her mind. With Jack and Samuel out of the frame, and assuming the locksmith was innocent, everything pointed to Yardley's other suspect, Elias Vale, or his business partner, Franklin Crabtree. "Jack, you said Franklin Crabtree felt guilty. What did you mean?"

Her question led to a long silence, during which Jack tied off the top of the sack and put it in a small rucksack he retrieved from the shelter. "If I tell you, will you talk to the police for me? Tell them I'm innocent."

"It would be better coming from you, Jack." Grace could see he was ready to run, and she desperately wanted to know what he knew, so she let it pass. "But yes, I will. I promise."

161

Jack's face screwed up as if he wasn't sure how to share his thoughts, or whether he should say anything at all. "I don't know anything for sure. It's only a feeling I had that Mr Crabtree knew who had forced Gus into doing the burglaries. He never said so, but it seemed odd that he was so determined to make amends to me for being wrongly accused. Elias Vale was the most obvious person for Mr Crabtree to suspect, because he was a fearsome man who demanded absolute obedience from the cadets. If he'd told Gus to climb the nets and jump from the top, Gus would have done it."

"And yet, you don't seem completely convinced."

Again, Jack hesitated before speaking. "Elias Vale was scary, but he was also … I'm not sure how to put it. Fair, I suppose, by his own rigid standards. He'd push you to the limit and beyond without mercy, but I don't think he was the type of man to break the law, at least not by stealing other people's possessions. I could be wrong. Vale was a hard man to judge, and I tried to stay out of his reach. I preferred Mr Crabtree, who was strict on discipline but kinder in his ways. You could see he cared for the cadets and wanted to do his best for us."

Grace waited for Jack to continue, but his expression only showed increasing doubt and reluctance to speak. It occurred to her that Jack could be protecting the man who had protected him all those years ago. "Do you think Franklin Crabtree might have been behind the burglaries, Jack?"

His shocked reaction put an end to that train of thought. If Franklin Crabtree was their man, Jack was unaware of it. "Then who, Jack?"

"I wondered if Mr Crabtree was protecting someone close to him. He never said anything or even hinted, but … he seemed deeply troubled by what happened, especially the locksmith's death, and yet he told the police he knew nothing."

"Someone close?" Grace prompted.

"I don't know. I suppose I wondered about his son, Barnabas. Doctor Crabtree, as he is now." Jack fastened the last strap on the

162

rucksack. "I shouldn't have said anything. It's wrong to accuse another man with no proof. The police will think I'm just trying to pass the blame."

"I understand, but it's vital for us to hear your impressions because you are one of the few people who knew the potential suspects for the previous burglaries. Why do you think Barnabas Crabtree could have been the one to force Gus into helping him?"

"I couldn't say. I didn't know Barnabas back then, or now for that matter, but I do remember overhearing Gus saying he was a useful lad to have by your side in a scrape. Gus claimed Barnabas had put a boy in hospital, but that was probably just one of Gus's tall tales." Jack slung the rucksack over his shoulder, looking cold, miserable, and resolute. "You want to be more careful who you're alone with, Mrs Penrose Pyke. Whoever you're after is a vicious killer. I heard what happened to Gus, and I don't want either of us to be next."

Grace shivered. Jack was right. It had been a foolish risk to trust him on instinct out here in an isolated thicket on her own, but that trust had paid off with his honesty. "Can I ask one last question, please, Jack? Where did you go after the auction on Friday night?"

"Back to my room in the boarding house. Nobody saw me, as far as I know. I was worn out after a long day's work and went straight to sleep." Without a backward glance, Jack Turner slid through a narrow gap between the branches as silently as a forest sprite. In an instant, he was gone.

Grace shivered again. She hadn't realised how cold she had become sitting in the chill of the thicket, with her knees and rear end damp from contact with the ground. She longed to go home or back to the comforting familiarity of Doctor Harvey's surgery, but Grace knew she must confess her sins at the police station. She could only hope that the new information from Jack would make up for letting a wanted man escape. Not that she had much choice. Jack might be of slight build, but there was no missing the bulge of his biceps as he lifted the rucksack.

163

A fraught discussion at the police station wasn't something she could face in her current state. A warm cup of tea and a hot meal would settle her empty stomach before she talked to Detective Inspector Wallace. It was vital to be properly fed when with child, she told herself, and nothing at all to do with letting Jack get a good head-start.

Detective Sergeant Declan Kelly didn't take the news of Jack Turner's escape well. Grace sat in Wallace's office, with Blaze's head on her knee, while Declan paced up and down, muttering unrepeatable Irish curses under his breath.

"So, Turner was hiding out in the Town Belt all the time," Declan fumed. "Darn it. That was the first place I wanted to search with Blaze, but I kept getting reports of sightings of him elsewhere, from people who knew him well enough to be sure it was him. First at the Octagon, then over at the Southern Cemetery, and finally out near the railway station in Caversham. The pattern was so clear, I felt sure he was planning to escape south by train to avoid the main railway station in town."

"Who were these witnesses?" Wallace asked.

"Mrs MacDonnell's maid, for one," Declan said. "And then a maid with a mop of curly hair who worked for a Mrs Atkinson in York Place. She swore the man she had seen was Jack. Then there was a housekeeper in Mornington."

Grace failed to bite back a chuckle. "Jack Turner may not be a handsome lad, but he has a way with all creatures great and small, and he is very popular with the female servants in the households he worked for. Mrs Atkinson's maid, Ellie, is particularly sweet on him."

Declan groaned and allowed a spectacularly descriptive, if anatomically impossible, curse to slip from his lips. "Apologies, Grace. It's been a frustrating day."

164

Grace dismissed the apology with a wave of her hand. "That's nothing compared to what the surgeons say when their assistants fail to produce the required instrument at the right time. Anyway, I am the one who should apologise, for letting Jack get away."

Wallace's lip ticked up on one side, a sure sign he was laughing inside. "You've been duped by pretty faces, Kelly. I suppose it speaks well of Turner that he is so admired. What's your opinion of his honesty, Grace?"

Grace considered the question carefully, not wishing to let her instinct derail a murder investigation. But no matter which way she looked at her conversation with Jack, she hadn't spotted a single sly flicker of eyes that might indicate a lie.

"I'll get down on my knees and beg your forgiveness if Jack Turner is anything other than a socially awkward but truthful man who fears being wrongfully accused of the burglaries. The fine reports of his character cannot all be wrong. Anyway, he had no access to the keys for the burgled households. Jack didn't work for all the victims either, although he did help Mrs MacDonnell pick up the auction donations. However, I understand you will still need to speak to him."

Wallace appeared surprisingly unperturbed. "I'm glad you stopped him from fleeing long enough to talk to him, Grace. His impression that Franklin Crabtree knew the man behind the previous burglaries was interesting. Elias Vale was always a strong suspect, but Barnabas Crabtree's name was unexpected. Sergeant Yardley said he was at boarding school at the time of the earlier burglaries."

"Yardley was misinformed, sir," said a familiar voice by the door.

165

Lancaster

Charlie heard enough of the discussion about Jack Turner to know that Grace had talked to him on her own. He was about to demand details of this foolhardy meeting when Grace and Blaze leapt upon him, getting tangled in their haste. Wallace's lip ticked up, while Declan rolled his eyes and went to get another chair.

Charlie sat, but he kept one hand on Grace and the other on Blaze as he outlined the appalling circumstances of Barnabas Crabtree's expulsion from boarding school and the ignominious departure of Matthew Vale not long after, when his father failed to pay his fees. "Therefore, both boys were in Dunedin when the first series of burglaries occurred. Matthew's sister told me both Matthew and Barnabas got up to mischief with Gus Fenton when they were children, while helping Mr Elias Vale collect rent from his tenants."

"Presumably they could have visited the locksmith too," Wallace said, "since Tillman was also Vale's tenant."

"Correct. According to Matthew's sister, the boys were fascinated by locks. She also said that Rosannah Vale, or Rosannah Crabtree as she was a decade ago, shared their interest. Rosannah was known as a clever and headstrong young lass who slipped out of the house to wander about town, visiting both the bakery and the locksmith."

"I overheard Rosannah Vale and her brother Barnabas arguing about money," Grace said. "Matthew Vale's property business is in financial trouble, as it was in his father's time. Barnabas refused to give his sister any financial assistance. As soon as his father dies, he plans to sell up and leave Dunedin, which might explain his lack of concern for his patients. Barnabas made it clear his father's death couldn't come soon enough."

Wallace got up to pace the room, as he did when he was considering fresh evidence. When pacing proved impossible, the office being crammed with four people and a border collie, he sat again, taking his frustration out on an innocent pencil. "I don't like the cut of Doctor Barnabas Crabtree's jib. He sounds like the worst kind of charming swindler to me, with a taste for violence as well. Nasty business beating a boy like that. If he is behind these burglaries and Gus Fenton's murder, I'm not surprised he is eager to move on. Is his father on his deathbed?"

"Franklin Crabtree suffered brain damage and partial paralysis from an apoplectic seizure several months ago," Grace said, "but he is not at death's door by any means. In fact, he does have lucid periods, so it might be worth talking to him. You'd have to take it gently. I can give you advice on how to gain the trust of a man in his condition."

Wallace gave the pencil a final stab, breaking the tip through a pile of papers stamped "urgent". "I fear for Franklin Crabtree's safety if his son is hovering over him, waiting for him to die. If Barnabas Crabtree killed Gus Fenton, he has nothing to lose by hastening another man's meeting with his maker."

"If we are to talk to Franklin," Declan said, "we'll have to get him away from the house, in case his son overhears."

Grace nodded her agreement. "Lancaster, the butler, who also acts as Franklin's carer and valet, is taking his employer for a walk at two o'clock. Detective Inspector Wallace, I wonder if Franklin Crabtree might respond better to a woman, because he would feel completely safe in the hands of a sweet, harmless lass like me."

The snort of laughter that burst from Charlie was echoed by the response of the two policemen.

Grace waited until they recovered. "If you gentlemen are quite finished maligning my sweet, innocent nature, I have another idea to throw in the cauldron."

"Please proceed, dear lady," Wallace said. "A gentleman must not ignore the entreaties of delicate, retiring wee lassies such as yourself, whom others are foolish enough to overlook."

Grace ignored the jibe, but she looked pleased all the same. "When we went for Lily's consultation with Doctor Crabtree, our valuables were left in a locked cabinet in the waiting room, in case metallic objects such as coins and keys interfered with the electrical treatment. All three of us were in the consulting room for an extended period, but both Doctor Crabtree and Rosannah Vale left for periods of time. It cannot be a coincidence that each of the burglary victims was also a patient and thus presumably did the same."

Wallace caught on immediately. "One of them could have taken an impression of the patients' house keys in wax to make duplicate keys for the burglaries. Who else had access to the locked cabinet?"

"Lancaster had a key. I don't know about the housekeeper or the other servants. Presumably, Mr Crabtree Senior has access to all the keys to his own house, although I suppose it is possible his son installed the locked cabinet when he set up the consulting rooms."

Wallace's palms rasped together with glee. "Doctor Crabtree looks more suspicious by the minute."

"Rosannah Vale also had access to the keys," Declan said, "and she was one of the auction organisers. Matthew and Rosannah both knew Gus, and Matthew Vale's business is failing, which means they are desperate for money. They would have to be working together, because Matthew had no access to the patients' keys."

"Actually, he might," Charlie said. "Matthew Vale conducts his business meetings in a hire-by-the-hour office in the city, which means he might be at home during many of the patient consultations. It would be easy enough for him to unlock the cabinet while the patients were busy with Doctor Crabtree. Rosannah's character is of interest too. Matthew's sister implied Rosannah came by the money to buy cream buns using her 'sticky fingers', which I presume means she wasn't above dipping into her parents' purses as a child."

Grace had her keys out of her bag, examining them. "No traces of wax. Not surprising perhaps, since the burglary mastermind would be lying low at present. However, the hair I placed across the clasp of my purse is gone. Someone has been prying through my possessions."

Charlie reached out to stop her hand. "Don't touch that calling card case."

Grace held the edges with the tips of her fingers. "Well, what do you know? A nice clear fingerprint. A smaller hand than mine. Mrs Rosannah Vale has some explaining to do. A shame – she seemed such a nice lady. Fortunately, I made sure I only had an old card with me, in my maiden name, so as not to be associated with a well-known private detective."

Charlie groaned. "I gave my name as Mr Penrose to Matthew Vale, but I had to give my full name when he became suspicious. They'll make the connection soon enough, I expect, especially if Matthew and Rosannah Vale are working together. Grace and I should talk to Franklin Crabtree and the butler as soon as possible, before word spreads of our interest in the household."

"Excellent," Wallace said. "At this stage, I don't want to give our game away by bringing any of them in for a formal interview at the police station until we have solid evidence. Kelly, you'll still need to track down Jack Turner, because we cannot rule out anyone at this stage. Visit the Crabtrees' house first to ask if any of them have seen the lad, being sure to emphasise that Turner is the prime suspect in a series of burglaries."

Declan was already on his feet, raring to arrest the troublesome fugitive. "Clever move, sir. Crabtree won't panic and run if he thinks we are focusing on somebody else."

"Take Blaze," Charlie said, making a fuss of his border collie so she knew she would be missed.

169

When Declan departed, Wallace turned back to Grace. "How is your investigation of Barnabas Crabtree's medical practice going? It would make my day if you gave me sufficient grounds to question him about possible medical malpractice."

"I need to consult Doctor Harvey and talk to Lily about her experience. Expect to hear from me later today. But now, we must hurry if we are to catch Franklin Crabtree on his walk."

Charlie left the police station in a sombre mood. He didn't want his wife to venture within a mile of any of the residents of York Place on her own, but an elderly invalid struggling to keep his grip on life ought to be safe enough if he stayed close.

They were each occupied with their own thoughts until they reached the Roslyn Cable Car, which would take them up the hill to the Imperial Ground. When they were seated, Charlie leaned close to his wife and said, "Grace, what did I miss in relation to Jack Turner? Declan seemed uncharacteristically out of sorts."

"DS Kelly was given the run-around by Jack's admirers, the maids at his various workplaces. That lad may be a quiet one, but he has his charms. Not like Doctor Barnabas Crabtree, whose charms are laid on with a trowel but stop at the outer layer of his epidermis."

"Favouring the underdog, as always, Grace. I can't complain about that."

"It's not that I favour the underdog, but rather that I prefer men whose charms come from an honest, caring place within. I don't object to a handsome exterior, as my choice of husband shows, but I prefer a man who doesn't realise he's attractive, not a blood-brother to Narcissus."

The sweetness of his wife's words and the soft swirl of her fingertips on his palm almost caused Charlie to overlook the critical point, as she probably intended. "I heard enough of the discussion in Wallace's office to know you talked to Jack Turner, even though he is the subject of a manhunt and a potential murderer. Please tell me my irreplaceable wife and baby were not alone with him."

170

Grace wriggled against him beguilingly. "You agreed Jack Turner was innocent. And I didn't seek him out. I followed Lancaster discreetly, because he was acting suspiciously by sneaking out of the house carrying a bulging sack. You would have done the same if you had been there."

"That's different."

"Why is it different, Charlie? I'm part of the investigation team, am I not? Lancaster has about as much fight in him as a cream puff, and I was careful to keep my distance. How was I to know that he was taking food to Jack, who was living rough in the Town Belt?"

Charlie counted to ten and then added another twenty for good measure. "You followed a potential suspect to a clandestine meeting with a wanted fugitive in a secluded spot, then wandered over to pass the time of day with them both?"

"You make it sound far more reckless than it was." Grace looked up at him with doe eyes. "I hope you don't think I am going to turn into a subservient, housebound wife just because we might be having a baby in a few months' time."

Whichever way Charlie replied to that, he knew he was on quicksand. Of course he didn't want his wife to change, but wasn't a degree of change inevitable when she became a mother? Fortunately, Grace treated the question as rhetorical and carried on speaking.

"Anyway, I waited until Lancaster left, so I wouldn't be seen. Unfortunately, Jack heard me before I could sneak away. He's harmless, honestly, but he's also terrified he'll be suspected and put through the wringer by the police again."

"How can you be absolutely certain Jack Turner is innocent?" Charlie asked. "Franklin Crabtree might be shielding Jack because he is complicit in the crimes too."

Grace trailed a soft finger up his wrist. "It's just as well we're going to talk to Franklin then, isn't it, my love?"

"For the sake of your poor, fearful husband," Charlie said, capturing her wandering fingers in his fist before he could give in

171

to her persuasive techniques, "perhaps you could refrain from meeting potential suspects alone in the future."

"I'll try, Charlie. Truly, I have no desire to take any unnecessary risks."

Her other hand slid down to her belly, which told him she understood the risks and meant what she said. However, the precise definition of "unnecessary risks" might have to be the subject of further discussion. Meanwhile, they had interviews to conduct.

"While you talk to Crabtree Senior, I'll have a word with his manservant. What's Lancaster like, Grace?"

"Devoted to Franklin Crabtree. Lancaster does whatever his employer demands of him. If you treat him with sympathy and respect, you might get him to open up. He is a quiet fellow. Aloof, but caring. My bet is that Lancaster knows far more about what is going on in that house than anyone realises. Matthew and Barnabas seem like the sort of people who would talk openly in front of the servants over dinner without registering their presence. Rosannah isn't so bad when not under her husband's gaze or her brother's thumb."

"Thanks for the tip. You look tired, my love. Why don't you go home after this? I can relay our findings to Wallace."

"I wish I could, but I must get back to Doctor Harvey's surgery. He asked me to investigate and allowed me time off to do so, but I don't wish to try his patience too far."

The cable car rattled up the steep slope through the Town Belt and shuddered to a halt at the Imperial Ground.

Charlie hadn't met either Lancaster or Franklin Crabtree, but he didn't need to be a detective to spot the lop-sided gait of an older man who was being gently guided around the ground at a snail's pace by a younger man. They stood out like a pair of dark clouds on a sunny day amongst the young boys playing football and a scattering of ladies and nannies with young children. Once he saw Lancaster's distinctive round figure, Charlie recalled him from the auction, taking coats from Mr and Mrs Vale in the foyer.

172

The pair approached a bench that had a view of both the cable car and the football. Lancaster wrapped his charge in the woollen blanket he was carrying, before helping Franklin Crabtree to sit. Before Lancaster could sit too, Charlie drew him aside, introduced himself as a private detective, and asked if he might have a quick word about a confidential matter.

"I have been asked to investigate a complaint by one of Doctor Crabtree's patients," Charlie said. "You can imagine my dilemma. I have no wish to confront Doctor Crabtree directly and cause embarrassment if there is no substance to the allegation. As a man of discretion with an oversight of the Crabtrees' household, I thought it prudent to seek your advice, Mr Lancaster."

Lancaster stared at him with the bland expression of a man who has perfected the art of seeing everything and saying nothing. However, he couldn't stop the tiny twitch that pulled at his left eye when the doctor was mentioned. "I have no knowledge of the doctor's practice, sir. My only role is to greet patients at the front door and see them to the waiting room." Lancaster saw Charlie glance at the invalid. "This gentleman is not a patient. He is my employer, Doctor Crabtree's father."

"I'll be frank with you, Mr Lancaster. I've made preliminary inquiries, which indicate that you are an exemplary employee of long standing, whose loyalties lie with Mr Crabtree Senior. I understand your reluctance to speak to me, but your employer's fine reputation is at risk too, if his son is found to be at fault."

Charlie held his breath, but it seemed he hadn't misread Lancaster's allegiance to his employer and dislike of his employer's son. "I'll only take a few minutes of your time. My wife will sit with Mr Crabtree."

Lancaster noticed Grace for the first time. "Ah, I see. The young lady who visited the surgery this morning. You're that private detective fellow who has been in the newspapers, aren't you? It must be a serious complaint for your services to be engaged. One moment please, Mr Penrose Pyke."

173

After returning to ensure his employer's hat, scarf and blanket were snug, Lancaster walked far enough away that they would not be overheard. He kept his eyes on his employer, who seemed not to have noticed his absence. Lancaster sighed. "Mr Crabtree enjoys watching the cable car come and go. Alas, it is one of his few remaining pleasures, aside from a glass or two of port in the evening and having the newspaper read to him."

Charlie smoothed his face into a bland imitation of the man before him. "Mr Crabtree has his adult children for company as well."

Lancaster's expression didn't change. "Of course. Mrs Vale has been a devoted daughter through good times and bad."

Lancaster left a pause, which Charlie didn't fill with an unnecessary query about the manservant's failure to mention the son. He had never quite understood how a person could remain expressionless and yet express disdain at the same time. Lancaster was a master of the art.

"You mentioned a patient with a complaint, Mr Penrose Pyke?" Lancaster prompted.

"The patient was concerned that her possessions had been tampered with during her consultation with Doctor Crabtree, despite her valuables being locked in a cabinet. She did not wish to make a fuss, but nor did she wish to ignore it."

Lancaster held Charlie's gaze. The allegation had not caught him by surprise. Finally, he blinked. "Just between ourselves, Doctor Crabtree insists on verifying the identity of patients. I believe there were instances in his London practice of patients giving a false name and not paying the consultation fee. Mrs Vale is obliged to follow his orders, but she is no thief, if that is what your client is insinuating."

"Ah, that explains it. My client will be relieved, I'm sure. Doctor Crabtree has a fine reputation, which might make him a target for cheats." Again, Lancaster twitched. Charlie continued as if he hadn't noticed. "I expect it cost Mr Franklin Crabtree a great deal to put his son through medical school in London." He waited for Lancaster to nod. "Doctor Crabtree's current occupation is perhaps not …"

Lancaster filled the pause with the slightest of smiles and a deviation from protocol. "… not a line of work of which his father would approve? Quite so. I hate to see my employer brought so low by his illness, but at least he has been spared a full understanding of his son's descent to the ungodly fringes of medical practice."

"Has Mr Crabtree's brain been so badly affected by his condition that he is unaware of what is happening around him?"

"He has good days and bad days. I confess I consider it a kindness to pretend that Doctor Crabtree is an esteemed medical specialist. His son was a great disappointment to Mr Crabtree in his youth, and thus it gives him pleasure to believe his son has redeemed himself. In fairness to the doctor, I have heard that his patients are generous with their praise for his cures. None of them have complained about his services, as far as I know, so perhaps it was wrong of me to imply that his methods are no more than outright quackery."

Charlie wanted to ask Lancaster's views on the other household members, but he doubted a direct question would be answered. Instead, he went for sympathy and a soft approach, as per Grace's tip. "It must be hard to see your employer so unwell. I do hope you will have the opportunity to stay on to work for the next generation, when the time comes."

Lancaster took several seconds to frame his response. "Mr Crabtree has been uncommonly good to me. However, when he passes on to heaven, as he could at any time, I feel it is safe to say I shall not remain in my current post once I have paid my final respects at his graveside."

A masterly understatement, Charlie thought, which spoke volumes of Lancaster's feelings without openly criticising his employer's nearest and dearest. "Is Mr Franklin Crabtree that unwell?"

175

"Mrs Vale took him to a proper doctor, who said he could have a fatal recurrence at any time. Then again, he might outlive all of us. Mr *Franklin* Crabtree is not one to give in to weakness."

"You are still a young man, Mr Lancaster. With your experience, I'm sure you will be in demand." Charlie found it hard to guess his age, but Lancaster was probably younger than thirty, despite his receding hair and rotund shape. A hint of redness about the nose suggested Lancaster might join his employer in a glass or two of port in the evening.

Lancaster appeared unperturbed about his future prospects. "Whatever happens, I have savings set aside, and Mr Crabtree has indicated there will be a modest legacy in his will to recognise my service ... assuming there is anything left of his estate by the time he passes."

There were many more questions Charlie wanted to ask, but Lancaster had been as forthcoming as he could be without being blatantly indiscreet. Charlie reached for his pocketbook, uncertain whether a tip would be accepted, but the butler-caregiver shook his head and walked back to his employer.

Charlie hurried after him, because Grace had risen from the bench seat, white-faced and unsteady on her feet. He took her arm to steady her and expressed his thanks to Lancaster quickly. As soon as he had guided his wife out of earshot, Charlie asked if she was feeling unwell.

Grace shook her head and hurried on towards the cable car, which was about to leave. Charlie settled her on a seat and draped his coat around her shivering body. "I'll take you straight home. You shouldn't be outside in this weather."

"It's not the weather, Charlie. Give me a moment to collect myself. Tell me what Lancaster said."

Charlie put his arm around her and pulled her close, both to comfort her and to keep their conversation private. "Lancaster seems an honest, decent sort of man, as you told me. He dislikes and mistrusts Doctor Barnabas Crabtree and hinted that he was spending his inheritance prematurely. Lancaster also believed Rosannah was only looking through the patients' possessions to check their credentials on her brother's orders. He seems to have no suspicions about any serious wrongdoing in the household, beyond his distrust of what he sees as quackery. However, he is also remarkably adept at disguising his views. Lancaster thinks his employer may not have long to live. What's your opinion, Grace?"

"Franklin's doctor would have warned the family that he could have a fatal bleed into his brain at any time. On the other hand, Franklin might live for many years yet, although his condition will probably deteriorate. Lancaster is doing a fine job of keeping him active and engaged, which will help. However, I don't think Franklin's condition is as serious as it may appear from his loss of movement on one side of his body. His children talked of him as if he had the mental competence of an infant, but that is far from the case."

"Were you able to get him talking?" Charlie whispered.

"He was eager to talk, and his speech is easily comprehensible if you listen closely. Franklin confuses past and present, but he hasn't lost his memory. He talked about the 'new' cable car, for instance, when the cable tramway has been operating for over a decade. He can move around by himself, as he demonstrated the night he accosted me outside his house, albeit with difficulty."

Charlie could feel her shivering against him, and he wasn't sure if it was her condition or a reaction to Franklin Crabtree. "Grace, what's the matter? Did Franklin upset you?"

"I'm fine," she said, huddling into his warmth. "I don't wish to read too much into his words, which may be based on muddled memories. Franklin mistook me for his dear departed wife, Rosie. He was so happy to see me, I felt awful for encouraging him to speak of the past. When I mentioned the burglaries, he became extremely agitated."

"Did he say why?"

"He wasn't very coherent. He said he would never forgive himself for Tillman's death. Arthur Tillman, the locksmith whose death was ruled as a suicide, I presume. Franklin said: 'I should have spoken up. I was afraid.' When I asked why he was afraid, he mumbled something about being worried about the children. 'Too much to lose', he said, and then, 'forgive me, Rosie.' His words were disjointed, but I couldn't help but take them as a confession of sorts."

Charlie lifted her head off his shoulder so he could look her in the eyes and understand what had left her so disturbed. "Do you think Franklin felt guilty simply because he guessed it wasn't suicide but didn't share his suspicions with the police? Or do you think he actually knew who killed Arthur Tillman and kept silent to protect the killer? Someone close to him, presumably. Someone he was afraid *for*, or perhaps someone he was afraid *of*."

"I don't know. Franklin acted like a man waking from a nightmare, recalling the feeling of terror but not the details of what had frightened him. My first thought was that Franklin suspected Elias Vale, but he kept quiet because he was afraid of bringing shame and suffering to their wives and children. But he stared at me with the strangest look on his face and with the whites of his eyes showing, as if he was still frightened. He said: 'Killing a man is a terrible sin, an unbearable weight upon the soul. Should such a crime ever be forgiven, my dear Rosie?'"

Tears formed in the corners of Grace's eyes. "When Franklin said those words, he grasped my arm with his right hand with such strength it shocked me. The power of his grip forced me back against the seat, unable to shake him off. In that instant, I felt him entirely capable of pushing a man's face into a mound of dough and holding it there."

Enthralled

Grace insisted on returning to Doctor Harvey's surgery to see if he needed her assistance. She was, after all, supposed to be completing her general practice placement with him, although her medical studies seemed like nothing more than a smoky haze on the horizon after the last few days.

Charlie agreed, but only if she went home if Harvey didn't need her. He promised to return to her as soon as he passed the new information on to the police team.

As soon as Grace arrived at the surgery, Doctor Harvey sat her down with a strong cup of tea and a blanket for her shoulders. He told her to wait while he attended to the next two patients, after which they would talk.

The time ticked past slowly, yet Grace could not recall what she thought about in Harvey's absence, other than the comforting sound of murmuring voices in the room next door.

"Slow day today," Doctor Harvey said, when he had resumed his seat beside her and stretched his aging limbs. "I've been winding down my practice before I retire. My sons are both specialists with no interest in taking over the care of geriatrics, wheezy children and expectant mothers, as they so charmingly describe my practice. What I need is another doctor who is good with women and children, to take on part of the workload and perhaps build the practice up again. The role would suit a doctor who has limited hours to spare from her other activities."

His use of the female pronoun jolted Grace out of her daze. A smile spread over her lips and beyond, lighting up her face. "You would take on a newly qualified woman doctor, despite the prevailing wisdom of not trusting a woman to do a man's job?"

Part of the reason Grace had pursued her interest in pathology was because she was sure no doctor would take her into their general practice, other than her father, who lived far away in Wellington. Thus, Doctor Harvey's offer had knocked her for six, in the best possible way.

"You have proved you are more than capable, Grace, if rather unconventional. I find it refreshing, to be honest. However, I should warn you that you might not be quite so free as you have been to pursue your investigative career. Don't feel you are under any pressure to accept. I could not offer you any hope of a partnership unless my sons agree."

"A position as a doctor is more than I had dared hope for. As for investigating, I would be willing to leave that to my husband. Or mostly to him. However, there is one potential complication, of which you should be aware. I believe I may be with child, due around the end of November, shortly after I complete my final exams."

"Splendid news, Grace," Doctor Harvey said, clapping his hands in delight. "Simply marvellous. I promise not to breathe a word. However, you are wrong to see a baby as a complication, although it is undoubtedly a factor to consider. My wife, who used to manage the practice, brought our children into the surgery when they were little. As a family practice, I think it sends a good message that we understand the demands of having children. You could adjust your hours to suit, and the income would allow you to employ a nanny if you wished."

Grace hoped she wasn't about to burst into tears. Her emotions seemed to have taken on a life of their own lately. "Doctor Harvey, I cannot thank you enough for your exceptional kindness. May I discuss your generous offer with my husband? I want to fling my arms around you and say yes right away, but the concept of having a baby is so new to us, we haven't had a chance to plan for the future. We'd given up hope of having a child, to be honest."

"Take all the time you need. And Grace, I think it's about time you called me Andrew if we are to be working together."

"I'd be honoured, Andrew."

"Splendid. Now, if you feel well enough, I'd like to discuss the investigation into Barnabas Crabtree. I had a concerning reply to my telegram to London this morning. It seems Crabtree never completed his medical degree, and thus he has no right to call himself a doctor. Furthermore, he left London under a cloud, with a malpractice lawsuit lodged against him."

"That's marvellous news ... Andrew. The investigation has widened to a criminal matter since we last spoke. The police are eager to speak to Crabtree, and they are looking for a reason to bring him in for questioning. What more compelling reason than the fact he is committing fraud by passing himself off as a qualified doctor? I saw a framed medical qualification on his waiting room wall, so he cannot deny the deception. And a lawsuit too. No wonder Barnabas Crabtree returned to Dunedin with money worries."

Grace would have given anything to stay in that cozy space chatting to Doctor Harvey about the future, but this was news that couldn't wait. Before she could rise from the chair, the outer door opened, and two voices could be heard in the waiting room, one of them belonging to her husband.

Charlie knocked and entered. "Grace, good to see you looking better. Afternoon, Doctor Harvey. A messenger delivered this note for you. He's waiting for a reply." He handed over the note, which Doctor Harvey read and passed to Grace.

"It's from Alistair," Grace said. "He's worried about Lily and asks if he can bring her to the surgery. Nothing urgent, he says, but it is relevant to our investigation."

Doctor Harvey rose. "I'll send a reply to Mr Stewart telling him to come straight in."

Grace sent Charlie back to the police station to pass on the vital news about Crabtree falsifying his medical degree and being sued

181

in London, while she awaited Lily's arrival nervously, praying her friend had suffered no complications from the electrical belt.

If anyone had asked her plans at that moment, she might well have thrown her long-held ambitions to the wind and pleaded to be more like the mothers she had seen this afternoon, laughing and playing with their children in the park, seemingly without a care in the world. The contents of her stomach forced their way upward again, making her grateful for the time alone before the next crisis hit.

Lily and Alistair arrived half an hour later, when Grace had regained her composure, with Charlie hard on their heels. Lily looked well, but Alistair's deep frown lines had Grace on edge. All five of them crowded into Andrew Harvey's consulting room.

"How are you feeling, Lily?" Grace asked.

"That's the problem," Lily said. "I've never felt better. As you know, I was nervous about visiting Doctor Crabtree, because I believed him to be a charlatan. However, the treatment he gave me was in no way unpleasant. Quite the opposite. I feel renewed and revitalised, and my pain has completely vanished."

Grace looked into her old friend's eyes and saw no sign that Lily was anything other than in earnest. "Lily, you don't have sciatica. You have never had it. It was a story we made up as an excuse to consult Doctor Crabtree."

"I know that, Grace. But I'm not a young woman any longer, and I do have aches and pains, even if I don't mention them. And now they're gone. Don't look at me like that, Alistair. How can Doctor Crabtree cure me of pain I never had?" Lily's nervous laugh receded into silence as she saw their serious expressions. "I'm starting to believe we underestimated Doctor Crabtree's galvanic therapy."

Grace was at a loss to know what to do, so she passed the baton to the more experienced doctor. "Any thoughts, Andrew?"

Harvey examined Lily's eyes and tested her reflexes. "Can you show me where the pain was, Mrs Stewart?"

Lily appeared confused, before waving her hands vaguely. "The usual aches that come with age. My upper leg and pelvis were sore this morning."

"Probably from your theatrical limping on that leg," Alistair said. "Charlie, you've researched electricity. Can it cause confusion in the brain?"

"Don't be ridiculous, dearest," Lily said. "I'm not *confused. I'm cured.*"

"I've never heard of electricity befuddling the brain," Charlie said, "but I'm no expert. It's possible, I suppose. Alistair, could you take us through what happened this morning during and after the consultation."

"Crabtree talked a lot," Alistair said. "The usual sort of hyperbole from a man wanting to sell his wares at an exorbitant price. Having said that, he did make a convincing case, and his file of testimonials appeared genuine. He talked Lily through what to expect and what further treatments he could offer, before he fitted her with one of the electrical belts. Crabtree tested it on the spot, and Lily said it was working. We'd agreed in advance that she would play along with whatever the doctor said. That's all, although it took the best part of an hour. We left, and Lily hasn't stopped talking about how wonderful she feels now her pain is gone."

"Have you worn the belt again, Lily?" Grace asked.

Lily looked down at her hands, leaving her husband to reply. "Twice. I took it off her in case it was causing her irrational behaviour."

"Alistair, dearest," his wife said. "It's entirely rational to want to feel well. There was no harm done. At least, I don't think so. Is it so hard to accept a new therapy, simply because it is not yet standard medical practice?"

183

"I understand what you are saying, Lily, but I tried the belt myself and felt nothing more than the slightest tingle. How can it be a cure?" Alistair held out the electrical device for all to see. "I suppose it's possible that only people who are experiencing pain feel the electrical current."

Charlie took it over to the light of the window to examine it more closely. When he was finished, he offered it to Lily. "Try it again, Aunt Lily, and tell us what you feel."

Alistair looked at Charlie as if he were mad, but Lily took the belt eagerly and went behind the curtain to put it on. When she pulled the curtain back, her face glowed. "It feels wonderful."

Charlie had his head perked to one side, watching Lily's reaction. "I disabled the electrical circuit by detaching a wire. It is physically impossible for you to feel even the faintest trace of an electric current."

"You did? But –" Lily disappeared behind the curtain again, looking puzzled.

"Interesting," Doctor Harvey said. "I have an idea of what might cause this strange reaction. Mr Stewart, how did Crabtree interact with your wife when he was explaining the effect she would feel. Describe his words, his tone of voice, and his actions precisely, if you would."

"I'm not sure how to describe it. He had his back turned to me, so I couldn't see his actions. What I recall most was his voice, which was very soothing and persuasive." Alistair demonstrated a lilting croon, such as one might use to lull a crying baby to sleep. "He assured Lily she would feel a blissful buzzing sensation that would banish her pain and make her feel renewed and filled with wonderful vitality, as many others had before her."

Harvey nodded along, as if that's what he expected. "I think the self-styled world-leading Professor of Galvanism may be a clever charlatan. Have you heard of hypnotism, or mesmerism, as it is often called. A trained person can induce a kind of trance, in which the target can be persuaded to respond to his commands."

"I saw it demonstrated once as part of a stage show," Charlie said. "The showman used his impressive powers of suggestion to convince gullible members of the audience to follow his orders, starting with simple actions, such as feeling sleepy. By the end of the show, the volunteers were flapping their arms and quacking like ducks. Amusing in a way, I suppose, but I confess I found it disturbing."

"Lily is far from gullible," Alistair said. "She's one of the cleverest, sanest people I've had the privilege of knowing."

"It seems you're wrong, Alistair," Lily said, her voice almost too low to hear. She had removed the belt during their discussion, and was now sitting down again, examining the disconnected wire. "I really didn't feel anything, did I? I could have sworn I felt a tingling. Crabtree kept saying, 'You cannot feel pain' over and over, and I didn't feel pain. How foolish I feel."

Doctor Harvey leaned forward to take the belt off her. "On the contrary, Mrs Stewart. You must have exceptional intelligence to recognise your confusion over the results and seek guidance. The power of suggestion, when applied by an experienced practitioner, is hard to resist. The stage show version is used purely for entertainment, of course. However, the technique has been used successfully by some doctors, especially those dealing with psychiatric and behavioural problems."

"Are you saying Doctor Crabtree was using a legitimate medical technique?" Charlie asked.

Harvey examined the belt with arthritic fingers, before flinging it onto his desk. "Not at all. Hypnotism must be used only with the express consent and full understanding of the patient, under controlled conditions. Anything else is grossly unethical."

Grace didn't know what to believe about the efficacy of hypnotism, but she was in full agreement that Crabtree's use of it was unethical. The man was a master of manipulation. Even so, she doubted he could have made Lily believe in him if she hadn't gone into the consultation determined to play the role of a patient in

185

unbearable pain with sciatica, with the avowed intention of being open to trying everything Crabtree offered.

"He truly made me believe I would feel a wonderful vitality," Lily said. "I suppose I wanted to recapture that feeling by wearing the belt again."

Grace threw her arms around her friend. "You played your role brilliantly, Lily. It's all my fault for asking you to take my place at the consultation."

"Dearest Grace, of course I couldn't let you do it in your condition." Lily's hand flew to her mouth. "Oh, I shouldn't have said that."

"You wouldn't be the first to give the game away," Charlie said. "We should have known that medically trained investigators like you and Anne would be one step ahead of us."

When the congratulations died down, Alistair cleared his throat. "I'm sorry to spoil the joy of the happy news, but there are still serious issues to consider, such as what to do about Crabtree's other patients. How were people with genuine conditions fooled into believing they were cured?"

"The mind has an extraordinary ability to believe, Mr Stewart," Doctor Harvey said. "We doctors have long known that a dose of sugar water can relieve real symptoms when there is no known medical treatment to help a patient. It also works for patients who wrongly believe they are ill when they are not. There may even be a genuine improvement, since the tension and anxiety caused by worrying about an illness can themselves cause pain and other symptoms. Any relief positively reinforces the patient's belief in the cure."

The simmering anger within Alistair boiled over. "If you are suggesting that you approve of Crabtree's use of quackery and mind tricks to create the appearance of a miracle cure, I can tell you I won't stand for it. He's charging a fortune for his electrical devices. That is outright fraud in my book."

186

"I agree, Alistair," Grace said. "Whatever good he thinks he is doing, Crabtree is not a qualified doctor, and his patients ought to be under proper care. He will be dealt with to the full extent of the law."

"And the judgment of his medical peers," Harvey said. "I agree he is a despicable charlatan and outright fraudster of the worst type, Mr Stewart. He may have helped people who believe they are ill when they aren't, but his callous duplicity has caused patients with genuine, treatable conditions to halt their prescribed medical treatments in the belief they are miraculously cured. Eventually, someone will suffer a serious complication or death. He must be stopped."

Alistair leaped to his feet, ready to charge out to stop the fake doctor personally, at the end of a fist if necessary.

Charlie's face was tight with anger too, but he put a restraining hand on his partner's shoulder. "Detective Inspector Wallace is planning to question Crabtree tomorrow morning, Alistair. You can be sure we will inform him of the so-called doctor's offences. The scoundrel will be shut down immediately and charged with fraud."

Duly Noted

After the fresh revelations of medical trickery, Doctor Harvey insisted they go home. Charlie escorted Lily and Grace, leaving Alistair to inform the police of the latest outrage.

When they entered their house, feet dragging, Mrs Brown took one look at Grace and said she'd run a hot bath. "You oughtn't to be running around after dangerous criminals, Mrs Penrose Pyke. Not in your condition. Oh. I mean … not when you're so busy with work."

Grace laughed. "The secret is out, it would seem. I'm beginning to think I was the last to know."

"It's only a few people, so far," Charlie said. "However, it might be time to tell our parents the wonderful news before they find out via the bush telegraph."

Mrs Brown grasped Grace's hands in her own, her face beaming. "So, it's true? Oh, my dears, I am so happy for you both."

"Early days, Mrs Brown," Grace said, failing to hide her delight. "I didn't want to say anything for another few weeks, just to be sure."

"Of course, my dear. You may rely on my discretion. Now, a hot bath and an early dinner, I think. Two messages arrived while you were out. One for each of you. I do hope you won't have to go out again this evening, because you both look like you've been knocked from pillar to post, and back again."

Charlie hoped so too, because he wasn't at all sure he could face another interview or meeting now that he had reached the warmth and comfort of home. He needed a restful evening of calm reflection to get his thoughts in order after a chaotic three days, and Grace needed to be tucked up in a warm bed.

He took both messages and opened the one addressed to him. Fortunately, it only contained additional information from Mr Burton, the schoolmaster he had spoken to briefly earlier in the day. Too briefly, it seemed, because Mr Burton had written to apologise for his lack of time earlier, which hadn't allowed him to give a full account of Barnabas Crabtree's expulsion from school.

The note read: *My conscience is troubling me, because I fear I left you with the impression that Barnabas Crabtree was a vicious brute. While it is true that the beating was an appalling act of violence, I must also add a disclaimer that I was not absolutely convinced that Crabtree was the guilty party. That said, the decision to expel him was unanimous and based on compelling evidence, including statements from the injured boy and from several boys who witnessed the assault. Also, the school had been plagued by unpleasant incidents of nasty pranks and bullying since Crabtree joined our ranks, and those incidents stopped after he left, which further indicated his guilt.*

Crabtree was not well liked by either pupils or teachers because of his arrogance and sense of entitlement. However, I had not thought him capable of such vicious behaviour as the beating. Nor did I see him as the type of boy who would act in an underhanded way to get what he wanted. He was always forthright in his demands for attention and never tried to disguise his bouts of ill-temper. A schoolmaster learns to read a room, and it never seemed to me that Barnabas Crabtree was feared by his peers.

I could not say the same for another pupil, who left the school shortly afterwards, not because he was expelled, but because his father could not afford to pay the fees. The boy was admired by many masters as a model student, but I had my doubts. I might add that the pupil in question was firm friends with the group of boys who came forward as witnesses to the beating. A clever and high-spirited group of young men, none of whom were ever caught for major infractions of school rules, largely, I suspect, because other pupils feared to speak out against them. These are simply my impressions. You must judge Barnabas Crabtree as you find him now. Yours sincerely, K. R. Burton.

The boy who left when his fees went unpaid could well be Matthew Vale. The very man who was so eager to draw Charlie's attention to Barnabas's disgraceful past. Perhaps the apple hadn't fallen far from the Vale tree after all. If so, Matthew had kept his vicious nature far better disguised than his father, Elias Vale.

Much as Charlie appreciated Mr Burton's conscience, the note only muddied already murky waters. On one hand, the unanimous verdict that Barnabas Crabtree had been guilty of the beating was a black mark against him. His own father obviously believed his son was at fault. On the other hand, the schoolmaster's intuition that Matthew Vale was feared couldn't be ignored. If nothing else, the note reinforced Charlie's impression that both men would do whatever it took to achieve their goals, whether by force or deception.

Charlie changed into more comfortable clothes and came downstairs to find the fire stoked and a glass of whisky by his favourite armchair. With his wife merrily humming in the bath, all he now required was Blaze at his feet and he would be the picture of contentment. His gratitude for Mrs Brown's thoughtfulness spilled into thoughts of the caring nature of Lancaster and thus onto Franklin Crabtree.

Grace wasn't an easy woman to unnerve, which made her reaction to Franklin Crabtree extremely concerning. Franklin was a clever and wealthy man, who was admired by cadets like Jack and Gus, and who knew the locksmith, all of which left him as a potential suspect in the original burglaries. At first glance, he seemed too frail and unwell to be a suspect in the recent spate of burglaries, but he was not so disabled that he couldn't leave the house to accost Grace in the garden. Grace had clearly been shocked by his strength today, as well as concerned about Franklin's guilty conscience.

Thus, the obvious question was whether Franklin Crabtree was still capable of masterminding a burglary scheme, despite his apparent frailties. Grace had been left in no doubt that he was strong enough to have taken Gus by surprise in the bakery, especially if Gus had been expecting a frail old man to collect the haul of stolen goods from the charity-auction burglaries. Indeed, Franklin may not have needed to do the evil deed himself, depending on how devoted a servant he had in Lancaster.

And that thought brought Charlie back to the quiet, apparently devoted manservant and the possibility Lancaster either assisted his employer or masterminded the recent spate of burglaries to provide himself with a golden nest egg before he lost his position as a butler.

Any of them – Franklin, Lancaster, Rosannah, Barnabas and Matthew – could have accessed the victims' house keys in the locked waiting-room cabinet, making the burglaries as easy as walking through a door while the owners were known to be out. Each of them knew about the auction and, with the possible exception of Lancaster, each knew the burglar, Gus Fenton, and the locksmith whose keys were used a decade ago. The younger generation needed money and thus had a motive. The problem was that it could have been any of them, alone or in combination, or none of them. By rights, Charlie should have added Jack Turner to the list, but he trusted Grace's judgement.

The solution would have to wait until tomorrow's interviews with the Crabtree household, which Detective Inspector Wallace would conduct in an official capacity, demanding answers that would not be given to a private investigator. Right now, Charlie was looking forward to sharing a quiet dinner with his wife and hearing her thoughts on the suspects. They'd hardly had a minute of quiet time alone since –

A brisk knock at the front door interrupted his thoughts. For a fleeting second, Charlie considered hiding from the visitor, but he could already hear Mrs Brown's footsteps down the hall. The next thing he knew, a black and white fur ball burst into the room and leaped onto his lap, smothering him with slobbery affection.

191

"Nice to see you, too, Blaze," he murmured at the damp nose thrust into his face. "Apprehended any fugitives lately?"

"Your bloodhound sniffed out Jack Turner all right." Declan Kelly flopped into the chair beside Charlie and helped himself to a whisky. "But I'm not sure I'd use the word 'apprehended'. When I caught up to Blaze, she was rolling on her back, having her belly rubbed by the murder suspect. You'll have to train that dog to corner her target and snarl at them, or the police force's tough reputation will be in tatters."

Charlie scratched Blaze's ears. "She only snarls at people she doesn't like. Blaze is an excellent judge of character."

"Maybe we should put her on jury duty," Declan said. "Anyway, Turner is cooling his heels in a police cell, thanks to Grace's tip and Blaze's exceptional nose, but not before the devil led us on a merry dance through bush and bog. While you sat in comfort in front of a cosy fire drinking whisky, it seems. Oh, to be an armchair detective."

Charlie raised his glass to his friend and stretched out his legs towards the fire with a satisfied sigh. "Ah yes, 'tis a grand life, Declan, my lad. Honestly, I don't know why I bother to get out of bed with so many helpers at my beck and call."

"Perhaps I ought to buy you a pair of slippers for your imminent retirement, so you can leave the real detectives to get on with the work." Declan settled back, taking a large glug of amber medicine. "Ah, now, that hit the spot. Talking of real detectives, thank you for lending me Blaze. You're lucky to have her back. You'd think I'd broken my children's hearts the way they clung to her this morning, begging to keep her. Not that we have room for a dog, unless you'd like to swap Blaze for one of my children."

Charlie ruffled the border collie's fur, not bothering to dignify Declan's jest with a response. "Get anything out of Jack Turner?"

"Less than he told Grace. However, I interviewed every person at Turner's boarding house, which is one of the more respectable ones. The man in the next room saw him return on Friday night

192

after the auction. The witness said Turner was too exhausted to notice him in the gloom of the corridor. Jack went directly into his room and was heard snoring his head off through the thin walls after that, keeping his irate neighbour awake. When I explained the situation, the witness said he was willing to swear that Jack Turner never left his room after nine-thirty in the evening."

"Jack could have slipped out when the neighbour dozed off. We know it was only Gus who committed the actual burglaries, so Jack's alibi is only relevant for the early hours of the morning when Gus was murdered."

Declan shook his head. "Gus was killed when he was making the first batch of dough, which would have been between midnight and one o'clock, according to his father. Turner's neighbour recalls checking the time shortly after midnight and banging on the wall to stop the snoring about an hour later. It's as close to a solid alibi as we'll get, assuming the neighbour hasn't been paid off. He seemed genuine. I'd have released Turner from custody if he hadn't been snoring fit to rattle the bars by the time I returned. Can't have been pleasant sleeping outside in the cold and damp."

"Excellent, one suspect down, at least five to go. I'd like to think we're making progress, but I expect the Chief Inspector won't coil his whip until we have someone in irons, preferably having confessed and returned the loot."

Declan drained the contents of his glass and set it down by the bottle. "Better have a top-up. I've got a lot to catch up on, it seems."

Charlie topped up his own glass too, since it was rude to let a guest drink alone. Then he summarised the results of his and Grace's investigations.

Grace joined them shortly after, fresh from her bath and unaware they had company. Wrapped in a thick dressing gown, with her hair down around her waist, she looked both vulnerable and wildly beautiful. She took her usual seat, Declan Kelly being a close enough friend to forgive her disarranged state.

"Evening, Grace. And may I say how radiant you look." Declan sat back in his armchair with a sentimental sigh and took a slug of whisky. "Reminds me of my lovely wife when she was ..." Declan coughed, pretending it was the whisky. "As I was saying, when Moira is fresh out of a hot bath, she has the same lovely glow."

"How kind of you to say so, Declan," Grace said, rolling her eyes at her husband.

Charlie gave her a ghost of a smile in return. News was spreading fast. "Aside from proving Jack Turner's innocence, have you made any progress, Declan?"

"I had an interesting interview with Franklin Crabtree's solicitor. Wallace wanted a complete picture of the family's financial situation, beyond the information Alistair Stewart compiled on the Vale and Crabtree businesses."

"I overheard Rosannah asking her brother what provision their father had made for her in his will," Grace said, "but Barnabas Crabtree refused to say. She was worried she would only get the usual gifts to daughters, such as dinnerware and family memorabilia. Rosannah believed Barnabas had seen his father's will."

"Oh, her brother knew what was in the will all right." Declan's impish grin had them on the edge of their seats. "The solicitor told me that Doctor Barnabas Crabtree came to see him almost as soon as he arrived back in Dunedin. He asked about the will and also about obtaining a power of attorney, because his father was incapacitated. The solicitor was relieved to oblige, as he had been acting on behalf of Franklin Crabtree until the rightful heir returned."

"Ridiculous," Grace muttered, "that a smart woman like Rosannah was ignored. Giving her brother free rein is hardly likely to be in the best interests of anyone but Barnabas Crabtree."

"The solicitor was not unaware of the issue. He hinted that the son should have been grateful not to have been disinherited by his father."

"Did he say why, Declan?" Charlie asked.

"You know how these legal men are, not willing to admit the sky is blue if it might compromise confidentiality. However, when I pressed him, the solicitor revealed that Franklin Crabtree's previous will had been drawn up after his son's expulsion from boarding school. Franklin insisted that both Rosannah and Barnabas attend the signing of the will, which left everything to Rosannah until such time as the errant son proved himself worthy by taking up a suitable occupation."

"I take it that version of the will is not the current one," Grace said.

"Correct. Barnabas Crabtree returned to his father's favour once he sent proof of his medical qualification and documentation showing he had taken a lease on a Harley Street surgery in London."

"Which suggests that Franklin believed his son was reformed," Charlie said. "Very interesting indeed, after Grace's interview with Franklin earlier today. I presume Rosannah knew the previous will had been revoked."

"She did. Rosannah never asked the solicitor to reveal the specific provisions of the latest will, but she knew she was no longer the primary heir. The solicitor said her father had made it very clear to her that Barnabas's fall from favour would last only until his son redeemed himself. Even so, it must have been frustrating for her to be used as a pawn in the father-son argument."

Grace exchanged a glance with Charlie. "We found out this afternoon that Barnabas Crabtree falsified his medical qualifications and is being sued for malpractice in London. Would Rosannah be able to challenge the current will on the grounds that her father was misled?"

"I'm no legal expert," Declan said, "but the solicitor said the latest will was drawn up on the explicit understanding that Franklin's son was of good character. Franklin insisted on adding a codicil to that effect. Rosannah would definitely have a case for

195

challenging the will, but it would be one heck of a court battle if her brother contested the case, which he undoubtedly would. I take it Rosannah Vale is unaware of the falsified qualification at present?"

"As far as we know," Charlie said. "Grace overheard Rosannah begging her brother to help her, because she and her husband desperately needed money, which means Rosannah and Matthew had a strong motive for committing the burglaries. Barnabas has a motive too, if he is being sued for malpractice in London. He cannot risk his father or sister finding out his true situation, which means he needs money urgently to settle the lawsuit quickly and quietly."

"Squandering their own wealth is no excuse for taking it from others," Declan said, "especially as the entire family is still better off than most folk. It's fair to say the solicitor had grave doubts about Barnabas Crabtree. I would go so far as to say he seemed relieved to talk to me, to share the burden of his concerns."

"Concerns?" Charlie queried.

"After Barnabas's return from London, it quickly became obvious to the solicitor that he would not be a responsible steward of his father's estate. As soon as the power of attorney was invoked, Barnabas used his father's money to pay for equipment he had bought in England without telling his creditors he was about to leave the country. The solicitor had no option but to arrange the funds transfer, although he advised against further depletion of the estate for anything other than legitimate household expenses. Barnabas said the equipment was an investment that would be repaid a hundred times over and it was his choice to make, anyway."

"Typical," Grace said. "Don't keep us in suspense, Declan. Who benefits from the latest will?"

Declan flipped open his notebook. "The long-serving servants get the usual minor bequests. Lancaster will receive the most, but only £20 and a Chinese lacquered box. Seems rather miserly to me, after all he has done for Franklin Crabtree."

196

"The latest will was written before Franklin's illness," Charlie pointed out, "when Lancaster might have been no more than an ordinary manservant. I hope the family is more generous when it comes time to settle the estate."

"I doubt it. Barnabas specifically asked the solicitor about the Chinese box and its contents, demanding to know its value. Fortunately, Franklin Crabtree anticipated his son's avarice, and provided the solicitor with an independent valuation of the gift. The box was worth a couple of shillings at most and contained only a letter thanking Lancaster for his years of service. Franklin insisted the solicitor read the letter to show there was no skulduggery. The solicitor obviously shared your view that his client had been less than generous to Lancaster. Apparently, Franklin Crabtree was so miserly he put the letter into a used envelope rather than wasting money by using a new one."

"Rich men do not stay rich by being generous, I suppose," Grace said. "How are the remaining assets divided?"

"Rosannah will get …" Here Declan had to read from his notes. "The Spode dinner set and a set of silverware, located in the butler's pantry, and the contents of the family china cabinet, as well as two large Chinese vases, located in the family drawing room. Again, Franklin provided a list of items and their valuations, presumably to prevent the items going astray before his death. The Spode and silverware were from Rosannah's mother's dowry and thus rightly belong to Rosannah, as did the Staffordshire porcelain items in the family cabinet. The porcelain is of good quality, but not hugely valuable. The other items listed were largely items of sentimental value, such as childhood games, favourite books, a coin collection, and a set of miniatures containing portraits of family members."

Declan took another sip of his whisky before revealing the sting in the tail. "Rosannah will also inherit her father's share of the Vale property business. It would have been a very generous bequest at the time the will was written. If the business is now failing, it might be more of a burden than a blessing. In short, Rosannah was right to be worried about her future. Her brother Barnabas gets everything else, including the house."

"I feel sorry for her," Grace said. "I can't imagine it gives her anything but ulcers to now be at her brother's mercy, right down to the bed she sleeps in. She must be terrified Barnabas will sell the house from under her when her father dies, so he can return to the bright lights of London or New York. Unless Barnabas sells the house and gives his sister a share, Rosannah will be entirely dependent on her husband once her father dies."

Declan tucked his notebook away and took up his glass. "According to the solicitor, the house may be the only asset left by the time Franklin dies. Between his financial support for the Vale property business, the cost of medical studies and supporting Barnabas in London, and the drains on his purse now that he cannot work, Franklin has a fraction of the fortune he once had. Hence, the solicitor's concern that the money will soon run out if not used wisely."

They fell into silence, while each considered the effect of the will on the potential suspects. In Charlie's opinion, Rosannah was not the only one who might feel aggrieved. "When I talked to Lancaster, he told me he was expecting a legacy from his employer to see him through. I'm sure he believed it would be more than £20."

"Still a lot of money in my book." Declan drained his glass and set it down. "I'd best be heading home before my wife and children forget what I look like. Best of luck shaking the truth out of the Vale and Crabtree families tomorrow."

"Are you not joining us?" Charlie asked.

"Some of us have real policing work to do while you sip tea with the charming doctor. Wallace is reassigning me to a brutal assault on the wharves. Politically sensitive, given it's a clash between rival teams of dockworkers over pay negotiations. The victim was a government informant, and now there's talk of a strike." Declan rose from his chair with a groan. "You'll be going soft with all this drawing-room melodrama, Pyke."

"Ah, the life of a gentleman detective. I can't tell you how much I envy your assignment down on the wharves in the freezing cold, holding apart two warring gangs of thugs who want to bash my face in."

"At least you know where you are with thugs. They call a spade a spade before they hit you with it. Well, I must be off. Thanks for the whisky, and sorry that Franklin's last will and testament contained nothing useful to help untangle the unholy mess you're facing."

"Oh, but it did," Charlie said, slapping his friend on the back. "In fact, the solicitor's statement might be the jemmy we need to crack open this case. Tomorrow should prove very interesting indeed, if I'm not mistaken. Enjoy your fisticuffs on the wharf while we're bathing in the glory of the Chief Inspector's praise."

Charlie saw his friend out and returned with a smile on his face. The smile dropped away in an instant when he saw Grace's grim expression. She was reading the second letter that had arrived earlier, addressed to Mrs Grace Penrose Pyke.

Inside the envelope was a neatly clipped article from a newspaper, which described the horrible death of a linesman who touched high voltage wires, right down to the *blue tongues of flame sputtering and darting from all over his body* and *the finger tips rolling green balls that danced from wire to wire,* as *the victim was cooked from head to foot.*

Revulsion and anger surged through Charlie at the thought that someone could have sent such a hideous article to his wife. Grace handed him the note that came with the article, which was short and nasty in the extreme. It said: *Shocking things happen to women who meddle in other people's business.* The note was unsigned, not surprisingly, considering the sender could be arrested for threatening behaviour.

"Doctor Crabtree is warning me off," Grace said. "I recognise those wild loops and elaborate curls as his handwriting."

"Or somebody else is trying to make it appear as if he is threatening you. Crabtree would have to be an idiot not to disguise his handwriting. It looks to me like –"

Grace cut in angrily. "He's so darn arrogant and reckless, I doubt he even paused to think of the consequences. If we set the police on him, he'll probably say exactly what you just said, that someone else was trying to implicate him. Anyway, he did make some attempt to disguise his writing by toning down his natural flamboyance. Crabtree knows exactly what he's doing, though. By using my full name, he is telling me that he wasn't fooled by my giving my name as Miss Penrose at the consultation. He knows exactly who I am and where I live."

She thrust out her chin and glared at the note with such vehemence it was a wonder the paper didn't combust. "If he thinks such threats are going to deter me, he's even more of a fool than I thought."

And that was exactly what Charlie was afraid of.

Quackery

With the threatening note weighing on her mind, Grace slept poorly. She rose early to go to the hospital, leaving a note for her husband to tell him she would meet him at the police station.

Her contact at the hospital provided the reassurance she needed. With renewed determination, Grace joined the team at the police station to go over the plan for the interview of Barnabas Crabtree and his household. The interview strategy had been devised the previous afternoon, while Grace was working at Doctor Harvey's surgery, but the new information they had gathered since then required a revised strategy. Charlie, inevitably, had spotted connections others had missed.

Wallace leaned forward over his desk, rubbing his giant paws together at the doctor's lack of medical qualifications and his dubious use of hypnosis. "It warms my old bones to have cause to arrest Barnabas Crabtree for fraud and medical malpractice. Let's use that as a lever to press him on the connections between his medical practice and the burglaries. We'll get Crabtree's sister, Rosannah Vale, into the interview too. I want to see how she reacts to the news."

Charlie replaced the pile of papers the inspector had toppled off his desk in his enthusiasm. "Lancaster, too. I'll need everyone out of the way while I search the house."

"Oh yes, you can be certain I won't overlook the butler." Wallace shot a wolfish grin at Charlie. "You have exceeded my wildest hopes, for which I will be forever grateful. If we can make an arrest today, the Chief will be delighted. Or rather, he'll be back to his normal self rather than prowling the station like a bear with a splinter in its paw."

Grace held back a smile at this description, which better matched the lumbering bulk of Wallace than the Chief Inspector. For all their difference in size, Grace would rather face Wallace on a bad day than the Chief on any day, because Wallace had a heart far bigger than his ham fists.

Wallace rose from behind his desk. "If there are no more issues to discuss, let's go get 'em."

"Before we leave, you should be aware of another disturbing development." Charlie handed over the anonymous threatening note and the newspaper article featuring lurid details of an electrocution.

When Grace saw Wallace's reaction to the threat against her, she feared she might have another case of apoplexy to deal with. She rose and handed the inspector his hat and coat. "I'm sure you'll agree the note is an encouraging sign that our killer is getting desperate. The perfect time for us to strike. So, let's go get 'em."

Wallace looked at Charlie, expecting him to voice his opposition to exposing his wife to a deranged monster. Conflicting emotions darted across her husband's face, but all he said was that her presence would be essential, as long as she remained with either himself or Wallace at all times. She nodded her agreement and thanks, knowing what it cost Charlie to let her face the person who had threatened her with such a repulsive death.

Grace buzzed with excitement as the team left the police station. To her mind, the purported revitalising tingle of an electropathic belt was no match for the natural euphoria that came with closing in on a murderous criminal. Their plan seemed foolproof, but Grace knew better than to count on everything going to plan, especially when they were dealing with a clever and ruthless killer. That was why she had a backup plan in the form of a little surprise if the killer turned on them. And, as a backup to the backup, her trusty knife was strapped to her ankle.

She glanced at her husband, who had the intense look Blaze took on when following a scent trail. With a pang of regret, she realised that her life would change when they had a child. It was almost unbearable to contemplate a life without the thrill of investigating by her husband's side, but being a mother came first. Grace took some solace in the fact she wouldn't miss being threatened and attacked. She could be an armchair detective, if they weren't too exhausted to discuss cases in the evening. And they had access to plenty of willing child-minders if her medical expertise was needed.

The first wrinkle in their carefully thought-out plan occurred before they reached the Crabtrees' house. Wallace declared his dislike of trudging up hills when there was a convenient cableway. While waiting at the city terminus of the cable car, Charlie suddenly ducked his head. "That's Matthew Vale disembarking. The man with the blue cravat."

They had decided the best strategy was to remove Matthew Vale from the house while the initial interview was conducted, because Rosannah Vale and her brother would talk more freely in his absence. To that end, Alistair Stewart had arranged a meeting with Matthew, in which Alistair would play the role of a wealthy gentleman with money to invest in property.

Grace peered through the heads, not having her husband's height advantage. Most of the men had hats pulled low as they trudged to work. She couldn't see Matthew Vale, but she did spot two blue cravats. "The royal blue or the teal blue cravat?"

"Dark blue," he muttered. "It doesn't matter. Matthew looked in my direction, but he probably didn't see me because he hurried on his way. He must be eager to meet a wealthy potential investor. Alistair hinted that the sum he wanted to invest would make both their fortunes."

They boarded the cable car for the short uphill journey, arriving outside the Crabtrees' house not long after nine o'clock, which ought to be early enough to ensure everyone was at home. Wallace ordered the constable to stand guard at the gates, letting nobody out, no matter their reason for leaving. The only man who would be let in was Matthew Vale, when he returned from his appointment with Alistair. Vale would be in a buoyant mood, Grace thought, but they would soon pop that bubble.

Lancaster answered the door. If he was surprised by a visit from the police, he hid it behind his usual smooth mask, as befitted a well-trained butler.

Wallace introduced himself as a detective inspector and told the butler he would speak to the inhabitants of the house in the dining room, leaving no room for doubt that this was an order, not a polite request. Wallace told the rest of the servants to keep their mouths closed and take the morning off. They obeyed with startling speed, leaving a kettle steaming on the hob, stopping only to doff aprons and caps, and don coats and hats.

At first, Lancaster refused to leave Mr Crabtree, but the invalid was asleep, giving his carer no cause to miss the ordeal of the interview. Grace rather envied Franklin Crabtree, lying in a comfortable bed, oblivious to the worries of the world as he dozed in a patch of sun, a light breeze through the open window ruffling the curtains. Far too nice a day to be sitting down to interview people suspected of murder, burglary, and medical malpractice.

Charlie drew Grace aside before she entered the dining room. He didn't say a word aloud, simply taking her hands and holding them in his own, before he left to undertake a search of the house. She watched him go, his back rigid as he walked away. He was worried about her being here but trying not to let it show. His intuition was not to be dismissed lightly, but it was too late now for her to change her mind. She entered the dining room and shut the door behind her.

Grace observed the suspects with interest as they chose their seats at the dining table. Wallace took the chair at the head of the table nearest the serving hatch. Doctor Crabtree, or Mr Barnabas Crabtree, given his lack of qualifications, sat as far away as possible at the opposite end of the table. Predictably, Lancaster distanced himself by taking a seat halfway down the long side of the table, equidistant from the two authority figures.

Rosannah Vale was the only surprise. She passed behind the butler to open the window a crack – for which Grace was grateful, as the room was oppressively stuffy – then sat next to Lancaster. Rosannah's head gave way to gravity, leaving her face hidden and her shoulders tense. Did she know what was coming, Grace wondered, or was the mere presence of a policeman of Wallace's seniority enough to worry her?

As Grace sat in the seat nearest to the door on the other long side of the table, she saw a slight shifting of the butler's arm, as if he had reached out his hand under the table for a fleeting moment to comfort the woman beside him. Rosannah didn't react overtly, except for an easing of the tension in her shoulders.

Barnabas Crabtree did not wait for Detective Inspector Wallace to open proceedings. Instead, he plunged right in with a strident protest. "What right do you have to order a search of my house?"

"*Your* house?" Wallace raised a fluffy eyebrow. "I was under the impression your father owned this house."

Barnabas glared down his nose at the inspector's impertinence. "I have a legal obligation to manage my father's affairs now that he is incapable of doing so for himself."

"And I am a Detective Inspector in the New Zealand Police Force with the legal mandate to search this property." Wallace paused to let the authority in his voice hit home. "Mr Crabtree –"

"*Doctor* Crabtree."

"There is no reason to raise your voice. I am not deaf." Wallace opened a file and extracted a telegram. "The medical school you attended in London has informed us that you failed to complete your medical training, *Mister* Crabtree."

Rosannah's head snapped up. All signs of submissiveness vanished as she glared at her brother. "What? Is this true, Barnabas? After all the money our father poured into your medical training and upkeep in London. Were you expelled again, or did you never even begin to fulfil the solemn promise you made to him?"

"I left of my own volition," Barnabas said, in a voice that didn't quite reach a shout but still proclaimed him as a man with a short fuse. He glanced at Wallace and swallowed his anger. "If you must know, I attended a lecture at the Royal Society on the therapeutic uses of galvanism, which made me realise that this was the true future of medicine. Medical schools are hopelessly behind the times, still advocating the same old methods, which fail to recognise the advancements made in the field of electrotherapy. I completed a course of study under a specialist in the field, and thus I have every right to set up a medical practice."

Grace decided it was time to make her presence known. So far, Barnabas Crabtree had ignored her entirely, which was extremely aggravating, considering the vicious threat he had made against her only yesterday for interfering in his business. "Mister Crabtree, whatever training you undertook, you do not have the right to put a framed qualification from the medical school in your waiting room and tell your patients you are a qualified doctor."

"How dare you question my competence?" Barnabas peered at Grace as if he truly hadn't noticed her presence before. "Aren't you the girl who attended a consultation with the Chinese woman?" He turned to Wallace. "Have the police stooped to using girls to spy on reputable professional men, Inspector?"

Wallace remained imperturbable, as always. "Mrs Penrose Pyke is the assistant police surgeon. She is also a member of the investigation team hired by the police to look into various criminal matters of a serious nature. Fraudulent claims about medical qualifications are not the only concern we have."

Rosannah Vale's attention shifted to Grace at the mention of her full name and position. She was hard to read, but she looked interested rather than disbelieving or fearful. Not that Grace trusted any of them, because the residents of this house were actors and actresses worthy of the dazzling stages of London's West End.

In contrast, the bogus doctor's response bordered on incredulity. "You cannot expect me to believe this girl is an assistant to the police surgeon, Inspector. She couldn't even cope with a simple consultation without having to leave the room to settle her fragile nerves."

Rosannah's sharp gaze shifted to Grace's hands, which were resting unconsciously on the round of her belly. Grace moved her hands, but not before she saw a flash of understanding in Rosannah's eyes. Understanding, and perhaps a hint of regret. Grace had no problem recalling exactly how that felt.

"Really, brother, you should have more faith in the competence of the female sex," Rosannah said. "Mrs Penrose Pyke's nausea is the least of our worries, given the shocking accusation against you. The poor woman was simply feeling unwell and needed a breath of fresh air. Am I correct in thinking you are with child, my dear?"

"I believe so, Mrs Vale," Grace said.

This admission caused a momentary distraction for Wallace. His head swung her way with a wide smile of genuine delight, which transformed him into the doting grandfather he was, rather than the formidable policeman he usually portrayed. Even Lancaster managed a small smile, which was the first emotion he had betrayed since the interview began.

However, Barnabas Crabtree was far from delighted. After glaring at his sister, his eyes fixed on Grace, narrowing with suspicion. "Another ruse to deceive us, I expect. You left the consulting room to poke your nose into my private affairs, didn't you? You can be sure I will make a formal complaint to the medical authorities to protest your disgraceful behaviour, Miss Penrose. Or Mrs Penrose Pyke."

"Your sister is correct about my reason for leaving the consultation, Mr Crabtree," Grace said. "By all means make a complaint if you wish to cause yourself further embarrassment. My investigation was at the behest of the medical authorities, who harbour grave concerns about your conduct and its damaging effect on your patients."

"Outrageous slander!" Barnabas leaned across the table in Grace's direction, his knuckles white against the polished wood of the table. Being a tall man, with a powerful presence, he must have known his actions were intimidating. "I heal my patients in the most natural way possible, with no possibility of causing them harm, unlike the so-called establishment doctors with their dangerous pills and potions. I have hundreds of testimonials from patients who sing my praises for curing them."

Grace refused to be intimidated, outwardly at least. Inwardly, she had no problem visualising a chair leg clutched in his fist, meting out revenge against a fellow student for some real or imagined slight. She leaned forward too, her palms flat on the table. "Then how is it that Doctor Harvey and I were called to attend an emergency caused by one of your electrical devices? Mrs Eugenie Atkinson suffered severe heart palpitations and recovered only thanks to Doctor Harvey's quick intervention."

"Absolutely impossible," Crabtree retorted, slithering back into his chair and crossing his arms.

"In a normal, healthy person, perhaps," Grace said, leaning further forward. "But Mrs Atkinson was not healthy, as you would have known had you completed a full medical examination before selling her an electrical belt. Did you even ask your patient if she suffered from a serious heart condition? Does it not concern you that you were so convincing in your salesmanship that she stopped taking vital heart medication prescribed by a qualified doctor? For that matter, did you take account of her obesity or give her precise instructions about not using the device around water?"

Rosannah's hands went to her mouth to cover her shocked gasp. Even the imperturbable Lancaster expressed his horror by way of a slight widening of the eyes.

"If Mrs Atkinson had a heart condition, she failed to inform me of the fact," Crabtree spluttered. "I cannot be blamed for that."

"You failed in your medical duty to ask her," Wallace said. "A clear case of medical malpractice, punishable by a substantial penalty under the law of our land."

Barnabas Crabtree's arrogance deflated as he hunched into his chair, his face drained of colour. "The electrical current should not be strong enough to cause a serious adverse reaction," he mumbled.

"Quite so," Grace replied, "under normal circumstances. In fact, your belts have barely enough current to be detectable, Mr Crabtree. Indeed, I doubt you can justifiably claim any genuine therapeutic effect at all."

"In short," Wallace said, "you are a charlatan, Mr Crabtree, who is defrauding gullible patients for financial gain. Another serious offence."

A knock at the door interrupted them before Crabtree could respond. Wallace excused himself, warning them, in no uncertain terms, to stay in their seats or they would be arrested. He left a fraught silence behind, forgetting his promise not to leave Grace alone.

She allowed her gaze to wander over the suspects, never letting it linger on anyone too long. Unnerved by the high voltage glare Barnabas Crabtree was sending in her direction, Grace dropped her hand to her ankle, as if to scratch an itch, while surreptitiously loosening the strap that held her knife in place. She prayed Wallace would not be gone too long.

Hiding in Plain Sight

Charlie heard angry voices echoing down the hall soon after Wallace, Grace, and the suspects entered the dining room. His assigned task, searching the house, seemed far preferable to dealing with Barnabas Crabtree's outrage at having his brilliance questioned.

Two rooms were at the top of his target list, but first Charlie conducted a quick search of the other main rooms, not wishing to miss any obvious clues. Even though the weight of evidence was shifting the scales towards an arrest, they still lacked definitive proof.

Upstairs, Barnabas Crabtree had taken the best bedroom for himself. He had not stinted on the luxuries either, which meant he was making an excellent living as a Professor of Galvanism, or he was using his father's savings freely, or he had a profitable sideline in burglary. Presumably, the master bedroom had belonged to Franklin Crabtree before he moved into a downstairs room when his mobility became compromised by illness. Rosannah and Matthew had probably taken over the master bedroom until Barnabas returned from London. Another source of tension in this tensest of households.

Charlie was itching to search the bedroom and adjoining study from top to bottom, but time was against him. He conducted a cursory search, finding household and business account ledgers for the period since Barnabas's return from London. The ledgers confirmed two points: Barnabas had made rapid inroads into his father's dwindling fortune, and Grace was correct that his handwriting was a fairly close match to the note she received the previous night. Close, but not perfect. His usual style was an elaborate scrawl with flamboyant loops. The handwriting on the note was more restrained in both size and consistency, which might simply have been a feeble attempt to disguise his distinctive hand.

He moved on to the second-largest bedroom, which housed Matthew and Rosannah Vale. Charlie's eyes took a second to adjust to the gloom, because the room was on the shaded side of the house. The smell of damp hung in the air, disguised by a hefty application of lavender. Their possessions filled the bedroom and the adjoining dressing room, but their characteristic neatness saved the room from being cluttered. Charlie felt sure Rosannah would have been seething mad at having to cede the larger room to her unmarried brother when he came home, having already seen her chance at inheriting the house vanish.

With no obvious clues leaping to attention, Charlie moved on to the next room, which was an office.

A quick examination told him that Rosannah used the smaller desk to manage her social and charitable activities, while the larger desk was Matthew's primary place of business for Vale Holdings. Half of the room reeked of cigar smoke; the other half was heady with the scent of lavender. The cloying mix of the two smells would not have encouraged Charlie to linger even if he had time, much as he wanted to indulge his curiosity. He had to make do with a quick search through the locked drawers of each desk, which were no match for his lock picks.

Charlie found the older household account ledgers in Rosannah's desk drawers. She had managed the household for her father until her brother's return, writing in an elegant hand entirely unlike the handwriting of her brother or the note sent to Grace. Rosannah's management of household expenses was as precise and conservative as her style of writing.

Flipping back through the ledger quickly, he saw Rosannah hadn't been in charge for long. Franklin Crabtree had been almost as profligate in his spending as his son, having made large withdrawals from his rapidly diminishing bank balance before his seizure. Franklin's accounts did not itemise spending beyond the

211

general categories of wages, household expenses, and a mystifyingly large miscellaneous category, which concealed the reason for the large withdrawals.

Charlie glanced at his pocket watch, alarmed at how fast the time was ticking by. He had no wish to be caught rifling through the drawers when Matthew Vale arrived home from his appointment with Alistair Stewart. However, he did take the time to confirm the parlous state of Matthew Vale's property business. While the business was making a profit on most of the smaller holdings with long-term tenants, it was losing money hand over fist on a single larger building Matthew had purchased several months ago, which had required a costly refurbishment before it could be rented. Vale Holdings would soon be bankrupt without additional investment.

Matthew Vale's handwriting was not a good match to the threatening note. Not that it meant much, since Matthew, or anyone in the household, had ample opportunity to practice copying Barnabas's distinctive handwriting.

The only certainty was that there was no love lost between the brothers-in-law. From what Matthew's sister had said, there had always been an intense rivalry between them, and Barnabas's expulsion from boarding school had likely put an end to any residual friendship. The latest version of Franklin's will must have driven an even greater wedge between the two men. When Matthew married Rosannah, she had been the heiress to her father's fortune. Now, she would inherit only family memorabilia and half of a failing property business.

Charlie relocked the drawer and moved on to the room at the top of his search list, the family drawing room at the other end of the bedroom level.

The collection of family treasures mentioned in Franklin Crabtree's most recent will was exactly as the solicitor had described it to Declan Kelly. A large cabinet displayed the Staffordshire porcelain, along with the other items described in Franklin's bequest to his daughter, Rosannah. The childhood

212

memorabilia, including games, children's books and Franklin's coin collection, were crammed into a bottom drawer of the cabinet. He took a quick look through them, which was just as well. A wad of receipts fell out when he unpacked the drawer, explaining Franklin's excessive expenditure in the years leading up to his seizure.

Charlie found Franklin's bequest to Lancaster at the back of the top shelf of the cabinet, behind a porcelain figurine of a demure shepherdess with a lamb at her feet. A dainty little red lacquered box with a Chinese motif. He would have chosen the box over the porcelain if he'd had his pick, but not because the box was more valuable. It was a beautiful piece, but one could purchase something similar for a few coins in the Chinese emporium he and his Aunt Lily frequented. Charlie had been certain Franklin would give his devoted servant an item of value, likely choosing something that Barnabas would not recognise as valuable. Exactly as the solicitor had described, the only item inside the box was the old envelope, sealed with red wax. Holding it up to the light, Charlie could see the envelope held only a single sheet of paper – the letter of thanks to Lancaster. He closed the lid and tucked the box into his pocket.

The only other items mentioned in the will stood on either side of the fireplace in the form of two tall Chinese vases, exquisitely adorned with long-tailed birds sitting in a flowering tree. His Aunt Lily, who took great pride in her Chinese ancestry, had a similar pair, which he had admired many times. He removed the gold-edged top of the nearest vase and peered inside, noting that the vases had been weighted down.

Charlie went to get Wallace to act as a witness. If the vases contained what he hoped they contained, he wanted to cover himself so he couldn't be accused of planting evidence. The inspector said he'd join Charlie as soon as he'd had a quiet word with the suspects, to ensure they didn't move from their seats. The inspector's "quiet word" followed him down the corridor.

It took a frustrating few minutes for the two of them to extract the contents through the tapered necks of the vases without

213

breaking them. However, the effort was worth its weight in gold. Gold, both in solid lumps and as jewellery, packed tightly into sturdy leather pouches along with silver, diamonds, pearls and more, matching the descriptions of items stolen in the burglaries.

The end of Wallace's lip ticked up. "It'll be nice to have the Chief off my back."

A typical Wallace understatement, delivered with a raised eyebrow that Charlie interpreted as: *do we have proof of who did it?* And that was the problem. Gut feelings were not enough, especially as they hadn't definitively ruled out any of the suspects yet. Their only hope was to keep the questions coming until one or more of them gave the game away with a slip of the tongue, proving their guilt, or their innocence.

"I'll keep searching the house, sir," Charlie said. "I still need to confirm a couple of points."

"Hide the valuables for now, Pyke, while I continue the interview." Wallace clapped him on the back and presented Charlie with that rarest of gifts, a broad smile. "I believe congratulations are in order to you and your wife, and not only for the investigation. Don't worry, I won't share the wonderful news until you are ready."

"Thank you, sir." Charlie couldn't imagine the circumstances under which Grace would announce her condition to a group of murder suspects, but now was not the time to enquire. "How did the suspects react to Grace's presence?"

"I don't think Barnabas Crabtree sent the threatening note, because he gave a convincing impression of a man who didn't know who Grace was until I told him. I'd better get back." Wallace departed with uncharacteristic haste.

The second of the two rooms Charlie wanted to search belonged to the devoted butler – a man who had mastered the art of hiding secrets. He felt sure Lancaster would be close to his employer on the ground floor, rather than with the other servants. Sure enough, the butler-valet-caregiver's room was next door to Franklin Crabtree's bedroom, to which it was connected by a bellpull.

Lancaster had a larger room than Charlie would have expected, and it was far more sumptuously decorated than any servant's quarters he had seen before. The décor and the marks left where furniture had previously stood indicated that the room had been a lady's sitting room or parlour before Franklin moved downstairs. A magnificent painting still adorned one wall, and the remaining furniture would have graced any home in the city. Thick Oriental carpets and an ornate fireplace kept the room warm. Although Lancaster deserved the comfort after all he had done for his employer, Charlie wondered how Barnabas had reacted to this conspicuous display of splendour in a servant's room, if he had ever bothered to inspect the butler's quarters after his return from London.

Charlie's suspicions about Lancaster were rewarded when he noticed a small desk wedged into an alcove. Rows of books lined the shelves above the desk, which was neatly laid out with the usual pens, ink and paper, as well as tweezers and a magnifying glass. A few minutes of searching the shelves and desk drawers confirmed what he suspected.

It was time to throw a stick of dynamite into the already tense interview, preferably before Matthew Vale arrived home from his appointment in town. He could only hope that Alistair had delayed Matthew's return with a never-ending stream of questions on property investments, a subject on which Alistair was far more qualified than Charlie would ever be.

Allegations Fly

A few minutes after Wallace left Grace alone in the room, Barnabas Crabtree's scorching glare became too much for her to bear. She rose and went to the window, waiting impatiently for the inspector's return. She pretended to admire the autumn foliage, while attempting to listen to the whispered discussion between Rosannah and Lancaster, who were seated nearby.

Charlie had voiced his suspicions about Lancaster last night after Declan left. Franklin Crabtree must have known of the butler's deception all these years. Indeed, Franklin had likely been the instigator. Now, seeing Rosannah and the butler seated side by side, with their heads together sharing their thoughts, Grace realised Rosannah had been complicit in the deception too.

Rosannah Vale had impressed Grace at their first meeting with her combination of competence and compassion. However, she was not a woman to be underestimated. Although she had set aside her impetuous youth to take the traditional roles of supportive wife and dutiful daughter, a clever brain still lurked under the tranquil façade. Rosannah's life choices hadn't worked in her favour. Her husband's failing business and her brother's reinstatement as the principal heir had left her in a desperate state.

A waft of lavender and a voice near her ear startled Grace out of her musing.

"What are you really doing here, Mrs Penrose Pyke? The police do not send a detective inspector to query a faked medical qualification, even if there are concerns around minor medical malpractice." Rosannah spoke softly enough to ensure her brother could not eavesdrop, but not so softly that Lancaster couldn't hear.

Grace turned to face Rosannah, who was standing uncomfortably close to her back, blocking her view of the room.

216

When Grace tried to move away, Rosannah moved with her, until the windowsill prevented any further retreat. She leaned against the sill, forcing herself to remain calm. "Mrs Atkinson could have died from your brother's treatment regime. I'd hardly call that minor. And misrepresenting a professional qualification is outright fraud."

Rosannah swivelled her head towards the spot her brother had been sitting, and then towards the door. When Grace shifted to peer around her, she saw that Barnabas had left the room. Wallace would be furious. She'd have to redeem herself by getting information out of Rosannah.

"You showed no surprise at hearing my married name, Mrs Vale. When did you find out who I was?"

"I read the newspapers and the *Ladies' Journal*. The name Grace Penrose sounded familiar to me at the consultation, but I didn't make the connection until my husband said he had a visit from Mr Penrose Pyke, the well-known detective, who wanted to invest in property. Matthew was excited, hoping to use your husband's name to draw in other clients. It could have been the making of the business, had your husband truly been an investor. Not that it matters now, because we will be tarnished by my brother's infamy regardless of who invests with us. I suppose one must accept the vagaries of fate, but it seems unfair all the same."

"Did you tell your brother my married name?" Grace's thoughts were on the threatening note addressed to Mrs Penrose Pyke, when she had only used Miss Penrose at the medical consultation. It was a flaw in her theory that Barnabas Crabtree wrote the note, especially as he had put on a convincing show of not realising who Grace was until Wallace deliberately dropped her name into the interview.

"I didn't tell my brother anything about you, but he may have overheard Matthew and me talking about you and your detective husband over afternoon tea."

If they were discussing it over afternoon tea, Lancaster could have been there to serve them, Grace realised. All of them would have been suspicious at the coincidence of a private detective visiting Matthew Vale while his wife visited Crabtree's surgery, which meant they knew of the investigation in time to send the threatening note. She needed to tell Wallace before the interview resumed.

Rosannah continued impatiently. "I'll ask you again, Mrs Penrose Pyke. Why are you investigating my brother?"

"Detective Inspector Wallace will inform you when he returns, Mrs Vale." Grace heard the door open, so she stepped around Rosannah to have a word with Wallace. However, it was Lancaster, who must have sneaked out while they were talking. Grace would have suspected Rosannah of deliberately distracting her to allow him to leave if he hadn't returned carrying an innocent tea tray.

The butler placed the tray, bearing a small teapot and a single cup, in front of Rosannah's chair. That single cup struck Grace as an act of defiance. Lancaster might as well have stated openly that he no longer served Barnabas Crabtree, and he deemed the police team as undeserving of his care. The fact that he had not brought tea for himself told her that Lancaster still viewed himself as a servant.

Barnabas returned, noticing the single cup immediately. He glared at the butler. When Lancaster didn't react, Barnabas turned away, placing a framed certificate on the table and resuming his seat without further comment.

The inspector's heavy tread was now audible down the hall, at long last. Grace beat a hasty retreat to meet him outside the dining room, admitting the two men had left the room while Rosannah had her cornered. She also warned him they had known of the investigation yesterday afternoon, ending with a comment that Rosannah and Lancaster seemed unusually close for a mistress and servant.

Wallace nodded, as if he was unperturbed by the news. Indeed, he seemed unusually animated. One side of his lips curled up at the end, which Grace took as a sign that he was overjoyed by whatever Charlie had found during his search.

Wallace resumed his seat. He leafed through his notes as if he had forgotten the tension he had left behind. "I apologise for my brief absence," he said, glancing up. "My colleague is an enthusiast of all things Chinese. He was particularly taken with a lovely pair of Chinese vases, which he wanted my opinion on, because I am also a collector of Oriental artifacts."

Having seen Wallace's home, which might have been transported intact from Scotland, Grace knew this to be a fabrication, although, for the life of her, she could not figure out why. Wallace was watching their reactions like a hawk, so Grace did the same. Barnabas seemed annoyed by the frivolous distraction, while Lancaster showed no reaction beyond a glance at the clock, leaving Rosannah to fill the silence with what appeared to be baffled politeness.

"My father started life as a merchant seaman," Rosannah said. "He picked up many pieces around the world, although I believe the Chinese vases were purchased in Sydney rather than the Orient. Father told me they weren't worth much, because they were reproductions, but I have always loved them. He promised the vases would be mine one day."

Wallace gave a satisfied nod. "Now, where were we? Oh, yes. Fraud and malpractice. What have you to say for yourself, Mr Crabtree?"

The rapid switch of topic caught Barnabas Crabtree by surprise. He showed none of the bluster he had earlier, but he wasn't ready to concede defeat either. "I can assure you there was no fraud or malpractice, Inspector." He held up the framed certificate. "As you can see, I am qualified to practise galvanic therapy."

"Mrs Penrose Pyke informs me your lack of medical qualifications resulted in significant harm to a patient, Mr Crabtree," Wallace said.

Barnabas sent Grace a phony smile, which straddled the line between apologetic and superior. "Mrs Penrose Pyke can be excused for her lack of understanding of my innovative methods. She may well have experience assisting the police surgeon with filing or passing him instruments or whatever she does, but she is not a qualified doctor and she has no knowledge of the beneficial effects of electricity on the human body." He held up his hand to forestall Wallace's objection. "It is a specialist field, and I know I am the only qualified practitioner in Dunedin."

Grace could tell he had rehearsed the speech during Wallace's absence. Most policemen would have been nodding their agreement at Crabtree's assured professional tone, but Wallace knew her too well to doubt her account.

"Why don't you enlighten us?" Wallace glanced down at his file. "How do electric hairbrushes and belts with little or no electrical current effect the miraculous cures you claim?"

"The cures my patients swear by," Barnabas corrected. "The scientific explanation is simple, but none the less miraculous for that. A low current, correctly applied by a trained specialist, works gently to remove blockages within the body, removing the source of pain and enhancing vitality. It is one of the greatest medical advances of our time."

Wallace rocked backwards in his chair. "Is that so? Nothing to do with your use of hypnotic techniques to convince the patient they are cured?"

The shot hit home. Barnabas Crabtree stiffened as his face drained of colour.

"Hypnotism?" Rosannah said, in a voice hung with icicles. "Is that how you do it? If this becomes common knowledge, we'll be financially ruined and shamed in front of the entire city."

Barnabas shoved his chair back so forcefully it crashed to the floor. "Close down the damned practice for all I care. Do you think I wanted to come back to this one-horse town after the glory of

220

London? I'd have packed up and left already if the old man hadn't kept clinging to life, refusing to give in to the inevitable."

The fake doctor strode towards the door, ignoring the outraged gasps from Rosannah and Lancaster.

Wallace moved quickly to stop him from leaving. "Sit down, Mr Crabtree. Do I need to remind you that I am conducting a formal police interview? If you attempt to leave again, I will arrest you."

Grace was interested to note that Rosannah had put a hand on the butler's forearm to restrain him after her brother's outburst. She hadn't touched the tea Lancaster had poured for her, but now she picked up the cup and sipped. Her allegiance was clear, and it didn't lie with her brother.

When Barnabas resumed his seat, Wallace continued. "I doubt you would care to return to London, Mr Crabtree, since you are being sued for malpractice there. And you will not be leaving Dunedin until you have faced criminal charges over your so-called medical practices."

Rosannah and Lancaster both stiffened at the revelation of a lawsuit, but they kept silent. Barnabas held his tongue too, although he was on his feet again, shaking with anger.

"When did you return from London?" Wallace asked.

"Eight months ago. I had to return to my father's side after he had a severe apoplectic seizure. I assure you that if I had stayed in London, I would have had that entirely frivolous lawsuit dismissed in an instant."

Wallace glared at his suspect until he sank back into his chair. "You returned only two months before Dunedin suffered the first in a series of burglaries, culminating in six burglaries on the night of the hospital charity auction."

"What's that got to do with me?" Barnabas said, his sullen expression shifting to wariness. "If you are implying that I am involved in such a sordid scheme, I can assure you that I was the auctioneer that night, standing in front of a room full of witnesses."

Wallace leaned back to better take in the effect of his next statement. "But you know Gus Fenton, the man who committed the burglaries under orders from someone he knew and feared. Almost exactly like a similar string of burglaries a decade ago."

Barnabas, Rosannah and Lancaster all flinched. Grace was sure each of them knew exactly which past crimes Wallace was referring to. Lancaster flicked a glance at the woman beside him, but Rosannah stared straight ahead. When the butler's head turned, the light caught it, and Grace saw a sheen of sweat above his lips.

Wallace smiled. He'd seen their reactions too. "We have definitive proof that the person behind the burglaries lives in this house. That person murdered Gus Fenton in cold blood as soon as Gus completed the final six burglaries, which stripped the valuables from the houses of people attending the charity auction. Each of the victims also had a link to your dubious medical practice, Mr Crabtree. We believe the keys used to perpetrate the crimes were copied when the patients were asked to leave their valuables in the waiting room cabinet."

Rosannah and Lancaster stared at Wallace with either horror or terror distorting their faces. Grace wasn't sure which.

Barnabas Crabtree's expression went through incomprehension and confusion, before settling on anger. "How dare you suggest such a thing? I can categorically assure you that there is no link whatsoever between anyone in this house and these dreadful crimes."

"Oh, there's a link," Wallace assured him. "More than one, in fact. Gus Fenton was part of the cadet programme your father and Elias Vale ran until Vale's death. The cadet corps never really recovered from its link to a gang of burglars, did it?"

"How dare you imply my father was to blame? He and Mr Vale did their utmost to provide a better future for troubled young men. It wasn't their fault one lad reverted to his criminal ways."

"The cadet corps was disbanded because my father-in-law died," Rosannah said, "not because of the actions of a single delinquent youth."

Wallace turned to her. "I'm surprised your husband did not continue the programme so dear to his father's heart, Mrs Vale."

"Matthew was only eighteen when his father died," Rosannah said, with rather more force than was warranted by a simple query. "He was far too busy dealing with his father's financial affairs to run the cadet corps. Besides, Matthew was never involved in or had any interest in the corps."

"Ah, yes," Wallace said. "Our enquiries indicate the Vale property business was in serious financial trouble at the time of the first burglaries. Difficulties the business is facing again. Without financial support from your ailing father – or your brother, since he now holds the purse strings – Vale Holdings will soon be bankrupt, if it isn't already. In short, Mrs Vale, you and your husband are in desperate need of money once again."

All the fight went out of Rosannah at Wallace's unsubtle hint that the burglaries were committed to prop up their failing property business. She looked so close to fainting that Grace reached for her bag to get smelling salts.

But Rosannah rallied enough to choke out an explanation. "That may be true, but I can assure you we had neither the need nor the desire to turn to crime. Matthew has a strong portfolio of properties, only one of which is causing problems. I'm afraid my husband rather overextended our credit to fix the issue. All we need is a little extra investment to see the business through a difficult period. Indeed, my husband is recruiting an extremely wealthy potential investor as we speak."

Wallace was not about to let her off the hook. "Am I to assume your financial problems are the reason you go through the patients' possessions when they are busy in the consultation room?"

"I do not! I am offended you would suggest such a thing."

223

Grace took out her calling card case, which still showed the dust marks of a test for fingerprints. "In that case, Mrs Vale, you won't mind me taking your fingerprints to compare to the ones I found on this card case, which was left within the locked cabinet in the waiting room."

"Fingerprints?" Rosannah said. "I have no idea what you mean."

"Did you not know that it is possible to establish a person's unique identity from the patterns on the tips of their fingers?" Grace said. "However, I do not need to take a sample from you, because I can see that the fingerprints on the case are smaller than those of the only other people who had access to the cabinet."

Rosannah blinked back tears. "Barnabas asked me to confirm the identity of patients. He told me he had problems in the past from people undertaking consultations and then not paying. I didn't want to do it, but you have to understand that I must do as my brother tells me or I'll be destitute."

Barnabas cut her off. "This is all quite preposterous. I accept it was a little underhand, but one has to be tough to survive in business these days. Besides, my sister convinced me there was no need to continue the practice, because Dunedin is a small, insular community, unlike London. We haven't been checking identities for months and have never had a problem with payments."

"Then why are your fingerprints on the card case, Mrs Vale?" Wallace asked.

"As I said to Mrs Penrose Pyke earlier, I believed I had heard her name before, and something didn't seem quite right. I didn't say anything at the time because the name she gave matched the card. It wasn't until later that I realised who she was."

"Mrs Vale, did you continue to search all the patients' belongings after your brother told to stop?" Wallace's voice rose. "Did you copy the patients' house and safe keys?"

"No! Absolutely not."

Wallace turned his attention to the far end of the table, where Barnabas was gaping at his sister. "What about you, Mr Crabtree?"

"What? No, of course not."

"Lancaster?"

"Me? No." Lancaster shook his head vigorously, but he had the desperate look of a cornered man about him. Grace really hoped it wasn't him, but kindness to an invalid didn't exclude the possibility that he could also be tempted by ill-gotten riches.

"Don't be ridiculous," Rosannah said. "Lancaster wouldn't hurt a fly. He's so honest, he's been known to return a dropped penny."

"If you say so, Mrs Vale," Wallace said. "Talking of hurting flies, or the human equivalent, I am reliably informed that you were expelled from boarding school after beating a boy with a cane, Mr Crabtree."

"A chair leg, actually," Grace said, mentally reviewing resuscitation techniques as Barnabas Crabtree went from shocked to furious to apoplectic at Wallace's sudden change of tack.

"I did no such thing," he yelled at a volume hazardous to eardrums. "I was wrongly blamed after being set up by the sneakiest, most vicious little toad in the school. Your husband," he bellowed at Rosannah. "God knows I warned Father against Matthew Vale, but he was always blind to Matthew's rotten core, only seeing the charming exterior. The day Father told me he believed Matthew's word over mine about the expulsion was the day I knew I had to get out of this house."

"The incident was the subject of an inquiry by the school," Grace said. "The evidence supported the case against you, and the verdict was unanimous. That vicious assault put a fellow student in hospital."

Barnabas Crabtree rounded on Grace. "How dare you, you foul, meddlesome witch? I don't know what you've got against me, but you can stop your despicable interfering in my business and get out of my house now, before I throw you out."

Family Treasures

As Charlie hurried along the hall, he heard Barnabas Crabtree unleashing a furious tirade against Grace. He could only hope that the baby growing inside his wife hadn't yet developed its hearing, because the disgraceful insults being hurled at its mother were enough to curdle the wee mite's blood. His muscles tensed as he ran the last few steps to the door and burst into the dining room.

He jerked the fake doctor out of his chair. "If you ever speak to my wife like that again, I will throw you in the dampest, darkest, most vermin-infested cell I can find and throw away the key."

Whether it was the suddenness of the attack, the words, or the furious tone, it worked. Barnabas Crabtree let out a squeal and hung his head in silence. Charlie glimpsed Lancaster's brief spark of glee out of the corner of his eye. He could hardly blame the man, after years of servitude.

Charlie remained standing inches away from the object of his fury, his chest and shoulders at maximum expansion. "Well, have you nothing to say to my wife?"

"I apologise for my uncharacteristic loss of temper, Mrs Penrose Pyke. It was unforgivable."

It was a feeble attempt, but enough for Charlie to release his hold.

Grace dipped her head to Barnabas and brushed her fingers against Charlie's hand as he sat beside her. "Thank you for your gracious apology, Mr Crabtree," she said. "Believe it or not, I've heard worse."

Wallace gave Charlie a discreet nod, indicating he should begin the next phase of the interrogation.

Charlie looked across the table at Rosannah Vale, whose face was so tense her jaw must have been aching. "Mrs Vale, are you aware of the terms of your father's will?"

"What? No." Rosannah's focus was still on her brother. She was obviously appalled by his tirade against Grace, but not unduly surprised. Belatedly, Rosannah switched her attention back to Charlie. "My father promised to look after my interests, but my brother has chosen not to reveal whether that is the case."

"You might as well know now, I suppose," Barnabas said. "When the time comes, you will receive Mother's porcelain collection and Father's half of Vale Holdings." Perhaps to reassert his dominance, or because he couldn't resist thrusting the knife deeper, Barnabas accompanied the words with the sort of smirk that had everyone at the table narrowing their eyes and clenching their fists.

Barnabas upturned his hands. "Don't look at me like that, sister. It's hardly my fault that your useless husband has rendered our father's generous bequest utterly worthless."

Rosannah kept her head held high even as a tear tricked down the side of her nose. "We'll manage. Money isn't everything, Barnabas, and Father has the strongest constitution of any man I know. He will live for years, while you sink under a mantle of disgrace."

"In fact, your father is bequeathing you several other personal items, Mrs Vale, such as his chess set, children's books and games, and his coin collection." Charlie watched Rosannah closely and was rewarded with a widening of her eyes and a tiny flare of nostrils.

"That battered old chess set," Rosannah said, sighing. "He and I used to play together. How sweet of him to leave it to me. We were both fascinated by old coins too, when I was young and curious about the world. How long ago that seems. It's lovely that Father has recalled my childhood interests."

Rosannah's face was alight with joy, even if she did a good job of disguising it as pure sentimentality. Charlie knew nothing about old coins, but he'd glanced through the extensive collection and noted coins dating back to antiquity. According to the receipts from a local coin dealer he had found in the drawer, the coins were worth a small fortune. Franklin Crabtree, cunning old devil that he was, had found a clever way to reward his intelligent, loving daughter, no matter which version of the will was valid at the time of his death, depleting his fortune to do so.

Charlie wondered if Franklin ever regretted not making Rosannah his successor to the family business interests when it became clear his son was not the man he had hoped for. The idea had probably never occurred to him, but it was clear he wished to see his daughter well provided for in a way that wouldn't be obvious to her brother. Or to her husband, for that matter.

"Your father is a man who values sentiment over the more obvious gifts of wealth," Charlie said, so as not to reveal the secret in front of her brother. He drew the lacquered box out of his pocket. "Mr Crabtree is bequeathing this beautiful Chinese box to his devoted servant, Lancaster. I know it is not valuable, but perhaps it has sentimental value to you, sir."

Charlie handed the box to the butler. Unlike Rosannah, Lancaster failed to hide his excitement when he took the box. The contrast with his normal unemotional expression made him look like a different man from the dignified butler he had played for so long.

Barnabas saw it too. "Give me that box," he demanded.

Lancaster took the envelope out of the box before pushing the empty box down the table without a qualm. He unsealed the envelope with gentle fingers, removing the letter and setting it aside. While Barnabas prodded the box for hidden secrets, Lancaster and Rosannah grinned at each other over the used envelope, completely ignoring the letter that had been inside it. The envelope wasn't even addressed to him, or to Franklin Crabtree, or indeed to anyone living in New Zealand. It was adorned with a simple penny stamp.

Given Lancaster's obvious excitement, there seemed no point in being discreet, so Charlie sought confirmation of his suspicions. "It's a rare stamp, isn't it?"

"The stamp should never have been sold." Lancaster's voice trembled with emotion. "The plate was malformed, leading to imperfections in the printing. However, a few sheets left the printer by mistake and were sold before they could be recalled."

Charlie suspected something of the sort. A misprinted stamp seemed a strange sort of object to desire, but the philately books on Lancaster's shelves documented several such stamps that were now worth more money than a butler could hope to earn in several years of service.

"A policeman who investigated the series of burglaries a decade ago told us about a quiet boy who collected stamps," Charlie said. "I suspect one of his few friends was a young girl who shared his interests. She used to visit your father's locksmith shop, but only to see you, not to look at your father's locks as she pretended. I am right, aren't I? You're Samuel Tillman, and your oldest and dearest friend sits beside you."

Lancaster froze, fear showing in the whites of his eyes. Rosannah placed her hand over his and glared at Charlie defiantly.

Barnabas stared, slack-jawed, before erupting. "I knew you were one of my father's charity cases, but I didn't know you were the Tillman boy. The old man must have been insane to harbour a fugitive criminal in his house. Do something, Inspector."

"What did you have in mind?" Wallace asked.

"The butler did it!" Barnabas yelled, on his feet now and pointing his finger at Lancaster, or Samuel Tillman, as they now knew him to be. "Arrest him!"

Wallace didn't move a muscle. "The butler did what, exactly, Mr Crabtree?"

229

"He's the criminal you're looking for. Samuel Tillman was suspected of being part of the original burglary gang. His father took the blame and committed suicide. Samuel must be up to his old ways again, and now he's murdered Gus Fenton, too. Don't just sit there, Inspector."

Rosannah rose too, equally furious. "How dare you, Barnabas? Samuel was wrongly accused. Not a day passes that he doesn't regret the fact that his father died thinking his son guilty. Our father trusted Samuel. He believed in him and gave him the fresh start he deserved."

"You're a stupid, gullible fool if you believe that, Rosannah. We're not safe in our own home with him here. I cannot believe you knew all along and hid this man's true identity from me." Barnabas grabbed the letter from the table and retreated to his chair, no doubt hoping for an explanation of his father's actions.

His sister wasn't about to be dismissed so rudely. "Samuel is more of a gentleman that you will ever be. If I've been a fool, it's been in trusting you to do right by this family. Go back to London if you want to, Barnabas, but you won't be taking an inheritance with you. When Father dies, which I hope won't happen for many years, I will contest your right to inherit so much as a brass farthing. You've lied about everything and gotten away with it for far too long."

"And I will stand by Rosannah and her father every step of the way," Samuel said, with quiet dignity.

"I'm sure you will, Lancaster," Barnabas said. "You'll continue to weasel your way into this household until you get what you want, even if you have to kill to get it. But you won't get it while I'm in charge. Now, get out of my sight."

Rosannah addressed her next words to Wallace. "I beg you to disregard my brother's vile accusations, Inspector. Samuel Tillman was and is innocent of any crime. As Lancaster, Samuel has proved a thousand times over that he was worthy of my father's trust."

"Why was your father so certain that Samuel was innocent of the burglaries, Mrs Vale?" Wallace asked.

Rosannah appeared momentarily taken aback, as if she had never thought to question her friend's innocence. "Gus Fenton was a tough, streetwise lad. Dear, sweet Samuel would have more chance of bending an iron bar than bending Gus to do his bidding. Neither of us believed for a moment that Arthur Tillman or his son had committed any crime. We were shocked that Mr Tillman felt he had to take his own life to prevent his son being suspected."

"Did your father suspect anyone else?" Charlie asked.

Rosannah's cheeks flared. "Perhaps. But Father never said a word to me, and I never mentioned my doubts to anyone."

"You must have had your suspicions."

"Nothing certain. It was nothing more than a feeling. I shouldn't say this out of loyalty to my husband, but it did seem to me that my father never trusted Matthew's father in the same way after the burglaries came to light. However, the police found no evidence against Elias Vale, and Father had already taken a stake in his business, so if he had his doubts, he held his tongue."

"Balderdash," Barnabas said. "Elias Vale was a far better man than he was given credit for. Why did Samuel Tillman hide behind a false name if he was innocent?"

"Because people like you refuse to trust a man tainted by association, regardless of his innocence." Samuel held out his hand. "Give me back my letter. Perhaps your father admitted his suspicions in his final words to me."

Barnabas ignored his plea. Instead, he unfolded the letter and read it. His face tightened into a furious grimace. Then, he rose and walked stiffly towards the door, ripping up the letter and screwing the pieces into a ball as he went. "I'm going to see my father. Don't try to stop me."

Charlie placed his muscular bulk in front of the exit, holding out his hand for the ball of shredded paper. "For heaven's sake, Mr

231

Crabtree, don't be so petty. Just give it to me. The letter belongs to Samuel."

The family solicitor had told DS Kelly about it, so Charlie knew it was only a letter from Franklin Crabtree to Lancaster, thanking him for his service. Barnabas Crabtree was a pathetic excuse for a man if he was so jealous of his father's gratitude to a devoted servant that he would withhold it.

Barnabas tried to get past him, but Charlie was prepared to knock him flat if he disobeyed. In the end, he had to grab the man's wrist. Barnabas flung down the ball of paper and fled the room when Charlie scrambled to retrieve it.

The door slammed behind him. Charlie tossed the letter onto the table and raced after him, but the key turned in the lock before he could open the door. No amount of rattling the doorknob changed the fact that Barnabas Crabtree had deliberately locked them in. The solid oak door scarcely moved when Charlie set his shoulder to it with enough force to raise a bruise.

Wallace was on his feet in an instant, turning to Samuel and Rosannah. "Quick. Do you have another key?"

Samuel ignored the command. He had come around the table to get the letter and was concentrating on flattening it out and piecing it together.

Rosannah answered. "The only key I know of was the one in the lock. Samuel, do you have a spare key?"

The butler did not hear her, so intent was his focus on the letter. With the howl of a wounded animal, Samuel shoved Charlie aside and slammed his body into the door, as if he could break through it with sheer fury.

After a second of paralysed shock, Charlie lunged for the letter, at a loss over Samuel's reaction. The contents of the letter left him stunned. The solicitor's account of Franklin's letter had left out a crucial element. After thanking Lancaster for his faithful service, the letter begged his forgiveness for staying silent all these years when Franklin knew that his son Barnabas had killed Lancaster's father, Arthur Tillman.

Deadly Slumber

Grace couldn't hear herself think over the noise in the dining room. Rosannah screamed blue murder when she read the letter. Wallace ran to the partially open window, rattling and banging it to heave it fully open, only to find a catch prevented it from opening wide enough for a person to get in or out. Meanwhile, Charlie was attempting to force open the serving hatch into the butler's pantry.

Samuel was still pounding on the door. Grace grabbed his arm and shook it to get his attention. "Samuel, please stop and think. Is there a spare door key?"

"I suppose there must be, but I've never needed it. Maybe in the sideboard."

Samuel, Rosannah and Wallace joined forces to search the bulky sideboard for a spare key. Wallace turned out cutlery drawers with a clatter, while Rosannah flung linen napkins aside and Samuel went down on his knees to rummage behind the crockery. Charlie took one look at the chaos and went back to wrenching open the serving hatch.

Grace took her chance to read the shredded letter, finally understanding the sudden furore. No wonder Samuel had reacted with such uncharacteristic fury. His trusted employer had known all along that Barnabas had faked Mr Tillman's confession and suicide to frame him for the burglaries a decade ago. Grace could scarcely believe that Franklin Crabtree had put his family's reputation above justice. He'd simply shipped his murderous son off to medical school in England and offered Samuel Tillman a new life as Lancaster to salve his conscience.

Grace already despised Barnabas Crabtree for his greed and his shocking deception of the patients who trusted him, but this was another level of wickedness entirely.

In the seconds it took for the implications to strike home to her, Charlie broke open the serving hatch and was now squeezing his muscular frame through the narrow opening. Just when it seemed he had as much chance as squeezing a football through a croquet hoop, a sudden thump and crash of crockery heralded his success. Grace picked up her skirts and followed him, leaving the less agile Wallace trapped in the dining room. As she tumbled back-first into the shards of broken cups and saucers left behind by her husband, Grace hoped Wallace found the spare key quickly, because she and Charlie were about to face a ruthless killer.

By the time Grace reached the hall, Charlie was sprinting out the front door. "Barnabas has gone. See to his father," he yelled over his shoulder.

Grace found Franklin Crabtree lying in bed, absolutely still, his neck resting at an awkward angle. A stream of drool slid down from his mouth onto the fresh white linen of the pillowcase.

Gently, she corrected the angle of his neck to make it easier for him to breathe. She bent over him, her cheek to his mouth. If he was breathing at all, it was too faint to tell. Although his body was still warm, Grace couldn't feel a pulse at the wrist. She pressed two fingers into his neck. There it was, feeble but definitely signalling life. After conducting a careful examination, she made him comfortable, wishing Doctor Harvey was there to advise her.

The angry red marks on Franklin's wrinkled skin confirmed he had been deliberately attacked. Presumably, Barnabas had panicked, knowing how little time he had, and hadn't waited around to ensure his father had died.

Grace wasn't sure what to do. Her patient was better off in his own bed because moving him might cause more harm than good in his condition. However, Franklin might still be at risk if he stayed in this house, which left her with no safe option. She sat down on the bed as she considered the situation. The evidence seemed to point unequivocally to Barnabas Crabtree's guilt, but the admission in Franklin's letter seemed at odds with other facts. Specifically, why would Franklin have reinstated his son as his heir, if he had known Barnabas was a murderer? Had he truly believed his son had reformed?

Grace couldn't forget that another man had the opportunity to attack Franklin. Samuel Tillman, or Lancaster as he had been then, had left the dining room for a few minutes to make tea while Wallace was absent. Moreover, Rosannah had distracted Grace to prevent her from seeing his departure. They would both benefit from Franklin's death, particularly if they could put the blame on Barnabas by implicating him as a murderer.

A thunderous pounding down the hall told her the spare key had been found. The running footsteps stopped behind her, sending a chill down her spine. She pulled the blanket over Franklin's chest and turned to address the onlookers. Thankfully, Detective Inspector Wallace was with the two suspects.

Grace didn't wish to tip her hand in their presence, so she kept to a summary of the facts, leaving out crucial details. "Mr Crabtree is alive, but he is weak. He seems to have suffered another seizure."

Samuel, who was holding a weeping Rosannah in his arms, hushed his old friend. "Will he live?"

"It's too early to say for certain. I'd like to get him to the hospital, but it is a risk to move him."

"Do you have a telephone?" Wallace asked.

Samuel pointed up. "Doctor Crabtree insisted on installing one in his study."

Wallace herded them towards the door with his intimidating bulk, despite Rosannah's protests that she should stay with her father. "I'll call for help. You two will come with me. Mrs Penrose Pyke has the medical training to provide the best care for the patient."

Grace nodded, relieved, but not surprised, that the inspector had seen the potential danger. As soon as they left, she checked her patient again. Franklin was no longer as pale and clammy as he had been, and his pulse was stronger. A tough old fellow, thank

236

goodness. The improvement tipped the balance. For both his recovery and his safety, it would be better to move him to the hospital.

A commotion outside drew Grace to the window. A thrashing Barnabas Crabtree was being dragged back to the house between Charlie and the constable who had been guarding the gate. The tall, charismatic doctor she had come to know these last few days had descended into a feral state. Even his flowing mane of hair looked wild as it tumbled around his face. They passed into the porch and out of her view, but she heard them in the hall. Barnabas protested his innocence, loudly and repeatedly.

Grace was turning away from the window when she noticed a smear of dirt on the sill. By craning her head, she could see that somebody had dropped an oddly shaped object into the shrubs outside. When she returned from retrieving it, she found Charlie waiting for her in Franklin's room. He held his arms wide, inviting her into his warm embrace. He didn't have to ask twice.

"Wallace will need me back in a minute," he whispered. "Barnabas and Samuel are facing off like dockyard brawlers. I wanted to make sure you were safe, and Franklin, too. How unfortunate he had another seizure at the worst possible time."

"Not unfortunate, Charlie. Attempted murder." Grace slid out of his arms and showed him the red mark on the victim's neck and a second one on his chest above his heart. "I thought it was a scorch mark, and it seems I'm right."

"How did a burn trigger his seizure?"

"Franklin wasn't burned; he was electrocuted." Grace picked up the object she'd dropped on the floor. A long electrical cable snaked from her hand, with a pair of smooth pads dangling at the end. "These are the electrical probes Barnabas Crabtree uses for his advanced electrotherapy treatments. They attach to a series of batteries in his consulting room. I don't know how they could be used in this room, though."

237

Charlie examined the plug at the end of the cable. "It's been rewired to fit a light plug. The house wiring would cause a far greater shock than a battery. It's a miracle Franklin survived in his condition."

"Heart of an ox is my bet." Grace drew her husband out of earshot of the patient. "His survival is not a certainty, and I cannot say what state his brain will be in if he lives. What a hideous way to try to murder someone."

"The killer probably thought Franklin's death would be passed off as natural causes because of his frail condition. It was a huge risk to take."

"Charlie, I know the case against Barnabas seems overwhelming, but I can't help wondering if that letter was genuine. I simply can't see Franklin Crabtree concealing a murder, even to save his son." Grace glanced at the lifeless figure on the bed again. "Or perhaps he underestimated his son's wickedness."

"It cannot be the same letter Franklin's solicitor saw, because a legal professional would be obliged to report a confession of a murderer's identity to the police. Declan gave no indication the solicitor was perturbed by the letter."

Grace thought back to the encounter in the park. "He could have written a new letter, I suppose. Franklin told me he'd wanted to speak up, but he was afraid. If Barnabas threatened his father, it would explain why Franklin planned to reveal the killer only after his death."

"Possibly, but that doesn't explain Franklin's decision to change his will in his son's favour," Charlie said. "Instinct tells me the original letter has been switched for a forgery. Perhaps it's my natural distrust of easy solutions, but all along it has seemed as if somebody was setting up Barnabas Crabtree to take the blame for the murders and burglaries. Why send the threatening note to you, for example, drawing attention to electrocution? And why would Barnabas risk murdering his father right under the nose of a detective inspector, especially when he was the only one with the opportunity to do it?"

"Actually, he wasn't the only one with the opportunity and motive. Lancaster – Samuel – left to make tea while Wallace was with you. Rosannah and Samuel might have suspected Barnabas all along of Arthur Tillman's murder and resorted to forging the letter to prove their case. Although it seemed to me their reactions to the letter showed they were genuinely shocked by the contents."

"In this household, anything is possible," Charlie murmured, but his jade green eyes were focused far away, as his brain sorted through new combinations of the known facts.

Grace waited for his attention to return to her before she spoke again. "The killer had little time to arrange the electrocution, which suggests premeditation."

"Premeditation is a given, Grace, because the plug must have been rewired in advance. It was a risk, though, with us in the house. I can't help feeling we're being played by a maestro."

"Or maybe we're looking for trickery where none exists. Barnabas did try to escape, after all."

"Only one way to find out." Charlie returned the electrical cable. "Can you keep this while I help Wallace with the interrogation? I don't want the suspects to know yet that Franklin's seizure was attempted murder. You'll have to stay with him until help arrives."

"With pleasure. I've had quite enough of all of them. I'll yell if I need you." Grace pressed a kiss on his cheek to send her husband on his way.

Charlie lingered, holding her close. "I'm hoping Matthew Vale will be back soon. He is the crucial last piece of the puzzle. Send him straight through when he arrives."

Down the hallway, shouted accusations and threats poured from the dining room. Charlie sighed and raced away to help Wallace. Grace listened for a while, wondering if they needed help, but the crunch of wheels on the gravel driveway diverted her attention. Fortunately, it was the cavalry, in the form of Alistair Stewart.

239

Grace met him before he'd brought the buggy to a halt. Together, she and Alistair carried Franklin Crabtree's frail body, still wrapped in the blanket, and gently lifted him into the buggy. While they were settling the patient, Grace briefed Alistair on the morning's events as quickly as she could.

Alistair had news of his own, and it wasn't good. "You need to know that Matthew Vale may be a victim, too. He was sipping a cup of tea when I arrived for our meeting. I could see from his expression that something was wrong, but Vale dismissed my concern. He said the tea tasted unpleasantly metallic and put it down to tainted water. After a few minutes, the muscles in his face started to spasm, and he asked if we could reschedule our meeting."

"Muscle spasms?" Grace recalled the locksmith who had supposedly committed suicide after the first burglaries. That death had been strychnine poisoning, which had the symptoms Alistair described. "Could it have been strychnine?"

"That was my thought, too. If the tea was poisoned, it might have been an accident. It's happened on rare occasions, when strychnine is left on a kitchen shelf to poison rodents and one of the kitchen servants uses it by mistake. However, I'm sure you'll agree an accident is unlikely in this case. I insisted on taking Vale to the hospital immediately."

"Is Matthew Vale still alive, Alistair?"

"I expect so, but I don't know for certain. It took me a while to find somewhere to tether the horse after he went inside. I couldn't find Vale, but that's not too surprising in that rabbit warren of the hospital. He said he'd only taken a few sips of tea, and the symptoms weren't severe, so he should recover with proper care. I didn't waste time looking for him because I wanted to warn you as soon as possible."

Grace shivered. "It seems we have a homicidal maniac in our midst, or at least a person willing to do whatever it takes to cover his tracks."

"You be careful, Grace. Don't underestimate this person, especially after that threatening note addressed to you." Alistair dotted a fleeting kiss on her cheek before climbing back into the buggy. Before Grace could reply, he took up the reins and set off on his second mercy mission of the morning.

Alistair was through the gate when Grace realised that she'd forgotten to ask a crucial question. She called for him to stop and ran after him, out onto the street. "What time did you arrive at the hospital, Alistair?"

"Our meeting was at nine o'clock. Vale's spasms started soon after, and I didn't waste time asking questions. We arrived at the hospital within half an hour. I imagine they would have admitted Vale for urgent treatment as soon as he mentioned poison and then kept him in for observation." Alistair glanced at the figure in the wrapped blanket, who was groaning. "I'd better get Franklin Crabtree to the hospital. I'll find Matthew Vale and send a message to you as soon as I can. I'll get the tea in the flask analysed, too."

Grace watched the buggy disappear down York Place, wishing she could be with Alistair. She inhaled deeply to regain her composure, having read that stress was not good for growing babies. She needed time to think, because the pace of the morning's events had left her reeling from suspect to suspect and back again. This case was making her paranoid, searching for deception at every turn.

Ironically, Charlie had mistrusted Matthew Vale as much as Grace had mistrusted his charlatan brother-in-law. In Charlie's opinion, Matthew was too smooth with the patter, playing the respectable gentleman to perfection even as he lied about the soundness of his business. And now Matthew was another victim. Or so he claimed.

Grace was several deep breaths into her attempt at regaining her calm when she registered a man approaching the house from the other direction, coming up from the city via Russell Street. A wave of sympathy washed over her when she saw the way Matthew Vale

241

dragged his feet. His misery was evident from his dull expression and the sickly hue of his skin. Charlie had mentioned the elegance of his attire, but Matthew looked decidedly rumpled and grubby.

At the rate their suspects were dropping, the killer would be the only person left standing soon.

As Matthew approached, his gaze went straight past Grace to fix on the constable, who was now back on guard duty.

Grace stepped in front of him. "Mr Vale, I'm regret to inform you that your father-in-law has had another seizure."

He looked at her, uncomprehending, before the shock registered. He stopped, but his eyes were on the house beyond. "Oh, no. Is he …? Will he recover?"

"Your father-in-law's condition is extremely serious, Mr Vale. I've sent him to the hospital."

"The hospital?" He groaned. "I've just come from there. If only I'd known. Where's my wife?"

Grace nodded her head towards the house and told the constable to let him through.

"Thank you for your assistance." Matthew glanced at her face, uncertain, as if she might be vaguely familiar, but he couldn't recall her name. "Apologies, no time for introductions. Excuse me, I must comfort my wife." He bowed awkwardly and stumbled past Grace towards the house, stopping only to wipe his shoes on the mat, as a well-trained gentleman would.

Grace hoped the wife in question wasn't still being comforted in the arms of the butler. The last thing they needed was another murder. That is, if the suspects already inside the house hadn't killed each other before Matthew got to them.

She hurried after him, new possibilities swirling through her brain after hearing of the poisoning from Alistair and seeing Matthew dragging himself up the street. A nice, quiet position as a doctor in a general practice was looking extremely appealing.

242

Volatile Mix

Charlie left Grace with her patient and ran into the dining room in time to help Wallace pull Samuel Tillman off Barnabas Crabtree.

All signs of Lancaster, the unobtrusive butler, and Doctor Crabtree, the respected medical man, had vanished. Accusations flew with equal venom in both directions, accompanied by flying fists, despite one of Barnabas's wrists being handcuffed to a cast iron radiator. Rosannah added to the confusion by pummelling and cursing her brother. For a slight lady, she had a vicious right hook, Charlie noted, when one of her punches missed its intended target and connected with his gut.

"Sit," Wallace bellowed, when the trio were finally loosed from each other's throats.

They sat. Barnabas perched on the edge of a chair by the radiator at the far end of the dining table, nursing a bleeding nose, while Rosannah and Lancaster sat close together in the middle of the table.

Wallace slumped into his seat at the head of the table, wearing a wistful expression that suggested he was contemplating the merits of early retirement. He pointed at Barnabas. "You. Explain yourself. A calm and truthful account, please. If you shout or in any other way cause trouble, I won't hesitate to charge you with one count of attempted murder, two of murder, and multiple counts of burglary." Wallace turned to the other two suspects. "That goes for you two as well."

"I thought my father was fast asleep," Barnabas said, dabbing his bloody nose with a handkerchief and speaking in the strained voice of a man who has had the stuffing knocked out of him. "I locked you in the dining room because I wanted time alone with my father to ask how he could believe such lies about his son."

243

"Do you deny your father's accusation that you murdered Arthur Tillman?" Wallace asked, shooting a quelling glance at Samuel Tillman.

"I swear by all that's holy that I had nothing to do with Tillman's death or the burglaries, just as I did not beat that boy at school."

"What did you do to your father?"

"Nothing at all. Despite being deeply upset by what he had written about me, I didn't want to wake him. I simply stood by his bed, trying to decide whether to wait for an apology or to walk out of this house and never return. The latter seemed the best option in my distressed state. I'm fed up with being accused by people who should know better. So, I left. If I'd realised that my father had suffered another seizure, of course I would not have gone."

"But you did cut the telephone wire, so we couldn't call for help."

"No, I didn't."

The explanation sounded feeble. Charlie doubted that a man who claimed to have medical training could fail to see that his father was not merely sleeping. He was about to raise the issue when the door opened behind him. He stepped aside, assuming it was Grace, but it was Matthew Vale. Just what they needed, another volatile substance to add to the explosive mix.

Matthew walked past Charlie as if he didn't exist, his eyes on his wife. "Rosannah, dearest, I'm deeply sorry to hear your father has taken a turn for the worse." Belatedly, he recognised the man sitting beside his wife. "Lancaster, remove your hand from my wife's arm immediately. I do not tolerate inappropriate conduct from the servants."

Rosannah rose, then sat again. "Lancaster has been a great comfort in a dreadful situation, Matthew."

Quiet dignity oozed from every pore as Lancaster fixed an unblinking stare on Matthew. "I am not your servant, Vale. Indeed, I might be wealthier than you are, so perhaps you should bow and scrape to me for a change."

"How dare you speak to me like that?" The scarlet bloom on Matthew's previously pallid cheeks deepened to a furious crimson when his wife didn't intervene to reprimand the servant.

"Now is not the time, Matthew," Rosannah said. "If you had been here, you would understand."

Matthew moved towards them, only to be stopped by Wallace, who indicated he should sit in the seat nearest the door and furthest from the rest of the family. Matthew glared at Wallace. "Who the devil are you to order me about?"

"This gentleman is Detective Inspector Wallace," Barnabas said, "so you'd better be on your best behaviour, Matthew."

Matthew sat, but only after nodding apologetically to the inspector and scowling at his brother-in-law. Wallace nodded back but didn't speak. The plan had been to let the tensions in the household play out, with the occasional push when needed.

Grace's arrival broke the tension. Charlie would have been happier to see her if his wife hadn't looked so pale and unsteady on her feet. She must have been down on her knees, because there was mud on them and her skirt had caught on the top of her boot, exposing the haft of her concealed knife.

She beckoned him to follow her out to the hallway, where she whispered fresh revelations in his ear. After a rapid discussion, Charlie embraced his magnificent wife, then wiped the ear-to-ear grin off his face. They returned to an expectant hush. Detective Inspector Wallace must have picked up on Charlie's mood, because his lip twitched up.

Matthew stood and offered Grace his seat. Although Charlie was pleased somebody in the room had remembered his manners, he would have preferred if Matthew hadn't been standing so close to Grace. As if sensing his unease, Matthew stepped away, taking the remaining seat between Grace and Wallace. When nobody spoke, Matthew took up where he had left off, glaring at Lancaster.

"Why did you leave my father?" Rosannah asked Grace.

"His condition is improving," Grace replied. "I've sent him to the hospital."

Rosannah released a pent-up breath. She leaned towards her husband, her hand outstretched. "I owe you an explanation, Matthew. Lancaster is an old and dear friend of mine. It's to my great shame I haven't openly acknowledged it before, if only to preserve his secret."

"What secret?" Matthew asked. "Will somebody please tell me what is going on?"

Barnabas was quick with an answer. "It seems the police have discovered a killer hiding in our midst, disguised as a butler."

"Lancaster? A killer? You cannot be serious. He wouldn't say boo to a goose." Matthew's puzzled gaze drifted from his brother-in-law's handcuffed wrist to the servant who had taken liberties with his wife. His frown deepened into narrow-eyed suspicion. "I felt unwell this morning at my meeting. My client rushed me to the hospital, worried I might have been poisoned. I thought it an absurd overreaction at the time, but perhaps he was correct. What do you have to say for yourself, Lancaster? Did you poison my flask of tea?"

Rosannah blanched at the accusation of poisoning and visibly recoiled at the mention of the tea flask. "It must have been something you ate, Matthew, because I was the one who prepared your tea flask this morning. It cannot have contained anything untoward because I rinsed the flask first and poured tea from the same pot I drank from. How are you feeling, my darling? Shouldn't you have stayed in the hospital if poison was suspected?"

Matthew looked from his wife to Lancaster and back, as if unconvinced by her explanation. "I'm fine now. The doctor gave me a ghastly powder and made me wait until the spasms stopped before discharging me." He turned to Wallace. "What evidence do the police have that our butler is a killer, Inspector? It seems preposterous to me."

"Certain facts have come to light, but our inquiries are not yet complete," Wallace said.

Right on cue, Barnabas cut in. "Lancaster is the locksmith's son, Samuel Tillman. His father took the blame for his crimes, and then he tricked my father into taking him on as a servant under a new name."

"Samuel Tillman?" Matthew peered at Lancaster with fresh eyes. "I recall the investigation, of course, but I don't think I ever met the locksmith's son. A rather odd, reclusive boy. I remember Arthur Tillman, though. A fine man."

"Samuel used to hide every time you and I visited to collect the rent," Barnabas said, his voice sharp with spite, "presumably because he had the sense to recognise you for what you are, Matthew. Unscrupulous and vicious."

Matthew closed his eyes and exhaled a long sigh. "If this is about your expulsion again, I beg you to spare me your tired old excuses, Barnabas. It seems we have more important matters to discuss, such as why you are in handcuffs, and not Lancaster or Tillman or whoever he is."

"It's far more serious than expulsion from school, Mr Vale," Wallace said. "We are here to arrest the person who masterminded two sets of burglaries. The same person who murdered Gus Fenton three nights ago and Arthur Tillman a decade ago."

Again, Rosannah took the side of her old friend over her brother. "The Samuel I knew then and the Lancaster I know now would never do such a thing. He always believed his father had committed suicide to save him from being wrongly arrested for the burglaries. It was only today we learned it was Barnabas all along, and Father kept silent to save him."

A spasm of pain crossed Matthew Vale's face. He turned to his brother-in-law. "I'm sorry you've finally been caught, Barnabas. I did my best to protect you, if only to preserve your sister's reputation."

247

"Lies!" Barnabas cried, clanking his handcuffs against the radiator as he tried to get to Matthew.

Wallace motioned for him to be silent. "Please explain, Mr Vale."

Tears streaked down Rosannah's cheeks. "You knew my brother killed Arthur Tillman? Why didn't you tell me, Matthew?"

Matthew wiped a tear away at the sight of her distress. "My dearest wife, how could I cause you such pain? Your father decided it was best for both our families to say nothing."

"What about the Tillman family?" Rosannah asked. "Didn't they deserve to know the truth?"

"Your father only realised the true culprit after Arthur Tillman's death, when the family had already left town. He couldn't face sending his son to the gallows, nor the disgrace that would have ruined your chance of happiness, my dear. Franklin only told me much later, before we married, because he felt I should know the truth about the family I was marrying into. Of course, I told your father I would never allow your brother's sins to stop me from marrying you. With Barnabas thousands of miles away, there seemed no point is taking any further action."

Rosannah's anguish softened into gratitude when she realised her father and her husband had both done their best to protect her family. The tightness in Samuel Tillman's jaw suggested his forgiveness would not be so easily bought.

As for Barnabas, his glare could have cut through a diamond. "Don't listen to him, Rosannah. This is what Matthew does. Always blaming others for his crimes. He destroyed my life, and now he is destroying yours."

Charlie exchanged a glance with Wallace, who nodded for him to take over. Charlie held up the pair of probes attached to an electrical cable. "These were hidden in the undergrowth outside Mr Franklin Crabtree's bedroom window. These are your electrical devices, aren't they, Doctor Crabtree?"

"Yes, but I did not hide them in the bushes. Why would I?"

248

"Did you wire these probes to the type of plug used in a light socket?" Charlie asked, holding the plug for all to see. "Thereby delivering the much higher voltage used by the house wiring than the lower voltage from the battery they are normally used with. A voltage that was applied to your father as he slept in his bed."

The former Professor of Galvanism reacted as if he had been subjected to his own electrical device. "What? No! Absolutely not. Such a shock could be lethal to an elderly man weakened by illness." His voice trailed off as the implications struck home.

"Your father's death would leave you wealthy," Wallace said. "Wealthy enough to pay off your debts and start again. Somewhere far away from accusations of murder, not to mention malpractice, fraud, and burglary."

Rosannah rose to her feet with the slow deliberation of an ocean wave gathering height, ready to break. "Of all the terrible deeds I believed you capable of, Barnabas, I never believed you could stoop so low as to harm your own flesh and blood. And don't you dare try to deny it, because you were the only person who could have done this to Father. After reading his letter accusing you of being a murderer, I suppose you thought you had nothing left to lose."

"I didn't do it, Rosannah," Barnabas said. "Please believe me. I didn't do any of it."

His sister turned away from his entreaties. "Inspector Wallace, I beg you to arrest my disgraceful brother before I do something I will regret. Get him out of my sight."

"I was only in our father's room for a few seconds before I left the house. He could have been attacked before I got there." Barnabas pointed at the teacup. "Lancaster left the room while the inspector was absent. He could have done it. And Matthew could be lying about being poisoned."

"I was in a meeting with a client when the symptoms began, and he took me to the hospital." Matthew raised upturned palms. "Casting blame will not help you now, Barnabas. I want you to know I forgive your nasty insinuations, knowing how desperate you must be to escape your fate."

"Actually," Charlie said. "Your brother-in-law makes a good point, Mr Vale. You have tried to put the blame on your brother-in-law at every turn, playing the quiet, respectable businessman to perfection. I have met many persuasive liars in my time, but you are in a league of your own."

Matthew tilted his head to the side, as if bemused by the unexpected accusation. "I don't know what Barnabas has been saying about me, but I assure you, I have done nothing wrong. What evidence can you possibly have against me?"

"You forged the letter from Franklin Crabtree to Lancaster, which falsely revealed Barnabas as a murderer," Charlie said. "A big mistake. You saw a chance to make your fortune, by ruining your brother-in-law, thereby getting control of your father-in-law's estate. But you didn't know that Franklin Crabtree's solicitor had already told the police the letter was nothing more than a sincere expression of thanks to Lancaster for his service."

"A completely baseless accusation, which I deny absolutely. Obviously, my father-in-law must have written a new letter when his conscience got the better of him."

"But he didn't, did he? Franklin Crabtree was so appalled by his son's expulsion from school for a violent assault that he disinherited him until he proved himself worthy. Franklin would never have changed his mind and reinstated his son as his heir if he had believed him guilty of the far greater crime of murder. In fact, Franklin was as deceived as everyone else had been about the expulsion. Your old schoolmaster was the only one to see through your clever deception, Matthew. You assaulted that boy, and your friends agreed to point the finger at Barnabas."

Matthew didn't so much as flinch. "That's pure fantasy, Mr Penrose Pyke. My brother-in-law's expulsion followed a formal inquiry, which reached a unanimous verdict against him. I truly cannot imagine why you think so ill of me."

Barnabas had barely controlled his volatile temper while he listened, but Charlie could see he was about to explode again. Rosannah stared in open-mouthed disbelief at the accusations against her husband, while Samuel gripped her arm, still not quite believing what he was hearing.

"There's more," Charlie said, gesturing for Barnabas to sit. "You also sent a threatening note addressed to Mrs Penrose Pyke, my wife, making it appear to be from Doctor Crabtree, who was being investigated by her. However, it was clear from the interview this morning that the Barnabas Crabtree knew my wife only as Miss Penrose, not Mrs Penrose Pyke."

"I don't know your wife at all," Matthew said, the pitch of his voice rising slightly in the first sign of stress he had shown.

"But your wife told you all about her, didn't she? You knew we were investigating Doctor Crabtree's medical practice, and you saw your chance to use us to discredit him. Did you also know we were investigating a series of burglaries and the murder of Gus Fenton, which we had already linked to someone in this household?"

"Of course, I didn't," Matthew said. "And I had no part in any of it. I couldn't have had anything to do with the attack on my father-in-law, because I was in a business meeting and then at the hospital, as I said. After I was discharged, I came straight home."

Grace twisted in her chair to face Matthew. "More lies, Mr Vale. Do you ever tire of them? We know the business meeting never took place, because your 'symptoms' began immediately after your client arrived. You went into the hospital alone at about half-past nine, giving you ample time to leave via the side entrance and return home. I know the hospital well. Would you care to tell me exactly which room you were in and which doctor you saw? Should I take a sample of your saliva and test it for strychnine?"

Matthew glowered. Grace smiled. "No? I thought not. It would be easy enough to fake the symptoms of poisoning to give yourself an alibi, especially as you knew exactly how Mr Tillman reacted when you forced him to ingest strychnine a decade ago. Or perhaps you gave it to him in a nice cup of tea."

Samuel Tillman let out the feral moan of an animal in pain. Grace ignored him and continued to address Matthew. "How shocked you must have been when you overheard the latter stages of the interview through the partially open window of the dining room. If you didn't know the extent of our investigation beforehand, you certainly did then. It would have been a huge risk to murder your father-in-law, but the payoff was immense if you could implicate Barnabas."

"You know that's not true," Matthew said. "You saw me arriving at the house only a few minutes ago."

"I did. But that wasn't the first time you arrived home, was it? Your shoes and trousers were smeared with lichen, mud and leaves, as they would be if you had clambered over the fence and through the stand of trees that ring this property, to avoid being seen by the constable on the gate. Easy enough to exit the same way and keep a watch on the house until it was safe to return. I expect you waited until you saw Barnabas being frogmarched back. How you must have gloated to see your plan working perfectly."

Matthew showed the first glimmer of anger at being thwarted by a woman. Charlie took three steps forward to stand directly behind Grace's chair, in case Matthew lashed out.

However, Matthew was made of sterner stuff. He merely shrugged. "You make it sound plausible, but it is only speculation. You can't know any of this."

"Oh, but I do," Grace said. "Russell Street is an extremely indirect way to return from the hospital, especially for a man as unwell as you pretended to be. Why not simply take the cable car, as you did this morning going into the city? However, Russell Street makes sense as a way to return home after circling through the Town Belt. The mud did not just stick to your shoes, you see. There is a smear of mud on the windowsill of Franklin Crabtree's

252

bedroom, and another on the doorstep where you wiped your shoes before entering the house the second time."

Charlie took over, hoping to further unnerve their suspect. "You had plenty of time to climb through Franklin's open window and electrocute him while we were occupied elsewhere. You hid the probes so we would think Franklin had died of natural causes, but not so carefully that we wouldn't find them if we were suspicious. What a shame for you that Franklin Crabtree is tougher than he looks."

Matthew spread his arms wide, as if protesting wildly fanciful accusations. "You're mistaken. There are leaves and mud everywhere at this time of the year."

"True," Grace said, "but not all leaves are the same. There are several particularly fine specimens of lancewood on the border of this property. They do not grow on city streets. I found fragments of the distinctive leaves on the windowsill and doorstep. There are also marks underneath the open dining-room window, where somebody crouched, eavesdropping. Shall we check the soles of your shoes for lancewood fragments, Mr Vale?"

Charlie's focus hadn't left Matthew. He saw the instinctive glance at the incriminating shoes and felt the surge of elation that came with a suspect on the verge of breaking.

Matthew Vale prided himself on his superiority, so Charlie targeted the next blow at his vanity. "Your brother-in-law was not the only man who needed an urgent inheritance from Franklin Crabtree, was he? Your business was failing, and you needed money quickly. Why not simply steal the money by restarting your old burglary scheme? An easy solution for a man who lacks any trace of a conscience."

"Character is so important, isn't it?" Grace said. "Your old schoolmaster had you pegged as a sneaky, disagreeable boy, who was feared by his peers, and he was right. But I'll bet even he would be shocked that you went on to murder Arthur Tillman and Gus Fenton and attempted to murder your own father-in-law."

253

Charlie stared into the eyes of a cold-hearted killer wrapped in the trappings of a quiet, respectable gentleman, but Matthew refused to rise to the taunt. He crossed his arms defiantly. "You cannot prove it. I won't say another word without my lawyer present."

The stunned silence around the table dissolved into a collective gasp of outrage at his tacit admission of guilt. Detective Inspector Wallace rose to his feet with a second set of handcuffs at the ready, a gleam of triumph in his grey eyes. Barnabas let loose a barrage of curses for all the humiliation and anguish Matthew had brought down on him over the years. Rosannah wrapped her arms across her body, recoiling from the despicable stranger she'd known as her husband. Samuel stood beside her, fists clenched, fury distorting his features.

Seeing the odds stacked against him, Matthew jumped to his feet, his eyes seeking an escape route. With a guttural cry, Samuel sprang onto the table and scrambled across to get to his father's killer. Unfortunately, his lunge off the other side of the table was ill-judged. Grace was sent sprawling, deflecting the force of Samuel's momentum into Charlie.

When Charlie had untangled his limbs from Samuel, he saw Matthew Vale on the floor beside Grace, holding her ankle and tussling with her. Before Charlie could get to him, Matthew was on his feet again, dragging Grace up with him, and holding the knife from her ankle sheath against her throat with the steady, competent grip of an expert fencer.

Wallace froze in mid-stride. "Put the knife down, Vale, and let her go. The rest of you, stand back and leave this to us."

"For the love of God, Matthew," Rosannah pleaded, "do what the Inspector says. Hasn't there been enough bloodshed?" She paused, but her husband didn't obey. "Do it for me, Matthew, if not for yourself. Don't I deserve that much after all my father and I have done for you?"

The knife resting on Grace's carotid artery never wavered. "I've always treated you well, haven't I, Rosannah? I've always respected you and your father. You can have no complaints, but you also have no right to tell me what to do."

Rosannah held her head high and kept tears at bay by sheer force of willpower. "Our marriage was nothing but a convincing charade, wasn't it? You wanted my father's money, so you turned on your charm, as you would turn on a tap to get water. Did you ever love me, Matthew?"

Her husband gazed at her as if the question puzzled him. "Love? I don't see the point in it when there are more important goals to strive for."

Rosannah turned away from him – not simply her head, but her entire body – until the only view she had was of the beauty of the sun through autumn leaves in the garden. Samuel retreated around the table to join her, putting his arm around her for support. Barnabas followed their lead a second later, the handcuffs rattling on the iron radiator as he turned his back on the brother-in-law who had almost succeeded in sending him to the gallows.

Matthew seemed unfazed by the rejection. His shoulders twitched into a fleeting shrug, before he turned to Charlie. The absolute steadiness of his gaze and the faint smile that played over his lips might have been those of a person amused by a child's petulance.

Charlie knew he needed to regain a semblance of control, so he played the only ace he had. "Stop by the family drawing room on your way in, did you, Matthew?"

Matthew thrust his chin out, but he held his nerve. "You have one minute to return the contents of the Chinese vases to me, Pyke, or your wife dies."

Charlie caught Wallace's eye. With the evidence they had so far, proving the case against an outwardly respectable man like Matthew Vale was by no means guaranteed. Now, he had undeniably implicated himself by revealing his knowledge of the hiding place for the stash of stolen goods.

"The proceeds of your burglaries were taken away from the house by one of our men," Charlie said, "alongside the father-in-law you attempted to murder. It is not within my power to return them to you, Mr Vale. I suggest you cut your losses and surrender now."

"You're a liar, Pyke. As they say, it takes one to know one. Do you honestly care as little for your wife as I do for mine, that you would risk her life for a few baubles?"

Matthew waited for Charlie to answer. "No comment? Perhaps I can change your mind. I must admit, seeing the effect of electricity on the old man was unexpectedly thrilling. All that writhing and thrashing at the touch of a probe. I long to test it again. What better subject than your wife? She pretends to be as tough as a man, but I'd wager a sustained high-voltage electrical shock will break her, and you. I should so like to see blue tongues of flame sputtering and darting from all over her body."

Charlie lost his ability to speak at the description of electrocution from the newspaper clipping Grace had received yesterday, which ended with the victim being cooked from head to foot. What had he been thinking, trying to bargain with a man like Matthew Vale?

Wallace answered for him. "Pyke, get those bags. Now. Vale, if you let Mrs Penrose Pyke go, I swear I will allow you to leave this house a free man."

"Too late," Matthew said. "I want to see them suffer for interfering with my carefully laid plans." He pulled Grace towards the door. "Inspector, could you please oblige me by securing the butler to the radiator with the handcuffs. Put him next to my brother-in-law. I'm rather hoping they might kill each other and save me the bother."

Wallace hesitated as his shrewd eyes weighed up the odds. But only for a fraction of a second. With a last glance at the knife against Grace's throat, he did as he was told, handcuffing Samuel to the other end of the radiator. The two shackled men exchanged grim nods, recognising a common enemy.

Matthew gestured for Wallace and Rosannah to come to the door, keeping Grace between him and them, the knife steady against her throat. "Into the consulting room, please. And don't try anything stupid, or this woman's blood will be on your hands. Oh, and Pyke, do be a good fellow and bring those electrical probes with you."

In the Hot Seat

Charlie cursed himself for not having given Matthew the stolen valuables right from the start. It would have been infinitely better to have him on the run from the police than to risk the lives of Grace and their child.

Wallace escorted Rosannah out of the dining room ahead of him, using his bulk to shield her as they passed Matthew and Grace.

Rosannah broke free of him in the corridor, turning back to face her husband. "Matthew, you must let Mrs Penrose Pyke go. She is going to have a baby. Take me as your hostage instead."

"Brave of you, my dear, now that you know what I am capable of." Matthew flicked the tip of the knife against Grace's skin, causing a drop of blood to slide down her pale neck. "However, our police friends value this woman far more highly than you, while my sentiments tend in the other direction. But thank you for telling me there is a baby on the way. All the more reason for Pyke to obey me, with two precious lives at risk of being fried to a crisp."

The calmness he displayed – his tone polite and almost apologetic – should have reassured Charlie, but somehow it made Matthew's stone-cold heart all the more terrifying. It wasn't simply his inability to feel ordinary emotions; it was the obvious pleasure he took from inflicting pain and humiliation.

Charlie sent a last, longing look at Grace. His hopes of distracting and disarming her attacker receded when Matthew directed Wallace and Rosannah into the storeroom adjoining the consulting room. With the solid door locked, it was now two of them against an armed killer with everything to gain and nothing to lose.

It wasn't too late to concede defeat, especially as the frantic, but futile, hammering at the locked door suggested they would not have help from Wallace anytime soon.

"Let my wife go, Matthew," Charlie said. "I will show you where I stashed the valuables and not stand in the way of your departure. You'll need me to get you past the constable at the gate."

"I do not need your help, Pyke. What I need is to see you punished. You have a choice. Either you watch me strap your wife to the chair and test the effect of an electrical probe on your child, or you can take her place. I can't say fairer than that. Either way, you'll tell me where you hid the bags."

With the knife still hovering at Grace's throat, that was no choice at all. Charlie sat on the chair. Matthew ordered Grace to strap him in tightly. When she was finished, Grace gripped his hands in hers and pressed her lips against his cheek.

"Enough," Matthew said. He dragged Grace away to the side of the room, where he plugged the rewired probes into the house wiring. His smile had widened by the time he returned to face his next victim. "You're a fool, Pyke. Your strength was your best weapon, but now you've lost your advantage by sacrificing yourself for a weak woman. Putting sentiment over logic will never make you a winner. My father taught me that at the end of a cane, but only until I was strong enough to fight back."

When this was over, Charlie would ask the police surgeon to take a closer look at Elias Vale's premature death, but that was not a subject to raise now. He shrugged. "Better to die for love than live with a heart of ice."

Matthew snorted his contempt. He released Grace to free his hands to take up the electrical probes. She fell at his feet, begging him to spare her husband. Charlie couldn't bear to watch her pleading. Matthew kicked her away with a callousness that had his muscles straining against the tight leather straps, while Grace curled into a ball, protecting her belly. She stayed curled up, whimpering in a way Charlie had never seen before. Heart-wrenching as it was to see his wife so distressed, he was glad her instinct had been to save the baby instead of her husband.

Her tormentor watched on, his lip curled in disgust.

Charlie had to draw Matthew's attention back to himself, and what better way than to flatter him. "I have to hand it to you, Matthew. You've been clever. Throwing suspicion for the first series of burglaries onto the father you despised, while terrifying Gus Fenton into keeping his silence, all without anyone suspecting the quiet, well-behaved, studious son. Franklin Crabtree trusted you to marry his daughter and handed you control of the Vale property business. Rosannah remained loyal to you until the end. Your mother thought you were a little angel. But you won that trust and loyalty through deception."

Matthew nodded, clearly taking the words as a compliment. "People are so gullible. It was almost too easy. A woman's loyalty means nothing. Look at your wife, grovelling on the floor at the first sign of danger. She's not worth the trouble."

This insult failed to elicit a reaction from Grace. Although Charlie was glad his wife wasn't putting herself at risk, he was surprised she wasn't fighting back. She had sat through his speech, hunched over her belly with her back to them, never making a move towards Matthew. If pregnancy changed a woman so markedly, she had chosen a poor time to show it.

Even so, unlike his opponent, Charlie trusted her to come up with a brilliant rescue plan. He just hoped it would be soon. Wallace was still doing his best to break through the door, but it showed no signs of giving way.

Fortunately, Matthew was now ignoring Grace, assuming she posed no threat. He advanced on Charlie with the probes.

Charlie tried a new tack. "It must be galling that I am cleverer than you. I have built a successful business, while yours has failed despite your attempts to rescue it by stealing other people's treasures. And I was the one who saw through all your devious misdirection. In fact, it was easy –"

Matthew darted forward and lashed the probes across Charlie's face like a whip. "Silence. I'm the one in charge." He dangled the probes in front of Charlie's face. "I am really looking forward to seeing the effect of high voltage on you, Pyke. Did you know they use electricity to kill criminals in New York? A marvellous innovation. I rather think I will go there and see for myself."

All Charlie could do was deny him the pleasure that a bully derives from making others suffer. "They use a much higher voltage in New York, Matthew. What you have in this house wasn't sufficient to kill a sick old man, so I shall barely feel a tingle. Perhaps I will even feel as refreshed and revitalised as your dear brother-in-law promises with his treatments."

Matthew's fingers tightened on the probes, but he didn't rise to the bait. Charlie's field of vision narrowed. The probes were now inches from his neck and temple. He couldn't look away, but he prayed that if Grace had a plan, she would put into action now.

She didn't.

"Where are the valuables, Pyke?"

"In the storeroom, with the Inspector." Charlie figured it was his only chance of giving his old boss a chance to get their man.

"That's a shame. I'll have to kill him too." Suddenly, Matthew plunged the two probes deep into his neck, making Charlie jerk and yelp.

However, the jerk was not from the shock of electricity, but from the shock of realising he felt nothing at all, beyond the discomfort of the probes digging into his flesh. Not even a tingle.

Matthew ripped open Charlie's waistcoat and plunged the probes against him again, this time around his heart. Charlie closed his eyes and prayed, and again he felt nothing. When he opened his eyes, he saw that Grace had crawled up behind Matthew.

She flung her arms around his thighs. "Leave my husband alone, I beg you."

He yelped and flung her away. "By Lucifer, woman, you've got the talons of a hawk." His eyes followed the line of the electrical cable to where the plug sat loose on the floor. "Think you're clever, do you, unplugging the cable?"

Grace sat there, looking at Charlie with the slightest twitch of her lips, giving him renewed hope that the old Grace still had an ace up her sleeve, although he couldn't imagine how she would prevail against such odds.

Matthew plugged in the cable and took up the probes again. But this time he advanced on Grace, who took one look at the anger contorting his face and curled into a ball again. Charlie wrenched his arms up and sideways as hard as he could, but the straps still did not give way. He watched helplessly.

And then, agonisingly slowly, but surely, Matthew Vale's leg muscles failed him and he sank to the floor with the gracefulness of a sack of dead fish.

Grace calmly stood up and removed the electrical plug, before slicing through the cable with the knife she had liberated from Matthew's belt. "Back-up plan," she said, grinning and wiggling the knife at him, before binding the comatose killer's wrists and ankles with the cut cable. "Nice work distracting him, Charlie. What a loathsome man."

She checked Matthew's pulse and left him on his side so he wouldn't swallow his tongue. Ever the doctor, Charlie thought, even when the patient deserved no pity.

"Nice work yourself, my love. You had me worried. I was beginning to think roast detective was on the menu. Might I inquire how you disabled the delightful Mr Vale so effectively? I didn't see you plunging an electrical probe into him."

She undid the bindings around his wrists and ankles. "Do I look like Mrs Frankenstein? As I said earlier, everyone acts in tune with their character."

"You disabled him with kindness and compassion?" He took her in his arms, hoping she wouldn't notice how much he was trembling.

"We came expecting to encounter a killer who was clever, vicious, and unlikely to be swayed by either logic or pleading. Therefore, I stopped by the hospital this morning to find something more persuasive than my feminine charms." Grace removed an empty vial and syringe from the hidden pocket in her skirt. "Behold, a logic no man can ignore. Unfortunately, my hands were shaking so badly, it took me a while to fill the syringe. I feared I might be too late. Next time, I'll fill the syringe first."

She glanced over at her patient, frowning. "I hope I didn't overdo it. After some serious arm twisting, the hospital pharmacist let me have a vial of a new drug he'd told me about. I wasn't sure of the exact dose required, and I didn't wish to underestimate the amount. Perhaps best not to mention it to the medical authorities."

A medical solution, of course. Charlie would never have thought of disabling the villain with drugs, but it came as naturally to Grace as breathing. He crushed his wife to his chest, taking care not to squash the precious Bean. "I shall inform the authorities I disabled the scoundrel using my manly strength alone, to deflect any awkward questions."

Grace ran her hand over his biceps. "An excellent idea. Far more believable than a pathetic, weak woman overpowering the brilliant Matthew Vale."

"He was a fool for underestimating you, Doctor Penrose. That was his fatal error. He saw my strength as our greatest asset, rather than your brains and ingenuity. I chose to play the victim because Matthew's disregard for your talents gave you a better chance of saving us than I had."

Grace eyed him up. "Pure pragmatism then? Nothing to do with sacrificing yourself to save the life of your wife and child?"

"Maybe a little," he said, silencing her with a kiss that sent an electrical pulse to all corners of his body. Hers too, judging from her delectable reaction.

The thumping on the storeroom door had ceased and been replaced by a bellow, demanding to know what on earth was going on out there.

Grace pulled away with a sigh. "I suppose we ought to release Detective Inspector Wallace before he does himself an injury. But don't think you've escaped without thanking me properly, Pyke, preferably in the peace and quiet of our bedroom."

"Sounds perfect to me, my love. After the shocking day we've had, a little tranquillity is just what the doctor ordered."

Final Shock

As the weeks rolled into months, there was no denying Grace's pregnancy. There was also no denying her colossal ignorance of the practicalities of being pregnant. She lowered herself onto the chaise longue with a groan and propped her feet on a cushion, wondering how it was possible that she had failed to consider the consequences of having an unbalancing bump protruding from her midriff.

Charlie probably could have told her, because he had been studying books on pregnancy and childcare as if his life depended on it. His initial worries about how he would cope had eased to a tentative confidence. True to form, her husband had never doubted for a minute that she would cope with being a mother. Grace was glad one of them was so certain. Thankfully, Charlie had assured her that he was looking forward to helping with the baby. Their savings would allow for extra help, too. Somehow, they would cope, as they always did.

She jammed another cushion behind her back. Lying here wouldn't get her essays written, but she needed a rare moment of peace away from her busy schedule to catch her breath. She was glad she'd agreed to have no more involvement in active investigations, especially where there was an element of risk.

Grace lifted the loose tea gown she now wore in the comfort of their home and contemplated the bulge, which had expanded to the point her belly button had popped out. Deep within her body, she could feel the fluttering of butterflies, making her wonder how long it would be before the baby was big enough to kick. She longed to chase a little foot around her belly, tickling it and wondering what their child would be like.

The shocking events at the Crabtrees' house were now a distant memory, recalled only when Grace sat in the new nursery, as she did now, admiring the gorgeous gifts they had already received. Pride of place went to the mahogany cradle bought at the fateful auction by Anne and Kenneth Drummond. An equally beautiful rocking chair sat next to the cradle, gifted by a grateful Robbie Wallace, who had received a commendation from the Chief Inspector for solving multiple murders and burglaries in the space of a few days.

The gifts looked perfect in the newly decorated nursery, designed by Lily with exquisite taste, assisted by a liberal financial contribution from Alistair.

Doctor Harvey's wife had visited last week and offered a lovely set of red deer antlers to complete the décor. Horrified at the thought of her child playing under the sharp prongs of a dead animal, Grace made a desperate, but polite, attempt to refuse the gift. Mrs Harvey chortled merrily and handed her a beautifully wrapped box instead, containing two pairs of tiny, perfect booties.

Grace ought to have guessed Mrs Harvey was joking, because she knew Doctor Harvey loved those antlers, which reminded him of his childhood in Scotland. The much-maligned antlers had finally found their home, to the relief of the hospital charity committee. And Grace had found a home with Doctor Harvey too, having agreed to work limited hours at his surgery the following year. They would take it one step at a time, building up the practice slowly as Grace balanced being a mother and a doctor. She put that daunting thought aside, determined not to let Andrew Harvey down after all he had done for her.

These were not the only gifts they had received. Mrs MacDonnell sent a beautiful crystal decanter, along with a note pouring out her heartfelt thanks for the return of her heirloom ring. To Grace's surprise, she had also received a bulky envelope marked as Mrs Atkinson's personal stationery. However, the note inside was a semi-literate scrawl from Mrs Atkinson's maid. Ellie thanked them for clearing Jack's name and said she and Jack were about to leave town for positions at a country house with a grand garden.

She signed the letter as Mrs Jack Turner, enclosing a pair of colourful crocheted butterflies.

Grace was overjoyed to know that one of their suspects had found peace and happiness. It had been a difficult time for the other suspects, although that hadn't stopped Rosannah from sending a letter expressing her thanks for clearing Samuel's name, and wishing them well for the birth of their child. Charlie had been particularly touched that the letter arrived inside the Chinese lacquered box. Rosannah said her father was recovering gradually under Samuel's expert care. She did not mention her husband, who was awaiting trial, or her brother, who had fled the country before he could be tried for fraud.

With a contented sigh, Grace stretched out her legs, happy to have the weight off her feet. After extensive negotiations by telegram and post, she had convinced her overexcited mother to wait until the baby was born before rushing south from Wellington. Grace suggested a Christmas visit, which seemed a safe bet, since the baby was due in late November. She'd thought a month would be plenty of time to transition from novice to perfect mother, but now she had her doubts. As time passed, the desire to have her mother beside her grew stronger than her desire to show she could cope on her own.

Grace shifted position, unable to get comfortable and worried that she shouldn't be quite so like an elephant seal at this stage of her pregnancy. Her confidence about the due date was more wishful thinking than certainty. The alternative was too terrifying to contemplate. Her greatest fear was that the baby would arrive early, before or during final exams, but she was determined not to dwell on it. In fact, once she reflected upon the matter, a premature birth wasn't even close to her greatest fear. What if she was such a terrible mother that she forgot about the baby while engrossed in her work? What if she dropped the poor mite on its head while bathing it? She squashed those fears deep into the seething morass of other terrifying unknowns, telling herself she could always hand the infant over to its father, who would never do such stupid things.

267

To distract herself, Grace grabbed her stethoscope, hoping she would hear a heartbeat to reassure herself that all was well. After a minor contortion to get the angle right, she was certain she could hear a faint, rapid beat. Then, her brow furrowed and her heart lurched as she realised it didn't sound like the heartbeat she had heard so often while examining other mothers. Blood rushed to her head, inducing an overpowering dizziness. She toppled backwards onto the soft cushions with a whimper.

Charlie entered the room with Blaze in time to see her faint. The pair of them were at her side in an instant. "Grace, what's happened? Shall I get help? Water? Smelling salts? The book I read said to be alert for elevated blood pressure. Have you checked it lately?"

Grace pulled herself together and squeezed his hand, scrambling for a relatively neutral topic of conversation to calm him before she delivered the knockout blow. "I'm perfectly fine, my love. I hope you don't mind, but I've invited my parents for Christmas."

"Oh. I've invited my parents too. Perhaps we ought to have discussed it first."

"Never mind," Grace said. "They'll keep each other busy."

"We'll be lucky to see our baby at all, with both sets of doting grandparents here. We'll have to hope that Blaze doesn't have a litter of pups at the same time. But honestly, even if that happens, we'll cope, won't we, as we always do? After all, how much trouble can a few adorable puppies and a single adorable baby be?"

Grace raised an eyebrow. Lord save her, the place would be a madhouse. For all his reading, her sweet husband hadn't the least idea what he was facing, because he had grown up without brothers and sisters. She pulled him down beside her. "Would you like to listen to the heartbeat?"

She put the earpieces into his ears and placed the end of the stethoscope on her skin. His gasp came out in an awed rush of breath, and his eyes rounded in wonder. "The beat is so fast ... It's really happening, isn't it? What if I turn out to be the worst father

268

ever? What if I drop the baby on its head while I'm bathing it? What if –?"

"Nonsense, Charlie. You'll be a wonderful father." She moved the end of the stethoscope around her belly.

His eyebrows bunched together, as Grace's had. "That's odd. I can hear a heartbeat here too. Is it some sort of echo?"

Grace propped cushions behind his back to make sure he would be safe if he fainted. "Charlie, dearest heart, you know I have twin brothers, but I'm not sure I've ever said that my mother was a twin too."

She watched as the shock hit her husband like the blast of a double-barrelled shotgun. "Charlie! Head between your knees, breathe deeply."

He fell back against the cushions, whimpering. "Heaven help us. I'm not ready for this, Grace. What do I know about coping with one child, let alone two?"

"Poppycock. I've seen you dispatch two armed thugs without breaking into a sweat."

"Simple brute strength, over in an instant." He gripped her hand until her fingers throbbed. "Children are for life, not an instant, and there's probably a law against handcuffing them to restrain them."

Grace couldn't have put it better herself, except that she had more experience of the challenges they faced, having survived her twin brothers' antics over many years. Handcuffs would have come in handy back then.

She extracted her squashed fingers and patted his hand reassuringly. "Chin up, my love. There's no turning back now."

Read on

In Book 10, *Deadly Demands*, Grace and Charlie face another challenging investigation when a blackmailer's nasty insinuations trigger a tragic death. With final exams and the birth of the twins rapidly approaching, this is one investigation they would be happy to leave to the police. But that option becomes impossible when the blackmailer strikes an unexpected target much too close to their hearts to ignore.

Thank You

Thank you for reading this story. If you enjoyed it, I would be very grateful if you would leave a rating or review to help other readers discover it.

Find out about other books and sign up for notifications of new releases at https://RosePascoe.com

Historical Notes

It's almost impossible to imagine how amazing such everyday conveniences as electric lights must have seemed to people in the Victorian era, who read their books at night by dim gaslight or spluttering candles. Thus, electricity was seen as another giant technological step forward, and people would queue to visit shops with electric lights and wonders such as elevators.

On the other hand, electricity was more than a little frightening too. Since the eighteenth century, experimental attempts to restore corpses using electric currents had fascinated and horrified the populace. Mary Shelley used this to frightening effect in her 1818 novel, *Frankenstein*. The novel was inspired by what was then called Galvanism, after Galvani's early experiments on "animal electricity", the natural generation of electric current within humans and animals.

Newspapers regularly carried stories of accidental electrocutions and criminals deliberately executed by electric chair, which made many people fear going near electrical devices of any type. The gruesome account of a lineman's death sent to Grace in the story was taken directly, in all its gory details, from a Dunedin *Evening Star* article from the era.

But Victorians were always eager to try any and every marvellous new discovery too. The medical use of electricity flourished to an extraordinary extent alongside the domestic and industrial uses that transformed society. The therapeutic devices mentioned in the story were based on real, widely available, and heavily marketed devices of the late Victorian era.

Many devices sold for home use, such as the electrical belts and hairbrushes, were shown to be of little or no therapeutic value, and some of them did not even provide a measurable electrical current.

Not that this stopped their enthusiastic uptake. However, complaints rolled in too, leading to court cases and the eventual demise of the real Medical Battery Company, which had been a major player in the "electropathic belt" trade.

The use of medical batteries designed for use by physicians sat on the fence between quackery and medical therapy. A wide range of medical batteries designed by legitimate manufacturers were used by some qualified doctors and disparaged by others. They could be purchased in sizes ranging up to the wall cabinet battery array described in the story, complete with probes for *every* part of the body. Similarly, some reputable hospitals had departments devoted to electrical medicine.

Dunedin had more than one purveyor of medical electrical devices in the 1890s, who advertised their wares in the newspaper and conducted demonstrations. The scene where the "statical machine" is demonstrated was drawn from an *Otago Daily Times* article from the era, sourced from *Papers Past* (New Zealand National Library). However, Doctor Crabtree is fictional, as are the other characters in the story.

Likewise, while the locations are real, the Crabtrees' house is fictional. The electric lighting used in the house was inspired by innovative elements of the nearby Olveston historic house, which was built a decade later. Olveston is a wonderful place to visit, with thirty-five glorious rooms to explore (https://www.olveston.co.nz/). The house must have been even more of a marvel when first built, because it was powered by electricity from a gas-powered generator, boasting electric lights and other novelties such as central heating, a shower in each bathroom and heated towel rails, as well as an internal telephone system and service lift.

Anyone interested can find images of locations and early uses of electricity in the "Inspiration" section at the bottom of the *Shocking Deceptions* tab on my website, https://RosePascoe.com.

Acknowledgements

A huge thank you to my fabulous beta readers: Mary, Jenny, Kathy and Ross. Their continued enthusiasm is very much appreciated.

Two writing friends have joined the beta reading group: Bronnie Thomas and Tracy Chollet. Check out their books at: www.tracychollet.com and www.bronniethomas.com.

About the author

Rose Pascoe writes historical mysteries seasoned with medical mayhem, women's rights, and a dash of romance.

She lives in beautiful New Zealand, land of beaches and mountains, where long walks provide the perfect conditions for dreaming up evil plots, when she isn't plotting real-life adventures.

After a career in health, justice and social research, her passion is for stories about ordinary women who meet the challenges thrown at them with determination, ingenuity, and humour.

Visit her at: https://RosePascoe.com

www.ingramcontent.com/pod-product-compliance
Lightning Source LLC
Chambersburg PA
CBHW011444170626
46816CB00008B/2505